CONSORTING WITH DRAGONS

SERA TREVOR

CONSORTING WITH DRAGONS

by Sera Trevor

Special thanks to Chris for the inspiration, and to Kevin for his amazing proofreading skills

CHAPTER 1

*J*asen sensed the dragons before he saw them.

He couldn't have explained it if someone had asked him. One moment, he was dozing in the carriage, not quite able to fall asleep due to his father's monstrous snoring, and then a feeling of warmth blossomed in his chest. It radiated outward with each beat of his heart, until his whole body was filled with it. The feeling pulled him to the window. When he looked out, there they were—dragons. Or not *there*, exactly—they were off in the distance, flying over the city of Draethenper, their silhouettes dark and enormous. There were two of them, swirling together in an unearthly dance with a grace that should be impossible for creatures of their size. The sun was low in the sky, melting into oranges and reds as warm as the feeling in his chest.

Jasen was moved in a way he had never been before. For some unfathomable reason, he decided to try to share the moment with his father. "Dad," he said, nudging him. "Wake up!"

The man continued to snore. After poking him a few

more times, Jasen finally resorted to giving him a hard slap on his enormous stomach. He let out a snort as his eyes shot open. "Wha-what?" he slurred. "What is it?"

Jasen gestured out the window. "Come look."

Slowly, his father complied. It took a few moments, but a grin tugged at his lips at last. Jasen smiled, too, pleased to share a nice moment with his father for once, but then his father said, "A-ha! We're nearly at Draethenper, then! Excellent timing—we're almost out of wine!"

Jasen sighed. He should have known better than to try. "I meant the dragons. And we've only been on the road for two hours! How can you be out of wine already?"

"Well, a lot of it has spilled, hasn't it?" he said, a touch defensively. "It's damn difficult to pour wine with all this jostling and bumping."

"You're drinking it directly out of the bottle."

"Of course I am *now*. I've learned my lesson, haven't I? Now, where did that damn thing run off to?" He patted around until he found the bottle he'd been working on before he'd nodded off. "Ah, here it is!" After taking a swig, he offered it to Jasen.

Jasen looked at the last swallow in the bottle, no doubt made up of his father's spittle as much as wine. "No, thank you."

His father shrugged and finished it off. He smacked his lips. "How much longer before we're there, do you think?"

"I don't know. An hour or so. If it's any longer, I'm sure you could lick the floor—that ought to sate your thirst, at least for a little while."

His father put a hand over his heart and rolled his eyes to the heavens. "Ah! You wound me, son! Can you blame me for being nervous, sending my only child out into the world, all on his own?"

Jasen scowled. "This was your idea."

"You didn't exactly collapse in despair when I suggested it." He clapped Jasen on the arm. "Cheer up, son! This will be good for you."

"Oh yes, my best issues are at the front of your mind, I'm sure. The fact that you'll make a fortune auctioning me off is just a pleasant afterthought, right? It has nothing to do with the fact that you've gambled away our wealth."

"I'm going to win it back," his father sniffed. "It's true, my luck has slumped in recent days—"

"More like years," Jasen mumbled.

"These things come in cycles, my boy! The wheel will turn."

There was little sense in arguing about it with him, so Jasen said nothing. He rubbed his face, trying to banish his weariness. They were on the last part of a journey that had taken two weeks; their home in a back province of the kingdom of Grumhul was as rural a place as one could imagine. They had left their horses and more rustic cart at the last inn, since his father had insisted on renting a fancy carriage for their grand entrance into the city. Not that anyone was going to see them—his father had gotten so distracted by a game of cards that they left two hours later than they were supposed to.

They were journeying to Draethenper, the city at the heart of the Draelands, which was the largest kingdom of the Allied Realms. Each year, dozens of eligible young men and women of either noble birth or sufficient means arrived to find a noble husband or wife. Over a grueling two months, they would be poked, prodded, and polished to make them as attractive as possible to potential suitors, who would arrive in the third month to begin their search for a lord- or lady-consort to wed. It would all end in a grand ball, where all engagements were announced and marriage prices were negotiated.

3

And now, Jasen would be among them. It wasn't a thought he relished. Consorts weren't ordinary brides and grooms. As the spouse of a title-holding noble, their responsibilities were as much political as they were matrimonial. If a title-holder passed away without heirs, or with heirs who were still in their minority, their spouse was given the title. That was what had happened when Jasen's mother had died.

Now that Jasen was older, he could challenge his father for the title, but he didn't particularly want to be the earl of Hogas—who would? It was a dull, backward place where nothing ever happened. Besides, he didn't relish the responsibility. Nobles who preferred the company of their own sex could name a niece or nephew as their heir, but Jasen was an only child. Accepting the title meant that he would have to put aside his own natural inclinations toward men and marry a woman, which was not something he wanted to do —not that they could afford a bride, anyway. And so it seemed Jasen would die a bachelor, and their lands would be passed to someone else. It was just as well. Neither he nor his father were cut out to be in charge of anything.

Since he didn't plan on marriage, Jasen found nothing wrong with seeking his pleasure with as many people as he pleased. This might not have been too scandalous, except that his choice of partners tended to come from "common" stock. After a few unsatisfying affairs with fellow nobles, who were all snobs, he found himself preferring the company of those without titles. Out of deference to his mother's memory, Jasen tried to keep his affairs quiet, but that all ended one day when his father caught him on his knees in front of Hans, a stable hand.

To his surprise, his father was delighted at the discovery. Such a scandal must definitely be concealed, and what better way than to send Jasen off to the marriage market at Court, just as his father had suggested on many occasions? After all, it would have broken his poor mother's heart to see her son's name dragged through the mud, wouldn't it? In other words, it was blackmail.

Well, that wasn't completely fair. His father was right that Jasen hadn't put up much of a fight. He had grown uneasy in Grumhul—when he was a boy, he had run freely with the children of the common folk, but as he grew older, it was assumed that he must separate himself and become a proper noble. Even his lovers acted this way. He had tried to make Hans into something more than a bed partner, but Hans had laughed him off. After all, what kind of future could they possibly have? Hans was determined to marry a nice girl and make a family. Their dalliance was only a bit of fun.

But if Jasen didn't belong with the commoners, he also didn't belong with the upper class. After his mother had died when he was twelve, his education had ended, leaving him unqualified for pursuing any of the professions deemed suitable for men from noble families. Neither did he possess any magical abilities—almost no one in Grumhul did. His one advantage was his striking good looks: he had long, red hair of an unusually vivid hue, brilliant amber eyes, lithe limbs, and fine facial features with lips whose natural resting state was an alluring pout. He wanted out of Grumhul, and with beauty as his only advantageous trait, Court was his best bet. He doubted he belonged there, either, but it was worth a try.

They rode in silence for a little while longer. Jasen kept his eyes trained on the dragons, who remained soaring above the city until the light faded. They flew off once the sun had set. Jasen wondered where they had gone. Dragons were their own creatures, not under the control of men. They could go anywhere—anywhere at all. Jasen wondered what that was like. He shut his eyes briefly and imagined where he would go if he could fly like a dragon. Some place where he belonged, although he couldn't imagine where that would be.

"The sun's almost set," Jasen observed. "We'll be lucky to get into the city at all at this rate."

His father waved his hand. "It will be fine, I'm sure. Are you eager to get there?"

"I'm eager to get out of this carriage."

"Oh, come now! Surely you're at least a tad excited?"

"Not really."

"Ah, you're nervous. You shouldn't be. You'd be a fine catch for any suitor—I suspect you'll have your pick of them!" He stroked his beard. "I think you should try for an older man. Much older, in fact—someone who is up to his ears in gold and dying for someone to spend it on. And just think—if you find one old enough, you probably won't even have to bed him that often!"

Jasen groaned and put his hands over his face. "I don't want to talk about this with you."

"What? I'm just being practical." He stroked his beard some more. "Even if you find someone too old for frequent sexual congress, you might still want to emphasize your—ah, experience in bedroom matters. I imagine that would be exciting to a man looking for some fun in his twilight years. You could describe your exploits to him—send him to his grave a happy man!"

"Please stop talking," Jasen mumbled from behind his hands.

His father, apparently, did not hear him, for he continued on. "I know that traditionally, the Court promotes purity, but believe me when I say that there are plenty of nobles who have little interest in such things. Why, the very first day I met your mother, we—"

"Dad!" Jasen shouted, removing his hands from his face. "I have no desire to hear about whatever you and my mother got up to, and I also have no desire to talk about any of the rest of it, either!"

His father held up his hands. "Sorry, sorry," he said.

Jasen got to enjoy five whole minutes of silence until his father started up again. "If an old man doesn't appeal to you, you could always set your sights a little higher." He waggled his eyebrows.

"I have no idea what you're talking about."

"The king, my boy—the king!"

Jasen stared at him. "The king? You're mad!"

"Am I? He's still a virile young man—thirty years old at the most. And it's been two years since the queen consort's death. He must find a spouse."

He was right. King Rilvor held two titles—not only King of the Draelands, but also the Lord of Drae, the human who was linked most closely to the dragons, and who by virtue of that fact was the supreme leader of all ten of the Allied Realms. All human magic depended on that link. While all of the royal family shared in this connection, it was the Lord (or the Lady, when there was a queen) who bore the brunt of it. It was a position of incredible power, but also incredible strain. He needed a partner to help ease his burden. If the Lord of the Drae grew too weak, humans would lose their powers. It had already started to happen—those who were dragon-blessed with magical abilities reported a weakening of their powers. Pressure was mounting for him to remarry, and in all likelihood, he would find his future spouse in this season's Court.

Even so, the possibility that the king might choose him was laughable. "Yes, the queen consort is dead," Jasen said. "And she was a *woman*."

"So? There are many men who enjoy the favors of both men and women. And I've heard rumors."

"The Lord or Lady of the Drae always marries to the opposite sex. They have to produce heirs."

"He has four children already. And it's not unknown for a

7

Lord of the Drae to have a king consort instead of a queen consort, if his queen consort dies. There was King Reder."

"That was three hundred years ago, and it hasn't happened since! And even if he did have an interest in men, do you honestly think the king would choose a man of the lowest level of nobility from the most backward of the back kingdoms to be his king consort?"

"Don't sell yourself short, son!"

"This has nothing to do with selling myself short and everything to do with having a firm grasp on reality! The Lord of Drae hasn't had a male consort in three hundred years, and neither fire nor fate is going to change that any time soon! Now kindly drop the subject."

His father shrugged. "All right, son, as you say." And then he added, under his breath, "But stranger things have happened, is all I'm saying."

They lapsed into silence after that. Jasen looked out the window again, watching the sky where the dragons had been. His father's suggestion was ridiculous—and even if it were possible, Jasen was fairly certain he wouldn't want to be king consort, anyway. All the politics and diplomacy and being a public figure seemed overwhelming to him. On top of that, there were also four children who he would become a stepfather to. No, he was most certainly not interested in the king.

It took even longer to get into the city than Jasen had anticipated. His father had decided not to hire a driver for their expensive carriage in order to save money, figuring that their footmen, Rodrad and Garyild, could handle it well enough. He had been wrong. Garyild was partially blind and Rodrad's hands were arthritic, so they settled on a system in which Garyild held the reins and Rodrad shouted directions. It was amazing that they'd made it as far as they had already without an accident, but their luck eventually ran out and they ran straight into a mud-filled ditch. It took all four of them to free the carriage, and by the time they were done, they were all filthy from head to toe. They also discovered a wheel had been knocked out of place and had to be repaired. And since it was dark and none of them possessed magical ability, they had to do the whole thing by lantern light.

Miraculously, they were able to make the repairs, by which time it was two hours after sunset. After the carriage was repaired but before they got back on the road, Jasen and his father got into a shouting argument that had begun with Jasen insisting that he should take over the driving, which his father forbade on account that it would make them look unsophisticated. From there, Jasen demanded to know why his father had chosen their two oldest servants to accompany them. After some hemming and hawing, his father confessed that he didn't trust Jasen not to "lose control" of himself with the younger servants, which Jasen felt was ridiculous and insulting and…well, also somewhat true, because he actually had slept with quite a few of them—it wasn't his fault that there was nothing else to do in their backward hellhole of a province, and besides, he thought his father was thrilled that he was such a big slut. And then his father roared at him that Grumhul was the home of the best people in the world—so what if they weren't fancy, they had heart and he should be proud of his heritage. Jasen countered by pointing out that if his father was so proud of their heritage, why had he insisted on the fancy carriage in the first place… And so on, for another half an hour.

All told, it was well past ten in the evening by the time they arrived at the city gates. The guards almost didn't let them through—no one was supposed to be admitted after dark. His father blustered and threatened, throwing around his title of the earl of Hogas in the kingdom of Grumhul, as if that were somehow impressive. Incredibly, it worked, and soon their fancy carriage, now covered with mud, was on its way to Strengsend, the grand palace of Draethenper. The palace itself was only one part of Strengsend—there were dozens of different structures, gardens, and several acres of land known as a draemir, a sacred site set aside for any dragons that happened by.

The scene from the city gates played out again at the palace gates, but they made it through there, too. Entering the palace grounds was like stepping into a dream. Even though it was night, the whole place was lit by dragon lights —glowing globes that were enchanted by the dragon-blessed to provide light. He'd always imagined them to be something like torches, but the light they provided was a much softer, unearthly glow. Strange but beautiful trees, each of a unique shape, lined the main road, along with neat rows of the loveliest flowers Jasen had ever seen. He could only imagine what it all must look like in the light of day. In the distance, he could see the magnificent palace. And he knew that beyond the palace, out of sight and up against the Ashfell Mountains, was the draemir. Jasen wondered if the dragons he saw earlier were there now.

The four large structures that made up the palace were known as the wings. The consorts were housed in the East Wing. His father would spend the night in the West, which was set aside for stately visitors. He would only be there for the night, however. The next day, he would make his way back out of the city to stay with a cousin for a few nights before returning to Grumhul.

Once the carriage had stopped, Jasen made to get out, but his father put a hand on his arm. "Wait. I'd like to have a word with you, before we say good-bye."

Jasen resumed his seat and crossed his arms. "Well?"

His father sucked in a breath and let it out in a long puff. He looked at his feet, then at the ceiling, and then, quite forlornly, at the empty wine bottle. Jasen rolled his eyes and made to get up again, but at last, his father spoke. "I know I haven't been the best of fathers, especially after your mother passed, but—well, I did the best I could. Maybe it wasn't good enough, but there you have it. You're my son, and I want you to be happy."

At that, Jasen let out an incredulous scoff. "Oh, of course. And if I could be happy as well as netting you a fortune, so much the better. Am I right?"

"And what's wrong with wanting that? We need the money."

"*You* need the money. I bet the day you found me sucking Hans's cock was the best day of your life, because that meant you could sell me to fill your coffers. You pissed away Mother's fortune, and now you're using the next generation to do it again."

He expected his father to start in with excuses, but he said nothing, merely looking down at his hands folded in his lap. "You're so much like your mother," he murmured. "She was always right about me, too."

"Oh, masterfully done—self-deprecating, with a mention of Mother to boot." Jasen fastened his cloak. He'd cleaned the mud off of his face and hands as best he could, but his clothing was still a mess. He just hoped that his cloak would hide the worst of it. "Just so we understand each other—if I do manage to marry some rich old goat, you are not getting a single copper beyond the marriage price, no matter how much you blubber."

"Of course, son," he said, his shoulders still slumped. Just when Jasen began to feel a twinge of regret, his father continued. "I won't impinge on your generosity. Find a husband, and be happy. Don't spend even a single moment thinking of your poor old father, all alone in an old rotting castle, perhaps going hungry—starving, even…"

Jasen bundled up the ends of his cloak, shoved it against his face, and screamed. "You know, you almost had me there for a moment."

His father peeped upwards. "A little too much?"

"Just promise me you won't gamble away the marriage price before I even find someone."

"I swear on your mother's grave."

"Swear on that wine bottle. I'd believe you then."

Jasen swung open the door to make a dramatic exit—only to have it slam into Rodrad, who had been struggling to get Jasen's trunk from the top of the carriage. The trunk went sailing after him.

"Rodrad!" Jasen scrambled from the carriage. The man was laid out on the ground, moaning, with Garyild beside him. The trunk had burst open, its contents scattered everywhere. "Are you all right?" He turned to Garyild. "Did the trunk hit him?"

"No, m'lord. At least, I don't think so."

Rodrad struggled to sit up. "No, m'lord, it didn't hit me. Just had the breath knocked out of me. I'll be fine."

"Are you certain?"

"Yes, m'lord. Just need a little help getting up—"

Jasen went to his side, and together, he and Garyild helped him to his feet.

"Everything all right out there?" his father shouted out of the window.

"Why don't you get your fat ass out here and see for yourself!" Jasen shouted back.

And then he noticed that the doors of the hall had opened. A handsome young man in uniform stood staring at them. "Can I help you?" he asked.

Jasen tried to respond, but he felt as if he were choking on something. It was probably humiliation, if he had to take a guess.

While he tried to compose himself, his father burst forth from the carriage. "I am Draul, Earl of Hogas of the kingdom of Grumhul," he said. He sounded not the least bit embarrassed. "And this is my son, Lord Jasen. He's here for Court."

Remarkably, the man did not laugh or sneer at them. "Of course, my lord," he said with a bow. "We have been expecting Lord Jasen." He paused. "Although we didn't quite expect him at this time of night."

"We had carriage trouble, didn't we?" his father bellowed.

"Yes," said the man, looking over at the carriage and their filthy clothing. "I can see that."

"Then why are you so surprised we're late?" His father thrust his chest out and leveled his best haughty stare at the guard. "Well? Aren't you going to have someone see my son to his room?"

"Yes, my lord. I'll see Lord Jasen to his room myself. I imagine you and your servants will want to retire, now that you've seen Lord Jasen here. Don't worry about the trunk," he said to Garyild and Rodrad when he saw them trying and failing to clean up the mess. "We can take care of it. In fact, why don't I send someone up to show you the way to the West Wing? I know the grounds can be confusing."

"Grand, grand," his father said. He turned to Jasen. "Well, good night. I can come by in the morning to say good-bye."

"That won't be necessary," Jasen kept his tone as neutral as he could.

His father's face fell. "No, I suppose it won't. Good-bye, son."

Jasen made his way up the steps, where the man waited for him. He bowed again and gestured to the door. "After you."

When they entered the hall, they walked up a small staircase covered in pristine red carpet, which became considerably less pristine as Jasen tramped across it. At the top of those stairs was a room with two enormous pillars supporting a high ceiling, and even more stairs. A lot more stairs. There were two enormous staircases on either side that curved around in a grand arch. It seemed to Jasen that two staircases were excessive, given that they led to the same place.

"Welcome to the East Wing," the man said. "I am Larely, by the way. I am the junior officer in charge of security."

"Pleasure to meet you," Jasen mumbled, keeping his gaze on his dirty boots.

"Are you injured?" Larely asked.

Jasen furrowed his brow. "No. Why would you think that?"

"You were obviously thrown from your carriage."

"Oh—no, I wasn't. I had to get out to help when we got stuck in the mud."

The guard seemed surprised. "You helped?"

"Of course I did. We weren't about to get out of there otherwise, were we?"

"I suppose not. But most of the nobles I've met would rather sit in a carriage all night than get dirty."

"I suppose that's easier to do here in the Draelands, but in Grumhul, we don't have magic. Things don't get done with a snap of the finger! We have to rely on each other to—" Jasen stopped abruptly when he realized that he sounded exactly like his father. "Besides," he continued in a cooler tone, "maybe I like getting dirty."

Larely burst out laughing. "I hadn't considered that a possibility." He gestured to one of the chairs that was situated off to the side. "Please, have a seat. If you will excuse me, I need to see that your father and your things are taken care of. Won't take me but a moment."

Jasen was going to protest, given the state of his clothing, but the guard obviously knew and had offered him a seat anyway. Jasen did as he asked. Larely disappeared behind one of the doors.

Jasen fidgeted in the chair. Not that it was uncomfortable. Actually, it was a bit too comfortable. The furniture in his own home tended towards the hard and wooden side. The creak of the opening door startled Jasen out of his thoughts. Larely had meant it when he said he'd be quick, it seemed. "All settled," he said. "I'll show you to your room now."

"You're a guard, aren't you?" Jasen asked, eying his uniform.

"Of a sort."

"The sort who shows people to their rooms and arranges for carriages? It isn't generally what guards in our country do."

"Nor in ours, but it seems to be a quiet night, and I like to keep busy. Otherwise, I might end up like Captain Ingo."

"The senior officer of security?"

"Yes. He's a hopeless drunk. Not that I blame him—it can get a bit boring here." He gave him a sly look. "Although there is the occasional moment of excitement. I am called upon to rescue consorts sometimes."

Jasen eyed him skeptically. "From what?"

"From themselves." He winked. "Let's get you to your room."

They walked back to the staircases, ascending the one on the right. They walked down a long hallway, passing many doors along the way, before ascending yet another flight of stairs.

Jasen considered himself fit, but even he was a little winded by the time they reached the top. At long last, Larely stopped in front of a door. A small placard with his name hung on it. "Here we are," he said, opening the door. "I've arranged a bath for you, and your things should be sent up shortly. If you should need anything else, ring the bell."

"Thank you."

"Orientation is at three," Larely continued. "A valet will be up in the morning to help you dress. And if you ever need anything the servants can't provide, just ask for me."

"That's too kind."

"Not at all. Good night, my lord," he said with a bow.

Once he was gone, Jasen set about exploring his new lodgings. The room was lavishly decorated in reds and golds. There was a bed on his left, and a dressing screen and full-length mirror on his right. A small table with two chairs were placed by the window.

Behind the dressing screen, there was a copper tub with bottles of soaps and oils laid out on a table beside it, and a rack with a dressing gown and a few fresh towels. As he approached it, steaming hot water began to fill the tub. He jumped back, startled, but regained his composure. It wasn't as if he'd never seen magic before—it just had never been quite this casual. Magic was a rarity in Grumhul. Only people who were blessed by dragons gained magical abilities, and dragons didn't come to Grumhul. Ever since Grumhul became a member of the Allied Realms, Grummish parents were welcome to take their children to neighboring countries to seek a blessing. But the Grummish were historically suspicious of dragons and magic in general, and thus it was rare that anyone took advantage of the offer.

Jasen removed his clothing as the tub filled. Once it was finished, he eased into the water. It was heavenly—a hot bath was a rare treat. He reached for one of the bottles and dumped some of its contents into the water. A sweet floral smell filled the air. He washed himself, including his hair, and then lay back and enjoyed the warmth. When he was finished, he dried himself and put on the dressing gown. The water from the tub vanished.

There was a knock on the door. It was a servant; Jasen's

trunk floated behind him. Jasen tried not to stare as the servant directed his trunk into the room. He wondered if the servant was dragon-blessed, or if the trunk itself had been put under enchantment. The servant collected his muddy clothes and left.

When the servant was gone, he retrieved a night shirt from his trunk. After he slipped it on, he climbed into bed. He should have been tired enough to fall asleep right away, but his thoughts kept him awake for some time. He had been so sure he was ready to leave everything about Grumhul behind, but now that he was here at the palace, he missed it. Already he felt out of place. That was probably only going to get worse. He shut his eyes and tried not to think about it. Instead, he thought about the dragons, remembering their smooth, intricate dance in the sky. Gradually he relaxed, and soon he was asleep.

CHAPTER 2

*J*asen woke up just before sunup. He'd always been an early riser, and being in an unfamiliar environment made his sleep uneasy. Since there was no point in lying in bed, he pulled on his dressing gown and got up. He discovered a few sweet biscuits in a jar on his bedside table, so he grabbed a couple and sat down at the small table by the window. It might have been tiresome climbing all those stairs, but the view was spectacular. He was facing east, so he got to watch the sun slowly illuminate the palace grounds. His attention was drawn to the famous Bedrose Gardens, known throughout the realm for their fantastic array of exotic flowers, breathtaking fountains, and gallery of topiary wonders. He wanted to see it, so he decided to get dressed and go for a walk. The gardens were not far from the East Wing. Larely had mentioned a valet would be sent to help him prepare for the orientation, but he couldn't imagine him arriving for at least another two hours. Surely he'd be able to slip out and slip back in again without anyone noticing.

It didn't make much sense to get dressed up in finery just

for a walk, especially if he wanted to go exploring. He selected a loose shirt and long trousers from his trunk—the sort he wore when he went for hikes in the swamps of Grumhul. His cloak hadn't been returned to him, but it was summer. The morning air would surely be cool, but he'd warm up once he got moving. He tied his hair back, pulled on some boots, and then he was off.

He walked down the stairs as quietly as he could. He figured there had to be some way for the servants to get around, and after some searching, he discovered a partially hidden staircase that led down to the kitchen. The kitchen was already bustling—no doubt it took a lot of work to get the whole hall fed. A few servants looked at him in surprise, but he quickly escaped through a door which led outside.

Jasen headed toward the gardens, but on his way, he felt a strange pull. That warm feeling he'd had in his chest when he'd first seen the dragons bloomed inside him again, and almost before he knew it, he found himself heading towards the palace instead, and when he reached the palace, he kept going—up a trail and straight into the draemir.

It did not occur to him to question this decision, or even consider it strange, but neither was he in a trance. He made his way past the palace, up a path which led towards the base of Ashfell Mountain. It was a bit of a hike—a good three-quarters of an hour passed before he finally stopped walking as he reached a clearing. Just beyond him was a forest, and beyond that, the mountain. He bent down to drink from a brook that trickled across the land. As the cold, sweet water hit his stomach, he suddenly realized how strange it was for him to be here. Why had he climbed all this way?

He was starting to get a little disturbed about the whole situation when he saw something come towards him from the forest. There was a vibration in the ground that matched a rumble in his heart. He gasped as the fire in his chest bloomed again, much stronger than before. As the feeling washed over him, the enormous figure stepped out of the trees: a dragon, its scales shining as red and bright as rubies in the morning sun.

Jasen had known that dragons were large creatures, but now that he was standing near one, he realized that he had not truly appreciated what that meant. Never in his life had he felt so small, but at the same time, he felt as if his world had expanded a hundredfold. Every doubt and every petty fear of his life grew as small to him as he must seem to this dragon.

The dragon approached him slowly. He lowered his massive head until Jasen found himself looking into an enormous eye that was the same amber color as his own. At once, they knew each other's names.

Tasenred. That's what the dragon was called.

Jasen touched the dragon's snout. A jolt went through him, and every nerve in his body sang. The dragon folded his legs underneath him and lay down on with an earth-shaking thud. Jasen let out a startled laugh. "Are you tired?"

The dragon blinked. Jasen sank down as well, putting his arms around the dragon's neck, his face flush with the smooth, warm scales. It felt like the most natural thing in the world to do. "Me too," he said. "It's taken me so long to get here…"

Jasen turned over and leaned against Tasenred's neck, closing his eyes and soaking in the sunlight that grew stronger with each moment. Some time passed, but Jasen couldn't be sure how much. He was disturbed from his rest when the dragon lifted his head, turning his attention to something. Jasen sat up and looked as well.

There was a tall man at the edge of the clearing. His black hair hung loose to his shoulders, and his face was covered with a neatly trimmed beard. He wore a red tunic and breeches, over which he wore a Drae's cloak, which was a ceremonial garment. It had dragon's teeth on the shoulders and was clasped with a bright red jewel known as a dragon's tear, and lined with dragon scales. The elements of the cloak were gifts from dragons, as dragons shed their teeth and scales often. He was a draed, then. Draeds and draedesses lived in monasteries among the people, but they also ventured into the draemirs for meditation and communion with the dragons.

Jasen had no idea what to say. Fortunately, the man spoke first. "I've never seen him take to someone so quickly." He had a slight accent—something eastern, but Jasen was too ill-traveled to place it exactly.

Jasen continued to sit there stupidly for a moment, realizing that he should probably say something. "Am I in trouble?" was what he came up with.

"If Tasenred wants to meet you, who am I to tell him no?" He sat beside Jasen. Tasenred let out a rumble that sounded pleased and lay his head down again. Jasen examined the man more closely now that he was near. He had an aquiline nose and sharp cheek bones, giving his face a certain harshness, but his eyes were the same friendly blue of the sky on a clear summer day. Jasen couldn't quite guess his age. He seemed not too old, but there were a few streaks of gray in his hair.

"If someone had told me a week ago I'd be consorting with dragons, I would have laughed at them," Jasen said. "I'd never even seen a dragon until yesterday."

The man cocked his head. "You mean up close?"

"I mean at all. We don't see dragons very often where I'm from."

"Ah, I see. And what brings you to the Draelands?"

"I'm here for Court. What?" he said at the surprised look

that came across the man's face. "Why do you look so shocked? Am I that shabby-looking?"

"Not at all. It merely surprises me that you are here without an escort. Lady Isalei is strict about her charges."

"Who is Lady Isalei?"

The man's confused expression deepened. "She is the keeper of all the aspiring consorts. Surely you met her when you arrived?"

"I was late," Jasen mumbled. "I suppose that means I am in trouble, after all."

The man waved his hand. "Do not let it concern you."

"Oh, I won't. Being in trouble rarely concerns me."

"I am glad to hear it," the man said, laughing. "What's your name?"

"Jasen," he said. "Of Grumhul," he added quickly under his breath.

"Grumhul? You are far from home."

"And thank goodness for that."

"Why? I have always thought Grumhul was beautiful."

"You've been?" Jasen asked, surprised.

"Not for many years. But I do fly over it from time to time."

"What, on a dragon?" Just the thought of it set Jasen's heart racing. "Really? You do that?"

The man smiled. "Yes."

Jasen put his hand on Tasenred, feeling the slow rise and fall of his breath and the smoothness of his scales. He imagined climbing onto his back and soaring across the realms, seeing everything so small beneath him as they went anywhere, every-where… "Sometimes I almost wish I could become a draed."

"And why couldn't you? You have already passed the first test of the priesthood—a dragon has called you. And you are not yet married."

Jasen sighed. "There's just one problem."

"What is that?"

"I could never take a vow of celibacy."

The man laughed long and hard. "I admire your commitment to principle. There are many draeds who do not take that vow seriously."

Like you? Jasen almost asked, because Jasen thought he detected a hint of flirtation in his voice. Which wasn't entirely unwelcome, to be honest, but the last thing he wanted to do was be caught compromising the morals of a draed on his second day here.

Jasen settled back against the dragon and shut his eyes, enjoying the rise and fall of the dragon's breath. He could swear he felt his heart beat in sync with that breath, but that really would be insane. It had been ages since anything felt this right.

"We should get you back," the man said after a few moments. "They are probably looking for you."

Jasen was about to protest when Tasenred did it for him, letting out a long, low grumble.

"Apologies, Tasenred," the man murmured to the dragon. "Duty calls, for all of us."

The dragon let out a snort and began to move. Jasen and the man both got to their feet. Tasenred turned his head to Jasen once more, blinking his amber eyes. Jasen put a hand on his snout for one last touch. And then the dragon moved. Jasen nearly stumbled as he got out of the way. The man helped steady him. Tasenred only spread his wings when he was well clear of them. A moment later, he was in flight. The wind whipped into Jasen's eyes, causing them to tear up. At least, he blamed the wind.

"It is always hard to see them go," the man said.

Jasen gave his eyes a quick swipe, feeling a bit embarrassed. "All right. Let's go find out exactly how much trouble I've gotten myself into."

They began their hike back down the same path Jasen had come up earlier. The sun had climbed higher in the sky—it was mid-morning by now.

"Are you cold?" the man asked.

"No. I'm quite enjoying the weather, actually."

"But perhaps you would like to borrow my cloak, all the same."

"Why?"

The man cleared his throat. "You are a bit underdressed for a lord consort."

Jasen looked down at his clothes. "Am I supposed to get into full dress every time I want to take a walk? That doesn't seem sensible."

"I'm afraid we are preoccupied with ceremony in the Draelands, to our detriment. For a lord consort to be seen in nothing but a shirt might be considered a bit—" He searched for the right word, "—provocative."

"Oh." Jasen felt his face color a little. He didn't want to seem as if it bothered him too much, so he added, "I'm not usually provocative by accident."

The man raised an eyebrow. "You are sometimes provocative on purpose, then?"

Jasen gave him a sly grin in response. The man laughed. Their eyes met for a moment.

Jasen accepted the cloak. "Thank you," he said, breaking eye contact. He really didn't need to be flirting with a priest, but as usual, he couldn't seem to help himself. As he put the cloak over his shoulders, he felt a pulse of heat surge through him. He inhaled sharply.

"You felt something?" the man asked, surprised.

"Yes. Something warm…"

The man gave him a long, considering look. "That is very

interesting," he said finally. "Not everyone can feel it. Are you dragon-blessed?"

"No."

"Even the dragon-blessed don't always feel the power in a Drae's cloak," the man continued. "It usually takes someone of enormous power to connect to it."

Jasen looked down at the cloak. He touched the jewel clasp lightly and felt another pulse of heat. "Oh," he said stupidly, because he couldn't think of what to say. *Power? Him?* "Should I take it off?"

The man shook his head. "No. It suits you."

They continued their hike. As they moved, the power Jasen had felt initially faded. He had so many questions about what it all meant, but he wasn't sure how to articulate them even to himself. "Will he be back?" Jasen asked after a little while. "Tasenred, I mean."

The man cocked his head. "He always comes back."

"Will it be before I have to leave in three months?"

"And why are you so sure you will be leaving?"

Jasen snorted. "Oh yes, I'm sure the king will meet me, fall madly in love, and beg for me to be his consort. Then I'll spend the rest of my days splitting my time between frolicking about the draemir and lounging in the palace, eating strawberries."

"Stranger things have happened."

"Funny," Jasen muttered. "That's exactly what my father said."

"You disagree?"

"I'm sure stranger things have happened, but that doesn't make my likelihood of marrying a king any greater, does it? And frankly, I'm not sure I find the thought very appealing."

"Oh? I doubt your cohorts would share that opinion," the man said. "Especially this year," he added under his breath.

"They can have him."

They walked in silence for a little longer. "Have—" the man started to say. He broke off to clear his throat. "Has the king offended you in some manner?"

"What?"

"You said you found him unappealing."

"Oh, no!" Jasen said, suddenly aware of what that must have sounded like, especially to a draed. The king was also Lord of the Drae, after all, and therefore the head of the priesthood. "He's a wonderful ruler—I am his loyal and faithful subject, naturally!"

The man waved his hand. "Yes, yes, but you still would not marry him."

"Well, no. I mean—I'm sure he's a nice person."

"Perhaps you think he is ugly."

"I wouldn't know. I've only seen him once, from a distance. He came to Grumhul on his tour of the realms when he was crowned." Jasen remembered it only vaguely—he'd been only eight years old. He recalled thinking the king looked much too young. He was still a gawky teenager at the time, and he didn't seem very regal. In fact, he seemed terrified. "Besides," Jasen continued, "that was a long time ago. I'm sure he looks different now."

"Then frolicking in the draemir and eating strawberries does not appeal to you."

"Of course it appeals to me."

"Then why don't you want to marry him?"

"Well, it's an awful lot of responsibility, isn't it? I'm not sure I'm up for it."

"Why?"

"I grew up in Grumhul. The journey here has been the most I've ever seen of the world. I have no education to speak of, no manners, no experience in anything other than —" He was about to say in bed, but stopped himself. "Well, let's just say no experience in anything important. I can't even dress myself properly, apparently."

"I do not think any of those things would matter to the king."

"The issue is not whether or not I would want to marry him, is it?" Jasen liked the man, but he was starting to feel as if he were having a conversation with his father. "The question is whether *he* would want to marry *me*, and I doubt that very much. There hasn't been a male consort to the Lord of the Drae in over three hundred years. No, I won't marry a king. I probably won't even marry a lord. I'm not sure anyone would want me."

"That is not true. Anyone with eyes would desire you. Anyone with a heart would want to make you his. And anyone who would dismiss you because you do not conform to meaningless manners and rituals is a fool."

Jasen blinked, feeling almost dizzy at the sudden turn in the conversation. Certainly, there had been a few flirtatious moments between the two of them, but that last line had been surprisingly intense. He wasn't sure how to respond.

By that point, they had reached the palace grounds again. While Jasen was trying to think of some reply, he heard a shout. He saw several guards coming their way, moving at a swift pace. One of them was Larely. The man leading them was an older man with a bulbous red nose. Behind them trailed a well dressed man with sallow skin and a sour expression.

"That's him," he heard Larely tell the other two.

When the party reached them, they bowed deeply. "Your Majesty," the sallow- faced man said.

There was a split second when Jasen wondered why this man was calling him "your majesty" before the truth clicked. His mouth dropping open in shock.

The king made a motion for them to rise.

"I see Your Majesty has found our stray!" the red-nosed man said with forced joviality, but he looked a little frenzied. "I assure you, we are not in the business of losing consorts. I personally see to the safety of all of the consorts under my protection!"

The king waved his hand. "The fault lies with no one, Captain Ingo. The dragon called to Lord Jasen. I am certain Lady Isalei will understand."

The sallow-faced man stepped forward. "But of course, Your Majesty," he said, his voice much smoother than Jasen would expect from someone who looked like he spent all of his spare time sucking limes. "When a dragon calls, we must be attentive. I imagine that's why you yourself were unable to attend the meeting of the ministers this morning."

"Precisely so," he replied coolly. "I am sure that you were able to approve the proposed changes in the uniforms of the guards without my guidance, although if you were unable to manage it, we could meet this afternoon."

The sallow-faced man either smiled or grimaced—it was hard to tell. "I do not think that it will be necessary, although there are other matters that require your attention."

"Of course there are." The king turned to Jasen. "And now I must return to my duties, and you to yours. I have enjoyed our conversation."

Jasen stammered unintelligibly for a few moments, hoping he'd think of something to say, but his mind remained stubbornly blank. He fumbled with the clasp of the cloak. "Your cloak—you'll want it back—"

The king placed his hand over Jasen's, calming his fumbling fingers. "Keep it," he said with a smile. "You may return it when I see you again."

Jasen returned his smile, although it quickly faded when he noticed the way the other men were looking at him. Larely and the captain's eyes were widened in dumb shock, but the sallow-faced faced man's were narrowed into slits. He regarded Jasen with the expression of someone who had just found a spider in his bedchamber and was figuring out the best way to squash it.

Jasen bowed awkwardly. "Yes, Your Majesty," he said, trying his best to sound formal.

A touch of sadness came into the king's eyes at that. He and the sallow-faced man departed, leaving Jasen with the captain and Larely.

Once the king had retreated, Captain Ingo turned his gaze to Jasen. He seemed to have recovered from his surprise and now seemed quite nasty. "I see my lord has not been informed of the rules. You are not to leave the building without an escort. Ever. Do you realize how bad I would look if something were to happen to any of you?"

"Like what?"

"You could be kidnapped! Don't you realize what a ransom some rogue could get from snatching up a consort?"

He tried his best to look contrite. "I'm sorry, I didn't realize."

The captain humphed. "Well, Lady Isalei will straighten you out soon enough." He turned to Larely. "See him back to the East Wing, and make sure he stays there. I have other business to attend to."

"Yes, sir."

They set out their separate ways. When the captain was out of ear shot, Larely grinned at him. "Well, you certainly don't waste any time, do you?"

"It isn't like that! I thought he was a priest!" As soon as the words were out of his mouth, Jasen slapped a hand to his forehead. That didn't sound any better.

Larely laughed. "Might I ask why you are wearing the king's cloak?"

"I forgot mine," he mumbled.

Larely looked at him more closely. "Are you wearing anything under there?"

"A shirt and trousers, same as I wear when I'm at home," Jasen said defensively. "No one told me that I had to be dressed up for a simple walk!"

"Especially when you planned to get dirty."

"And what is *that* supposed to mean?"

Larely gestured to his trousers, which were smudged with dirt. "Your clothes."

Jasen's face grew hot. "Oh."

"Some advice—you don't have to wash behind your ears, but you ought to stay clean where people can see you. Especially people like Minister Adwig."

"That man with the horrible face?"

Larely chuckled. "That would be him. Best to stay out of his way entirely, if possible."

That sounded like good advice. Jasen certainly had no desire to see much of him.

They were now upon the East Wing, but before they got any closer, Larely pulled Jasen to the side of the road, behind a tree. "You should probably take that cloak off."

"Why?"

"If your, ah, competitors see you walk up in the king's cloak—well, we might as well paint a target on your back."

"...Target?"

"Oh, yes. It's a vicious crop this year, seeing as the king's up for grabs. Most of the consorts would give their left buttock to have a private audience with the king. If they catch on that you've already managed it, no telling what might happen."

Jasen hadn't even considered that. Numbly, he fumbled with the clasp. He felt a pang of loss as the cloak slipped from his shoulders, but he managed to hand it to Larely.

Larely undid his own cloak and handed it to Jasen. "Here

you are—you can wear mine. But next time you leave your room, make sure you're fully dressed!"

Instead of taking the cloak, Jasen leaned up against the tree. He dug the heels of his hands into his eyes.

He felt a gentle touch on his shoulder. "Here, now," Larely said, his teasing tone gone. "Are you all right?"

Jasen removed his hands. "I'm fine," he said, and tried to mean it. There were too many contradictory emotions running through him. The elation he'd felt with Tasenred had rapidly faded, leaving only embarrassment over his mistakes and confusion as to what his encounter with both the dragon and the king had meant.

"I might have overstated the danger a bit. They are just young lords and ladies, not throat-cutting assassins. No need to be frightened."

"I'm not frightened of them. I'm frightened of my own amazing capacity to make a complete fool of myself." Jasen gave his temples a vigorous rub. "How did I not know he was the king? He must think I'm an idiot."

Larely snorted. "With the way he was looking at you, I don't think 'idiot' was what was going through his head."

"That's almost worse," Jasen said with a groan. He liked the man well enough, but his kingly station was more than Jasen could handle.

Larely gave him a puzzled look, but didn't press him. "Let's get you inside." He offered the cloak to Jasen again. This time he put it on. Larely draped the king's cloak over one arm and gestured ahead of him with the other. Jasen took one last deep breath before marching toward the palace. He forced a sense confidence he didn't feel. He would walk into the East Wing as if he belonged there. No more mistakes from here on out. He would be proper. He would be well-behaved. And hopefully, the rest would work itself out.

CHAPTER 3

*J*asen and Larely entered the East Wing through the servants' entrance; Larely spirited him up to his room as discreetly as he could manage. Once he was in his room, Jasen discovered that someone had gone through his trunk and hung up all of his clothing. It was probably the work of the valet that Larely had mentioned would be sent to him, but there was no sign of the man.

A short time later, a young woman arrived with a tray of tea. There were biscuits, fresh fruit, two kinds of cheeses, and slices of thick, flavorful bread. As he ate, he began to relax. There was so much going through his head, but he did his best to mute it.

It was still several hours from orientation, so Jasen decided to take a nap. He was awoken by a knock on the door. The valet had returned. He was a serious young man by the name of Dennack, who had brought some additional clothes with him.

"What are those?" Jasen asked once he was in the room.

"I had taken the liberty of going through your wardrobe

when you were away. It appears my lord was missing a few vital articles of dress. I had heard there was an accident with your trunk. Perhaps they were lost?"

Jasen had gone through his trunk earlier and hadn't noticed anything missing. He examined of the items Dennack had brought with him, which included a jacket, shirt and breeches. "I know I have those items," he said. "They're hanging up in the closet!"

"Ah yes." Dennack seemed a little embarrassed. "I thought my lord might want to sample a few items that were a little more…modern."

And now Jasen felt embarrassed as well. He knew Grumhul tended to be a bit behind the times where fashion was concerned, but hadn't realized it was quite that bad. "Right," he muttered. "Well, let's get on with it, then."

Jasen stripped out of his shirt and trousers while Dennack arranged a few things. He was not used to being dressed. Grumhulians rarely stood on ceremony and tended to dress simply.

Once he was down to his smalls, Dennack approached him with something that took Jasen a moment to identify. "Is that a corset?"

"Yes, my lord."

"And I'm supposed to wear it." It was a stupid thing to say, but he was having a hard time wrapping his mind around the idea. Only women wore corsets in Grumhul.

"Yes, my lord." Dennack slipped it around him. Jasen allowed it—what else could he do? "My lord might want to hold onto something," Dennack said as he gathered the laces.

Jasen took a hold of the bed post as Dennack began to pull. After one overly enthusiastic tug, Jasen yelped. "Stop!" he wheezed. "I can hardly breathe!"

"My apologies, my lord."

"Loosen this immediately."

Dennack loosened the garment a little, and then a little more at Jasen's insistence. Next came the stockings, which were made of fine silk. After that was the shirt, which had more lace at the sleeves than Jasen had ever seen. It was patently ridiculous, but Jasen bore it as best he could. A beautifully embroidered waistcoat followed.

It was when they got to the breeches that they ran into trouble. As soon as they started to put them on, it became clear to Jasen that Dennack had not brought the proper size.

"I assure my lord that they are the correct size," Dennack protested. "I measured my lord's other clothing and had our dragon-blessed tailor make the adjustments—"

"Well, he made a mistake," Jasen snapped. "Obviously."

"If my lord will lie down on the bed, it will make it easier."

"I will do no such thing. I can barely move as it is! I'll wear my own breeches."

Dennack looked over at Jasen's clothing in dismay. "As my lord wishes. But then the other clothing will not match."

"Then I will just wear all of my things." He didn't care how unfashionable they were. Until he could get things to fit properly, he wasn't going to subject himself to torture.

He undressed as Dennack got his perfectly serviceable suit from the closet, which was made of a very nice brown velvet that was only a little worn in places that no one could see, really. When he was dressed, Dennack presented him with the most ridiculous pair of shoes Jasen had ever seen. They were impossibly high. "How am I supposed to walk in these?" Jasen asked.

"It takes some practice. Please, my lord."

Jasen was going to refuse them, but Dennack looked so miserable that he put them on. By the time all of this was finished, three o'clock had arrived. Dennack led Jasen down all of the complicated stairs to the first floor. A crowd of consorts were entering through the giant doors under the staircase. Dennack gave Jasen a bow and abandoned him to his fate.

Jasen followed the crowd past a long hallway. At the end were two larger doors which opened into the Great Hall. Servants circulated amongst them with trays of treats, but there was no place to sit down. At the back of the room was a platform that held the only furniture in the room—several fine chairs, on which sat a few distinguished looking older gentlemen and ladies.

As Jasen's gaze left the platform and went back around to his compatriots, he immediately regretted his choice to ignore Dennack's advice. Everyone was dressed in the highest of fashion. The women wore dresses with full, enormous skirts, which made their waists look impossibly small. The dresses were decorated with sashes of silk, ribbons, bows, beads, and even jewels. Their hairstyles were something to behold—tight, cascading curls for some, ridiculously tall hairstyles on others. Some wore wigs, while others seemed to have their natural hair, but it was all elaborately done.

As for the men, they wore fitted frockcoats that pinched in at their slim waists and flared outward into a full skirt. They had fussy lace cuffs and lace at their throats. Their breeches were, indeed, as tight as the ones Dennack had tried to persuade him to wear. Bows were tied at the knees of some. The men's hair was somewhat more subdued, although there were still wigs and curls here and there. Their shoes were heeled, some even higher than his own.

Absolutely none of them wore anything remotely in the style of Jasen's own clothing. It appeared that he wasn't the only one to notice how sorely he stood out. People were sneaking looks at him out of the corners of their eyes. Everyone seemed to have hand fans, which they would open as Jasen passed by in order to hide their faces and murmur to each other. He heard a few snickers. He tried to tell himself he didn't care, but it wasn't working very well. He wished he had a fan for himself so that he could hide his face at least.

He was trying to duck away from a particularly mean-looking crowd when he stumbled. He would have fallen to the ground, but instead he crashed into someone. A strong, feminine arm caught him and helped him regain his balance.

"I am so sorry!" he stammered. He looked up, expecting to see a sneering face, but the expression on the lady's face was more amused than anything else.

"No trouble," she said. "I'm sturdy."

And she was. She was tall for a lady—much taller than Jasen. She had a strong jaw and dark hair that was done up in a style so elaborate that he wasn't sure how the whole thing was possible. Her dark eyes sparkled with good humor.

"Thank you," he said.

"These shoes take a bit of getting used to. I was so terrible at walking in them as a girl that my governess didn't let me take them off at all for two whole months."

"Why do they insist on them?"

"I think it's because it makes it harder for you to run away if amorous suitors set their sights on you. It doesn't work, though—I can run faster in these things than most nobles can run at all."

"That's terrible," Jasen said. "About making it so you can't run."

"Welcome to courtly fashion."

"I wouldn't welcome me quite yet," he mumbled, gazing down at his own clothes.

She laughed. "You're Lord Jasen, aren't you?"

Jasen rubbed the back of his neck. "My reputation precedes me, I take it."

"Oh yes. Your entrance last night has been all that anyone can talk about."

"I was hoping that would escape notice."

"Nothing escapes notice around here. Speaking of which —is it true that you went into a trance, ran naked into the draemir and fell into a swoon in front of a dragon, and then the king had to carry you back draped in his Drae's cloak?"

"I wasn't naked!" Jasen protested. "And I didn't swoon!"

The lady let out a delighted gasp. "So it is true!"

Jasen was saved from having to answer by the blast of a trumpet. Everyone fell silent at once. After a brief fanfare, a short old woman in simple but elegant clothes mounted the platform, walking in front of the seated elders until she was front and center. Her mouth was a firm, thin line, and her dark gaze was as sharp as a dagger.

"Presenting the Lady Isalei!" the trumpet blower announced.

Everyone applauded enthusiastically. Once the applause had died down, the lady spoke. "My lords and ladies," she said in a deep, clear voice, "I am happy once again to greet you, and trust you have settled in."

There was a murmur of *Yes, my lady* from the crowd.

"I am pleased to hear it," she said. Her mouth did something—widened a little, turned up at the corners. Jasen thought it might be a smile. "You all come from the finest families in the Allied Realms. You have received the best training at the most prestigious schools. And truly, you are a fine-looking lot. Young. Beautiful. Fashionable."

There was a pause. Her mouth snapped back to its previous shape. "Well, I am here to tell you that none of that is good enough. You may have been the jewels of your little

realms and provinces, but this is Strengsend—the most spectacular palace the world has ever seen, and you are all as
temporary and unimportant as a daisy in the Bedrose
Gardens. It is true that you are new blooms, but blooms fade
—more quickly than any of you realize.

"And so, we have very little time to shape you into something less flimsy than a flower. The suitors arrive in two
months. They are expecting to be charmed, dazzled,
impressed. And they are looking for more than a pretty face.
A pretty face they could get at any of the finer brothels. No.
You are to be *consorts*. Those are positions of great responsibility, and I expect each and every one of you to take this
matter very, very seriously. The entire course of your life is
to be determined in these next few months. I will not be easy
on you, but in the end, you will thank me. No matter how
polished you think you are, I promise you, you still
need work."

"Some of us more than others."

Jasen turned his head to see who had spoken. It was a
pretty blonde girl at the center of that mean-looking crowd
he'd been avoiding. Their eyes were all on Jasen. There was a
smattering of laughter.

"Princess Polina," Lady Isalei said. "How nice to see you
again. This is your third year with us, yes?"

The blonde girl flushed and covered her face with her fan.

"When I ask a question, I expect an answer," Lady Isalei
said.

"Yes, my lady," she squeaked.

"Hm. Even the loveliest flower won't carry on for *four*
seasons. Something to think on before you make disparaging
remarks about others."

"Yes, my lady." As soon as Lady Isalei looked away,
Princess Polina shot Jasen a venomous glare, as if the
scolding she received was somehow his fault.

"We will now begin our assessments of your strengths and deficiencies." She gestured to the elders behind her. "This is my council. They are here out of the goodness of their own hearts in order to help you achieve what they have achieved. You will not disrespect them by telling them lies. Answer our questions honestly so that we can get you into the best position possible. The potential for failure is great—but the rewards of success are even greater. Once you have been evaluated, you may take your leave."

With that, the venerated ladies and gentlemen filed off the platform. Behind each of them floated a scroll and a quill.

"Lady Isalei likes to make herself seem more terrible than she really is," Jasen's companion said. He jumped at her voice. She laughed, but not unkindly. "You see? She's in your head already. Relax. It's not as dire as she makes it out. She acts like the nobles who come here looking for marriage are some god-like beings with lofty standards. Actually, most of them really *are* looking for a pretty face."

"Why all of this, then?"

"Because no one wants to admit that picking out a consort and picking out a whore are basically the same thing. That would make many noble families pimps, and we couldn't have that, could we?"

Jasen, as a Grumhulian, was not easily scandalized, but even he was shocked at her bluntness. "What's your name?" he asked her.

"I'm—"

"Lady Risyda," finished a stern voice from behind them. They whipped around to see Lady Isalei, her paper and quill floating behind her.

Lady Risyda curtsied. "Yes, my lady." If she was nervous that her last statement had been overheard, she didn't show it. "It's a pleasure to see you again."

"You know I detest lies," she said, but there was the

smallest hint of a smile at the corner of her lips. "I assume you still possess the many faults you exhibited at Court last year?"

"Oh yes," she said cheerfully. "In abundance."

Lady Isalei humphed. "Have you worked on expanding your magical talents?"

Lady Risyda nodded. A look of concentration came over her face. She thumped herself three times on the chest and opened her mouth. A small puff of smoke in the shape of a heart emerged from her lips.

"Clever," Lady Isalei said dryly. "I'm sure that will command the respect of your servants once you are head of a household."

"I can make it in the shape of a riding crop," she said. "Or maybe a dismissal with no references, although that might be a little abstract."

Lady Isalei sighed. The quill scraped on the page. "Your dress and bearing seem much improved this year. How is your archery?"

"Splendid. I won first prize at the Enoquan Archery Tournament last summer."

"Good, good. And your languages?"

Risyda made a long, incomprehensible reply that was to Lady Isalei's satisfaction. "And what about your licentious habits and poor attitude?"

"I've kept up with those as well, my lady."

"I know you think you're clever, and it's true you can be amusing. That's a fine quality to have. But if you are not careful, you are going to amuse yourself into a grim situation. This is your third year. You must make a match, or resign yourself for spinsterhood in your father's home. Which is it to be?"

Lady Risyda didn't answer right away. "I could always become a draedess?"

Lady Isalei snorted. She turned her terrifying attention to Jasen. "And you must be Lord Jasen."

Jasen bowed. "Yes, my lady." He hoped he didn't sound too stilted.

"Of Grumhul." She said it as if she had the same opinion of his homeland that Jasen had.

"Yes, my lady," he mumbled.

"That means you were educated at Rodkiner Academy, yes? That's the nearest, I think."

"Ah, no."

"Verar, then."

"No, my lady. I was educated at home." Which was partially true. He'd had tutors until he was twelve. Then his mother had died, and his father found better things to spend his money on.

"I see." She looked him up and down. "Hair, face and figure are good, although a complete new wardrobe is needed," she muttered to the floating quill, which scratched away on the parchment floating beside it. "Have you any special talents?" she asked, addressing Jasen again.

"Talents?"

"Perhaps you possess some magical ability."

"No."

"Athletic skills?"

"I'm good at mudball."

It took a moment for her to absorb that information. "Mudball is not quite what I had in mind. I mean something of a more sophisticated activity, such as riding, archery, or fencing."

"Oh. Then no, not really."

"Perhaps you are well-read and can converse on many interesting subjects."

"No." With every no, Jasen's voice got smaller and smaller.

"Musical aptitude? Painting? Dance, perhaps?"

Jasen shook his head to each one.

Lady Isalei pinched the bridge of her nose. "And how, then, did you make your way to us?"

"Someone lost a bet." Which was true. His father, in a rare instance of good luck, had beat one of the royal recruiters in a game of cards. The man had no money left, so he'd given him a place for Jasen at Court.

"A bet," the lady echoed. The quill quivered beside her expectantly. "Make sure his breeches are extra tight," she told it. The quill obediently scratched that down. "That will do for a start," she said to Jasen. "I would like to meet with you privately later on. You have a lot of catching up to do. I would also like to discuss some rumors I've heard."

Jasen felt a lump in his stomach. "Yes, my lady."

She nodded to both Risyda and Jasen. Jasen stared miserably at his horrible shoes. He was startled out of his self-pity when Risyda whacked him with her fan. "Bow," she said out of the corner of her mouth as she curtsied. Jasen did so with such force that he nearly toppled over. Risyda thrust a hand out and steadied him. When Jasen looked up, he saw Lady Isalei's lips curl up ever so slightly. "Good afternoon to you both," she said.

Jasen thought the torment was over, but Lady Isalei had not walked three steps when she was confronted with the blonde princess from earlier. "My lady," she said, curtsying. "I must apologize to you for my unseemly outburst. I don't know what came over me. The heat of the room, perhaps. It's making me dizzy—I am not myself!"

"Of course, Princess," Lady Isalei said coolly. "Perhaps you should apologize to Lord Jasen."

"Oh, yes, of course," she said. She curtsied in his direction. "My deepest apologies."

"Ah—thank you." Jasen hoped that was the right thing to say.

Lady Isalei nodded. "I'm sure I will hear no more of trouble between you—any of you," she said with a pointed look as Risyda.

"Yes, my lady," they all said in unison. The Lady Isalei nodded again and left.

Jasen glanced back over at the princess. He couldn't figure out why she was baring her teeth at him; then he realized it was probably meant to be a smile. "Silly me," she said. "We aren't even properly acquainted. I am Polina, princess of the realm of Intasnia."

"Fifth princess," Risyda said. "That is the proper address for your people, right, Polly? Because you have four older sisters. Older, successful sisters."

Even more of Polina's teeth became visible. "Yes, Lady Risyda, you are correct."

"Polly and I studied at Enoqua Academy together," Risyda continued.

"Yes, we are old friends," Polina said to Jasen. "And I so hope that you and I can be friends as well!"

"Of course."

"Well! So pleased we could have this little chat, but I must be off."

"Always a pleasure, Polly!" Risyda said. "Don't trip on your gown on your way across the room, like you did last year!"

The princess opened her fan with such force that it sounded like the crack of a whip and sauntered off across the room.

"I love winding her up," Risyda said with a grin. "No one spins quite as spectacularly as the princess if you do it just right." Before Jasen could respond to that, she took him by the arm. "And now that we've been evaluated, we are free to go, so you're coming up to my room."

"I— That is to say," Jasen stammered. "I'm flattered, but I don't think—"

She whacked him with her fan. "Not in that way. I need to hear every single detail of what happened this morning, and you are going to tell me."

Jasen wanted to protest, but he realized that it was probably futile. She was remarkably strong. Besides, he could not wait to get away from the crowd, and he didn't relish sitting in his room alone.

~

RISYDA'S ROOM was a bit larger than Jasen's own. In addition to the small table with two chairs that Jasen had in his room, there was also a lounging sofa.

The first thing Risyda did was sit down on the sofa and kick off her shoes. Jasen followed suit, taking one of the chairs.

She wiggled her toes. "The one nice thing about those blasted shoes is that they feel so good to take off."

Jasen made a sound of agreement and rubbed his foot. He already had a blister.

"Now if only I could undo my hair. And my corset. Not 'til the end of the day, sadly." She sighed. "Oh well." She gave Jasen a mischievous look that he was already growing accustomed to. "I do have something that will ease our discomfort a little."

She went over to her bed, got onto her knees, and pulled out a box from underneath it. She brought it back to the sofa and opened it. Inside was something that looked like a bottle, along with some long tubes. She screwed the tubes onto the bottle and set it on the floor.

"What is that?" Jasen asked.

"A hookah," she said. She pulled out a small pouch. "And this is kara weed. Have you ever tried it?"

"I've never even heard of it."

"You really are a rube, aren't you?"

Jasen didn't take offense. After all, he was.

"You're going to love it," she said, packing the contents of the purse into the contraption. She concentrated for a moment; a burst of flame sprang out of her finger and lit the weed. She sucked one of the tubes, inhaling the smoke. With a contented sigh, she lay back on the sofa as she exhaled the smoke through her nose. "Mmmm. Now that is much better." She offered one of the tubes to Jasen. "Your turn."

Jasen took the tube. "Could we get in trouble for this?"

"Don't tell me the man who sneaked out of his room to go frolicking with dragons is worried about a little kara weed."

She had a point. Jasen sucked in some of the smoke, and then fell into a coughing spasm.

Risyda got up and patted him on the back until it was over. "I probably should have given you a little more instruction. Here, like this..."

A few puffs later, Jasen got a handle on it. He felt wonderful all over. He'd never cared for wine or spirits, which always left him dizzy and sick. This, however, was just a comfortable buzzing feeling. He found himself sliding to the floor.

"Well? How do you like it?"

"I feel like I'm covered in bees," Jasen said. "Nice bees. Bees that feel good."

Risyda laughed. "See? I told you." She inhaled another puff and let it out in a few perfect rings. "All right, let's get the getting-to-know-you bits over with. This is me: rich merchant father, I'm the youngest daughter, we don't like each other, et cetera. He has been training me my whole life to fetch a good marriage price. I can't decide whether I want to marry so I can escape him or screw him out of the gold he so desperately wants. Now you."

"Dead mother, drunk and gambling- addicted father. Same sort of deal with the marriage."

She beamed. "I just knew we would have a lot in common." She rested her chin on her hand. "Now, to more interesting matters. Just what exactly happened this morning with you and the king?"

Jasen only hesitated for a moment before the whole thing came spilling out. He knew he should be more cautious over whom he trusted, but the kara weed made him feel so relaxed and he desperately needed to sort through what happened. When he was finished, Risyda puffed thoughtfully on her pipe for a few moments. "You're going to marry the king," she finally said.

Jasen groaned and fell back on the ground, one arm flung over his face. "I don't want to marry a king!"

"Why not?"

"I don't know anything about…well, anything! And to be king consort? To have the entire fate of the magic of the Allied Realms resting on whether or not I'm properly supportive? That's a nightmare, not a dream come true."

"But what can you do? He's already decided he wants you."

"You don't know that. You *can't* know that."

She waved her hand. "Of course I can. I have spent my whole life training to catch a suitor. I know the signs."

Jasen sat up and took a few morose puffs until he felt a little better. "What am I going to do?"

"You're going to have to make yourself utterly repulsive. Fortunately, I'm an expert on that as well."

Jasen frowned. "I don't want to be repulsive to him."

"Oh, no. Don't tell me you like him?" Jasen just gave her a

miserable look. She took a few more contemplative puffs. "Well. This is all deliciously complicated."

Their conversation was interrupted by a knock of a strange rhythm on the door. Jasen sat straight up, the pleasant buzzing feeling rapidly fading in panic. "Quick! Get that thing back in the box—"

Risyda waved her hand as she stood up. "Don't worry, it's fine." She weaved her way to the door and opened it a crack. "Hello!" she said cheerfully.

"Fucking hell, Risyda, I can smell you all the way down the hallway!" said a familiar voice. "I know you can control it, so why aren't you?" The door opened a little more, revealing Larely.

"Sorry," Risyda said. She waved her hand. The smoke swirled into a ball in the middle of the room. Another wave and it disappeared with a small pop. "Better?"

"Yes, but it isn't even dark yet. Can't you wait until everyone's asleep at the very least?"

"You worry too much. Everyone's still at orientation."

"Just the same, you could really get into…" He trailed off when he finally saw Jasen. "Oh no. The two of you are friends now?" He put a hand over his face and groaned. "My life is about to get exponentially more difficult, isn't it?"

Risyda batted her eyelashes. "Do you want to come in?"

Larely looked over his shoulder and then slipped in the door, shutting it behind him. "Just for a moment." He crossed his arms as he looked down at Jasen, who was still sprawled on the floor. "Haven't you already been in enough trouble today?"

"Don't let him lecture you about trouble," Risyda said. "He is a very naughty guard."

This struck Jasen as the height of hilarity. He tried and failed to suppress a surge of unmanly giggles. Risyda joined him.

"Oh, shut up, both of you," Larely said, but it was good-natured. He grabbed one of the hoses and took a quick puff.

"Keep it to—" he started, but had to stop as a coughing fit overcame him. That made Jasen laugh harder. "Keep it to night from now on," he finished after he got a hold of himself.

Risyda saluted. "Aye-aye, captain."

"I mean it," Larely said. "You could get sent home."

"We'll be good, I promise," Jasen said.

Larely scoffed. "Oh, I doubt that very much, but try not to get caught."

"Keep clean where they can see me," Jasen said, echoing Larely's earlier words. "Got it."

"At your service, as always," Larely said with an overly lavish bow. He winked at Risyda, which was interesting. Jasen had thought that Larely had been flirting with him earlier, but maybe he'd misjudged the situation. The two of them seemed awfully close.

"I should go," Jasen said, pushing himself off the floor. "I actually don't want to go back to Grumhul just yet." He fumbled for his shoes. It took him a few moments to get his balance when he stood.

Risyda helped steady him. "Are you sure you can get to your room all right?"

"'m fine," Jasen muttered. And he was, mostly.

But when he left her room, he almost immediately lost his sense of direction. He ended up going down when he should have gone up, and left when he should have gone right, and after wandering around for a little while, he realized he was hopelessly lost. The pleasant buzzing feeling had transformed into a raging headache.

He found a staircase and managed to get back up to the second floor, but only after nearly breaking his neck falling down. The thought of having to go up yet another set of stairs was too daunting to consider. He was just considering trying to make his way back to Risyda's room, possibly on his hands and knees, when he turned a corner and ran straight into Larely. Jasen stumbled and would have fallen, but Larely caught him. "Steady now," he said, helping him regain his footing.

"I hate these shoes," Jasen said passionately. "And all these stairs. Why are there so many? And these halls. And all these doors that look alike."

"You're lost, aren't you?"

"A little."

"Then I'll show you back," Larely said, linking his arm with Jasen's. Jasen was grateful for the support.

They reached Jasen's room. "Here you are. Again." Larely grinned at him. "This is the third time in twenty-four hours I've shown you to your room. Do you think it will stick this time?"

"I would say yes, but I really can't be sure."

Larely laughed. "That's fine. I don't mind rescuing you."

"*Rescuing* me?" Jasen scoffed. "Well, I wouldn't quite put it like that."

"Whatever you say, my lord," Larely said with an ironic little bow.

Jasen muttered his thanks and stepped through the door. Once inside, he took off his shoes and lay down face first on his bed. He rolled over eventually and rubbed his face vigorously. A thousand thoughts swirled in his head. He had thought that he wanted to be away from Grumhul and his father more than anything else, but this was turning out to be far more complicated than he had anticipated. He was barely sure he wanted to be a lord consort at all, let alone king consort.

At the same time, the king had been so handsome, and so

kind. Nothing like he expected. Even thinking of him now made his heart beat a little faster.

Eventually, he got up and splashed his face with some water, trying to banish the last of the kara weed's effects. He would be expected to dine in the dining hall tonight. The thought of facing all of the consorts again made him queasy, but at least he had Risyda now. He decided to try to put aside his larger doubts and just make it through the evening intact. He could worry about the rest of it tomorrow.

CHAPTER 4

*E*arly the next morning, Jasen was awoken by a knock on the door. Though he was an early riser, even he hadn't gotten out of bed yet; the sun was barely up. Groggily, Jasen pulled on his dressing gown and answered the door. An impeccably dressed servant stood before him. He was an older man, with large cheeks and bulging eyes that made Jasen think of a toad.

He gave Jasen a small bow. "Good morning, my lord. I am Rotheld, and I shall be your valet for the remainder of your stay."

"What happened to Dennack?"

"Lady Isalei determined he was not up for the challenge."

"Oh," Jasen said faintly.

The man stepped inside, brushing past Jasen. He snapped his fingers—a whole rack of clothing followed him. "Would my lord like to begin dressing for his morning appointments now?"

"Now?" Jasen said. "But the sun is barely up!"

Rotheld took a deep breath and let it out through puffed cheeks. "To dress properly takes time, my lord."

There was something about Rotheld that told Jasen arguing with him would be futile. "Of course," Jasen mumbled.

They started with a shave, which was actually rather relaxing. When they were finished, Rotheld searched through the rack of clothing, occasionally looking at Jasen as if he were an interesting problem to solve. He at last selected a deep emerald green suit. "I think this will do."

Jasen had to admit that the clothes looked good (although apparently his opinion didn't count for much since Rotheld didn't ask for it). He went behind the dressing screen to change out of his night shirt and into his smalls. When he was finished, he went back to Rotheld, who was holding the dreaded corset. "Is that really necessary?" he asked.

"A trim waist, a straight back, and strong shoulders are the ideal form of masculine beauty."

Jasen wanted to point out that his waist was already trim, but realized that it was probably futile. He subjected himself to the lacing. Fortunately, Rotheld was gentler than Dennack had been. It was still uncomfortable.

Next, Rotheld helped him into a white shirt. "I like this," Jasen said once he had it on. "Much less lace on the cuffs than what Dennack tried on me yesterday."

"My lord has a natural beauty," Rotheld said. "I think items of a more subdued style would be appropriate."

The stockings went on next, and then the breeches. It took five full minutes to squeeze him into them. While Rotheld was lacing them up in the back, Jasen had a thought. "How am I supposed to relieve myself in these?"

"With assistance."

The waistcoat and jacket were easy compared to the rest. Rotheld added a cravat of lace around his neck. Rotheld bade him to take a seat. He got out a brush from a kit he'd brought with him and ran it through Jasen's hair. Jasen was nervous about what he was planning to do with it, given the elaborate styles he'd seen yesterday, but after some thought, Rotheld merely tied it at the base of his neck with a simple ribbon.

Last were the hated shoes. He helped him up and steadied him when he wobbled. "We shall practice your walk later," Rotheld said.

"We shall?" Jasen asked with a sinking heart.

"We shall," Rotheld repeated firmly. He gave Jasen a gentle push towards the mirror. "Go see yourself," he said, his tone somewhat softer.

Jasen teetered over to the mirror and was stunned by what he saw. Gone was the unkempt boy from Grumhul. In his place stood a polished, beautiful young lord consort. He could barely believe it was him. For a moment, he didn't feel like an impostor.

Rotheld stepped behind him. "Is my lord satisfied?"

"Yes."

He handed him a fan, which fastened around his wrist. "Then it is time for your meeting with Lady Isalei."

"What, already?" His stomach did a flip. He took one last look at himself, trying to glean some confidence from the handsome young lord in the mirror. He wasn't sure if it worked.

They walked down to the main floor, where they went under the stairs and down the hall, stopping at the last door on the right. Rotheld led him inside, bowed, and took his leave. The room was a cozy parlor. There was refreshments set out for two. Jasen wasn't sure what he had been expecting, but this wasn't it. He felt as if he were there to catch up with a doting aunt rather than endure an interrogation.

The lady herself wasn't there, but she arrived shortly after. Jasen rose when she entered. "My lady," he said, bowing.

"Good morning, Lord Jasen," she said with a nod. "I trust you slept well?"

"Yes, my lady."

They took their seats. Jasen dredged up some ancient memories of etiquette and poured out the tea, as was expected of the younger person in a private setting. "So you do have some manners," she said. "I'm certainly glad to see it."

"Yes, my lady." He was too nauseated to drink himself, so he fiddled with his fan under the table.

She took a sip of tea. "If you grip that fan any tighter, it's going to break."

Jasen hastily released the fan. "Yes, my lady."

She waved a hand. "Let's dispense with the yes-my-ladys for the time being. You needn't be so nervous. I'm here to help you. You are not the first young consort who was rough around the edges. Tell me the education you do have, and we'll work from there."

"I had tutors in reading and religion, as well as courtly manners," he said. She raised an eyebrow. "Until I was twelve," he finished. "My mother died, and my father was somewhat lax in continuing my education."

"I see," she said. "And you've had nothing since then?"

He shook his head.

She sighed. "Well, it's a challenge, but I've worked with rougher. Let's have a spot to eat before we continue, shall we?"

Jasen thought he was too nauseated to eat, but he discovered that a few biscuits and a cup of tea helped settle him.

"Now, then," the lady said when they were finished. "I am going to ask you a few questions, and you must answer me with complete honesty. If you are not honest with me, I will have you on a carriage back to Grumhul before you have time to blink. Am I understood?"

The lump in Jasen's throat felt too great to speak, so he simply nodded.

"Were you really called by a dragon yesterday morning?"

"Yes, my lady. I had decided to take a walk in the gardens, but before I knew it, I found myself in the draemir. Tasenred was waiting for me."

"And then you met the king."

"Yes, my lady." He paused, and then the rest came tumbling out. "But I didn't know who he was at first, truly! I would have never spoken s-so carelessly to him if I had known. And it really isn't uncommon for men of noble birth to dress simply in Grumhul—I didn't know I'd be considered half-naked!"

The lady blinked at him in an expression Jasen couldn't quite pinpoint. "Well, Lord Jasen, you are either the most naive consort I've ever seen, or the cleverest. The king has already requested to see you."

"Oh."

"'*Oh?*' You have netted the largest, most sought after prize of the entire Court with barely any effort, and that's all you have to say?"

Jasen felt a surge of irritation at that word—*prize*. As if all of this were just a game, and none of them were people. "It wasn't 'barely' any effort," Jasen said. "It was no effort at all. I didn't set out to seduce the king. I went for a walk. I had a conversation with someone I met. That's all."

"I see," she said. "Am I to take it that the king's attention is not welcome?"

Jasen didn't know what to say. He felt like he was being asked to make a decision that would affect the rest of his life, and he simply wasn't prepared for that. He clasped at the fan again, gripping it so tightly his hand hurt. "I did not say that," he finally said.

The lady considered him for a moment. "I was going to

impress upon you that the role of king consort is not one to be taken lightly, but it seems to me that is something you don't need to be told."

"No, my lady," he said miserably.

"There is so much that rests on the shoulders of the king consort. It is not only the king's desires that matter. The fact that you are male is going to concern many people. The fact that you have no experience in courtly politics will concern even more." Lady Isalei's gaze shifted from Jasen to her tea cup. When she spoke again, it was more as if she were thinking out loud. "And then there's the Grummish angle. Goodness, what a mess."

At that, Jasen felt a rush of heat warm enough to melt away his timidity. "What does my nationality have to do with anything?"

She turned her attention back to him, seeming a little startled. "Grumhul is the only Allied Realm without dragons. Surely you can understand that there will be some skepticism that a marriage to a Grumhulian will rekindle the connection with the dragons."

The flame in Jasen grew. "Grumhul may not have dragons, but we are hard-working, honest people. And being from Grumhul is not my fault—nor is my inexperience or being male, for that matter! All I know is that a dragon called me, and a king found me. I don't know what it all means. The only thing I'm sure of is that it's as big of a mess for me as it is for you."

Lady Isalei leveled a cool gaze at him. Jasen's brief flame of courage was extinguished.

"F-forgive me, my lady," he stammered. "I don't know what came over me."

She returned her attention to her tea, which she drank with agonizing slowness. "You are a curious person, Lord Jasen," she said at last. "I feel I may have misjudged you."

"I don't think so, my lady," Jasen muttered.

"Are you quite certain that you want to question my judgment further?"

Jasen stomach dropped. "Oh! No, my lady! That's isn't what I— What I mean to say is that I—" He stammered some more, but found that he did not have an end for that particular sentence. He felt as if he were falling down a cliff; every time he thought it was over, the ground crumbled on him and he was sent tumbling once more.

Then the lady did something strange—she smiled at him. "I believe what you mean to say is that you trust my judgment in matters of the Court. In return, I will trust your judgment in the matters of your heart, which in my estimation is a good one. I think that we should be allies, don't you?"

"Allies?" he echoed. "You approve of me?"

She took a sip of her tea before replying. "Many of the king's other advisers are pushing for a more conventional choice—that is to say, a young lady from a prominent, dragon-blessed family. But I am of the opinion that the king's heart is the most important matter to consider. So, are we allies, then?"

"Yes, of course!" Jasen said quickly.

"Good. Our first priority will be to improve your etiquette. The rest of the lords and ladies have had years of training; their time here in the next two months is meant only to polish their skills. You, however, are going to have to have more extensive instruction. I will arrange for you to meet with private tutors."

"I will do my best to catch up."

The lady shook her head. "No. You will not 'do your best.' You will simply *do*. Have some confidence in yourself. A dragon did call you, after all, and you clearly have some fire in you. That's not a bad quality to have. It just needs to be refined."

She was right. Jasen straightened his spine. "Yes, my lady." He paused before he spoke again, but hadn't she just given him permission to be bolder? "And when I am caught up, I will see the king again?"

She smiled again. "Not right away. Generally speaking, courtships don't start until after the suitors arrive, although since the king himself is a suitor, that has...*complicated* things. There are certain personages—" and here she grimaced a little— "who wish for the king to start courting right away and make his choice as soon as possible, but I have advised the king to refrain from courting any consort for at least a month so that everyone can get properly settled. And since we are allies now, I think you will agree that you should put your best foot forward, which means we wait until I deem you ready. You may have made an impression on the king, but he isn't the only one you need to impress."

"What do you mean?"

"The king has the right to select his spouse, but his council must approve of the match. It would behoove you to give them no cause for complaint."

People like Minister Adwig, Jasen thought, but didn't say.

Lady Isalei rose. Jasen got to his feet as well, grateful that the interview was almost over.

"You may go refresh yourself now. Your first lesson starts in one hour. You will be meeting with Lady Toran, who will instruct you in the finer points of courtly manners. Rotheld will escort you to her."

Jasen bowed. "Thank you, my lady."

As Jasen returned to his room, he tried to sort through his emotions. Half of him wished fiercely to be back in the swamps of Grumhul, where nothing was expected of him. But the other half of him... Well, as Lady Isalei herself had just said, he was called by a dragon. He could *feel* it, like a flame in his heart. Even as a Grumhulian, he knew that that wasn't something you could just turn your back on. He would nurture that flame and see what it illuminated.

~

THE NEXT FOUR weeks passed by in a blur. There was not a single moment of Jasen's day that was not structured. He awoke at dawn to begin the long process of dressing and grooming, after which he met with Lady Toran for two hours to drill him on his etiquette. He had a brief break before music lessons, which he attended with several other lords and ladies. He'd never picked up a musical instrument in his life and couldn't begin to guess why this was a skill deemed important. After that was a quick luncheon, and then dance lessons, followed by diction, discourse and literature. He was equally inept at all of them.

Dinner afforded him a longer break, but it was not exactly a restful experience. Word of the king's interest in him had spread like wildfire, and just as Larely had predicted, it made him exceedingly unpopular. Princess Polina seemed especially put out. Jasen wasn't sure how to handle it all. He wasn't used to having to impress.

After dinner, he received more private tutoring, and then rounded off the night with "leisure" time, which was not actually leisure because consorts were expected to practice conversation during that time, or read aloud to one another from classic works of drama and poetry, or work on their needlepoint, or practice their dance, or any of the other dozen little ways in which proper consorts were supposed to amuse themselves and their suitors.

Finally, at nine in the evening, he was permitted to retire. Only he didn't, most nights. He waited for Rotheld to leave him, and then he would sneak to Risyda's room. Sometimes it was just the two of them, but occasionally, Larely would join them. Larely was an invaluable coconspirator—he always made sure their less savory pursuits went undetected.

He wasn't used to this much activity. In Grumhul, days passed by lazily with little happening. Here, every moment was bustling, as if there couldn't possibly be enough hours in the day to get everything done. The fact that it was all so senseless and shallow made the urgent nature of it surreal. If Jasen had even a minute to think about it, he might have rebelled, but there was no time to stop and consider anything. Perhaps that was the point.

But through it all, that little flame still burned in him. All these useless rituals seemed like strange fuel for that fire, but he tried to trust Lady Isalei. If she said this frivolity would light his path back to the king and the dragon, then he would submit to it, although at times he felt like it was extinguishing the fire rather than feeding it. But then he would remember the feeling of Tasenred's scales against his skin, and the feel of the king's heated gaze. He would grit his teeth and dive back in.

At last, the first month of training was over. Jasen waited eagerly for the king's invitation, but it didn't come. He didn't even receive a visit from Lady Isalei—surely she would want to see his progress? Unless his tutors had reported that he was a hopeless case. He tried to push that thought out of his mind and hold on to hope.

On the fifth week, however, that hope was abruptly shattered. He could even pinpoint the exact moment that it happened. It was during their evening socializing period. He and Risyda were in the Swan Parlor, pretending to read. Across the room were Princess Polina and a few of her cohorts. Jasen tried not to listen to them, but the inanity of their chatter was too annoying to ignore.

"I had another prophetic dream last night," Polina was saying.

Lord Banither, one of Polina's most ardent toadies, gasped. "Another one, Princess? You must tell us what it is!"

"I am lying in a field," she said. "The sky darkens—there is something passing above me..."

Lady Lalan, a dark-haired beauty from Westrona, put a hand to her breast. "A dragon, do you think?" she breathed.

"Yes," Polina said dramatically. "It was the same dragon that gave me the gift of prophecy when I was but a child. She lowered her noble head and looked into my eyes, and then suddenly I felt something on my brow—something heavy, but I couldn't see what it was..."

"A crown!" Banither said.

Polina fluttered her fan. "Oh, do you really think so?"

Risyda let out a snort of laughter. Polina glared over in their direction.

"It looks like it will rain tonight," Polina said loudly. "I certainly don't care for this unseasonably cold weather! Although I imagine it must be a comfort for you, Lord Jasen, as I hear it rains often in Grumhul. Tell me—is it true that your people bring their livestock into their homes when it rains?"

"Only when there might be mudslides," he mumbled.

Polina and her friends tittered.

"Why do you think that's so unusual, Polly?" Risyda said. "Don't you keep animals in your homes, too?"

"Animals in our castle? How ridiculous!"

"You were just regaling us earlier with stories of all your precious little doggies. You know, those fluffy little things that are always yapping and nipping at people's ankles. It's so cute the way they think they're threatening."

"That's different," she snapped.

"Even useless animals are still animals," Risyda said.

SERA TREVOR

Polina waved her fan so quickly that it was a blur. Risyda and Jasen shared a grin.

Silence descended upon the room. Polina's friends tentatively began to chatter again, but the foul mood of their leader made their talk strained. Eventually, Polina stood up and yawned dramatically. "Dear me, I am tired this evening. Perhaps I should retire early. After all, I want to look my best for my audience with the king tomorrow."

Jasen whipped his head up. Polina gave him a sly look out of the corner of her eye, but continued to address her friends. "Minister Adwig says that I am the exact image of the late queen consort."

Something inside him snapped. Tears pricked his eyes. Since he had no intention of letting Polina see how hurt he was, Jasen put his book down on a chair and left, heading back to his own room. For once he was glad of all the stairs— he imagined each stair was Polina's face. He was halfway up the first flight of stairs when Risyda caught up with him.

"You shouldn't let her bother you," she said. "The fact that the king is seeing her doesn't necessarily mean anything."

"I don't care."

"Right," Risyda said. "That's why your face is bright red and you're stomping up these stairs."

"Lady Isalei said that she supports me, and yet Polina of all people is meeting him before I do. Why?"

Risyda bit her lip. "Lady Isalei just wants you to make the best impression possible."

"Or maybe she's changed her mind." He couldn't believe he'd been naive enough to believe that Lady Isalei was truly his "ally." Of course she would prefer that the king settle with a princess. How could he have been so stupid? Then a worse thought came to him. "Or perhaps the king's mind is the one that changed," he said quietly. He resumed his march up the stairs.

Risyda followed him. "Well, maybe that's a relief," she said carefully. "You said you weren't sure you wanted to be king consort, didn't you?"

The flame in his heart flared at that, but he tempered it. "You're right, I don't. And I don't want to be here at all. I will never be any good at this! I might as well give up now. I'm going to arrange for a carriage tomorrow to go to my uncle's. My father can think of some other way to pay off his debts. Maybe he'd like to come here and win himself a rich spouse!"

Risyda put a hand on his shoulder. "Before we start sending for carriages, why don't we go back to my room and relax for a little bit."

Jasen let her lead him back to her room. She pulled out her hookah and let Jasen take a big puff. Some of his tension left. He lay on his back on the floor and stared at the smoke that swirled around them. The thing he liked best about kara weed was that it made anything other than the moment he was in seem unimportant. Risyda took her own puff and then spread out on the sofa, lying with her head hanging backwards off the edge.

Eventually, Jasen asked, "Is she really dragon-blessed with premonition?"

Risyda snorted. "Of course not. Premonition is the one dragon blessing that a person can claim without any proof. Most people who claim to have it are frauds."

Jasen watched Risyda puff different shapes of smoke out of her mouth for another few hazy moments. "What does it feel like to be dragon-blessed?"

"Do you mean in general or when it happened?"

"Both."

Risyda took a few moments to answer. "I don't know how to describe it. I was awfully young at the time—only six years old. The draeds took me to the draemir along with a few other children. We prayed for a while, but it didn't seem like any dragons were going to come. We were about to leave when she came—a small, green dragon. I felt a warmth like nothing else— it seemed to come from inside me. The draeds brought us up to the dragon and we all touched her. I felt a spark."

"And then you had your powers?"

"Not at first. It was a few weeks before they manifested. I set the tablecloth on fire at dinner one night. That was quite a disaster." Risyda rolled over and gave him a searching look. "Why are you asking? Did something like that happen to you?"

"I don't know," Jasen said. "Maybe. But don't you have to be a child to be blessed?"

Risyda shrugged. "I'm not an expert by any means, although there is a difference between being blessed by a dragon and being called by one. The experiences feel similar, but they mean different things. Being dragon-blessed means you're given an ability. Being dragon-called means that a dragon is requesting your service."

"Have you ever met anyone who was called?"

She hesitated for a moment. "I was, once."

"You were?"

"Yes, when I was fifteen. I woke up one morning, and before I knew what was happening, I grabbed my horse and rode straight to the nearest draemir. It was the same dragon that blessed me." She looked down at her hands, seeming uncomfortable for once. "I've never told anyone that before."

"Why not?"

"I didn't want to be a draedess. An austere life of self-sacrifice isn't something that I find very appealing." She lay back on the sofa again, staring at the ceiling as she puffed some more. "Then again, becoming a wife doesn't seem appealing to me, either."

They smoked gloomily for a while until there was a familiar knock on the door.

"Thank the heavens," Risyda said. "Maybe Larely can cheer us up."

Risyda opened the door to let him in. He was carrying a small bag.

"Well, you two look glum," Larely said. "Is the torturous existence of a noble wearing on you?"

"You have no idea," Risyda said. "What's in the bag?"

Larely pulled out a bottle. "Colderberry wine."

"Oh, I could kiss you!" Risyda said. And then she did—a wet, sloppy smack on the cheek. Larely blushed a little. Jasen supposed that answered the question of whether or not Larely was flirting with him. He felt relieved. Had he been in Grumhul, he could see himself in a romance with Larely, but the whole business with the king and his lessons and the dragon had left him too upside down for trysts.

They passed the bottle around as they chatted. Larely and Risyda seemed to not have any troubles, but after a couple of swigs, Jasen felt sick. He never could hold his liquor. "I'm going to bed," he said, struggling to his feet.

"Are you all right?" Larely asked. "I can help you back to your room."

Jasen waved him off. "No, I'm fine," he said. "You two have fun."

"Wait," Risyda said. She went to her bedside table and pulled out a small pouch. "Take this in the morning. I had it made by a dragon-blessed healer. It banishes wine-induced illness."

"Why don't I just take it right now?"

"Because I'm having a premonition," she said dramatically. She shut her eyes and put her fingers to her temple. "Yes, it's becoming clearer... I'm seeing you, tomorrow, desperately ill. Your valet will witness your illness and declare you unfit to go to lessons. So ill, in fact, that you must not be disturbed for the entire day. But maybe not too ill to sneak out for a while."

Jasen grinned. "My lady, your gift is truly awe-inspiring. I think you may be right."

CHAPTER 5

*T*he next morning, Jasen felt as ill as he'd imagined he would. He warned Rotheld, who insisted that getting up and walking around would make him feel better. He soon changed his opinion when he tried to lace Jasen's corset. On the first pull, Jasen was colorfully sick all over the floor. After having to clean that up, Rotheld retreated without further protest, nodding in agreement when Jasen said he didn't think he'd be up for lessons, or for taking any luncheon, either.

Once he was gone, Jasen mixed up the powder Risyda had given to him in a glass of water and drank it. He felt better almost immediately. He took out his forbidden shirt and trousers and got changed. He knew his flaming red hair made him too recognizable, so he added a knitted cap that laborers often wore; this wasn't the first time he had thought of escape, and so had asked Larely to smuggle him one earlier. Once he thought everyone was up and out for breakfast, he made his way down the stairs and out the servant's door, and just like that, he was free.

The day was bright and beautiful in the way it often is

after a good rain. He breathed in the cool, sweet air. As much as he loathed to admit it, Polina was right about one thing—it did remind him of home. He walked about aimlessly for a little while, not sure of what to do. Part of him wanted to go to the draemir, but he felt it was too chancy—he didn't want to draw attention to himself.

He decided to go for a walk in the Bedrose Gardens. While the lords and ladies were often allowed to take strolls in the gardens, there were many areas they weren't allowed to explore for fear of getting their fine clothes dirty. Back in Grumhul, Jasen spent a lot of his time outdoors, going wherever he pleased; no one was ever too fussed about getting dirty, because mud was an inescapable fact of life in Grumhul.

He left the path, climbing through bushes and trees to get to off the normal trails. To his surprise, he found a patch of beautifully chaotic wildflowers—very different from the rest of the orderly gardens. He lay down, immersing himself in the bright colors and sweet fragrance. For awhile, he was content to watch birds flit above him, singing songs that Jasen had never heard before. He wasn't sure how long he lay there, but when he finally stood again, he felt refreshed. After leaving the wildflowers, he wandered until he found the orchards, which had trees bearing several kinds of colorful fruit. He grabbed a few for a snack before heading off to explore some more.

Eventually, he made it back to the more well-trod area of the gardens. He heard young voices calling to one another. Curious, he followed the sounds until he came upon a field, where twenty or so finely dressed children were playing a game. All of them except for one: a girl who looked to be about eight years old sat on the edge of the field near a pile of rackets and balls. She had hair so blonde it was nearly white and large blue eyes, currently wet with tears.

Jasen approached her. "What's the matter?" he asked.

She eyed him warily. "They won't let me play," she said. "They say I'm too little."

Jasen looked over at the other children, who were using delicate rackets to bat a tiny ball back and forth over a net. "It doesn't look much fun to me, anyway," Jasen said.

"I wanted to play catch-a-ball, but they say that it's a game for babies."

"I'll play with you."

She wiped her nose with the back of her arm. "Really?"

"Really."

The girl got to her feet and picked up a medium-sized leather ball.

"So how do you play?"

"You don't know how to play catch-a-ball?" she asked, her earlier wariness returning.

"I'm not from around here," he said, which was true enough.

That seemed to satisfy her. "You throw this ball to each other, but you back up a little every time so it gets harder. Whoever misses a catch or doesn't throw the ball far enough loses."

That didn't sound like a much more interesting game than the racket one, but Jasen didn't say so. The girl tossed the ball to him, which he easily caught. It was a little lighter than the balls they used in Grumhul to play mudball, but about the same size. He dropped it on the ground, rolled it into the crook between his foot and ankle, and then popped it into the air, catching it on his back between his shoulders.

The little girl's mouth dropped open in astonishment. "That was amazing!"

Jasen grinned. "Thanks," he said as he let the ball roll off his shoulder.

"Do it again."

So he did. After that, he juggled the ball between his knees before sending it sailing up into the air again. He bounced the ball off his head before catching it in his hand. The girl applauded, and he took a bow.

"Can you teach me how to do that?" she asked.

"Well, unfortunately it takes a bit of practice. But I can show you the basics of mudball, if you want."

"Mudball?" she said, screwing up her nose. "What a terrible name for a game."

"Names can be deceiving," he said.

"And what's your name, then?"

Jasen hesitated. "It's Jay." He hoped she wouldn't ask where he was from—he'd like to make sure it didn't get back to anyone that he'd been here.

"That's a good name," she decided. "My name is Erada, and I'm eight years old."

The name sounded vaguely familiar, but he couldn't quite place it. "It's nice to meet you," Jasen said. "Come on—let's go to that end of the field there."

Jasen taught her basic volleys and kicks. Fortunately, her shoes and her dress were much more sensible than the usual courtly clothing. She was a quick study, and soon they had a good volley going back and forth. She tired of it eventually and asked him to start doing tricks again. He was happy to oblige her. Back in Grumhul, he used to play mudball often, but he'd abandoned it during the last year or so. He hadn't realized how much he had missed it.

After a little while, Jasen became aware that all of the other children had stopped their game and had crossed the field to watch him. He did an exceptionally tricky kick. They all oooh'd appreciatively.

"What are you playing?" asked one tall, serious-faced boy of twelve. He resembled Erada, so Jasen guessed that he was her brother.

"It's called mudball," Erada said loftily.

"Can we play?" asked a dark-haired girl.

"What do you think?" Jasen asked Erada. "Should we teach them?"

Erada gave it some serious thought. "All right, I suppose so"

Jasen marked out two goals and explained the game, and after briefly teaching them a few moves, they began to play. It was awkward and slow-going at first, but the children caught on with surprising quickness. Soon they were laughing and running along the field. Jasen forgot about his worries and lost himself in the game.

After some time, they all stopped to rest. Jasen learned a few of their names—the serious boy was called Ados and was indeed Erada's brother. They thankfully didn't express a lot of curiosity as to Jasen's identity.

"Why is it called mudball?" Ados asked as they all got up to resume their game.

"Where I'm from, there's a lot of mud. Usually, we coat the ball in mud to make it more difficult to kick, and the field's usually muddy, which also makes things slippery."

"That sounds like fun!" Erada said.

Jasen grinned. "It is."

Ados looked thoughtful. He raised his hands, and a cloud appeared above the field, a little ways off from their position. He made a gesture, and water came crashing down. He picked up the ball and rolled it in the newly-created mud. "There," he said, his face deadpan. "Now it's mudball."

Jasen couldn't help but laugh. They all rushed out again, getting themselves thoroughly muddy as they played. The children shrieked with joy as they slipped in the mess. Jasen hoped they wouldn't get into too much trouble for soiling their clothes, but what kind of monsters would deny children the joy of getting well and truly dirty once in a while?

The game soon devolved into a mud fight. They were having so much fun that none of them noticed they were being watched. Erada had just pounced on Jasen and was smearing mud onto his face when Jasen heard a throat being cleared. There, standing beside them was an older woman who looked as if she was about to explode with outrage—and the king. Jasen froze.

Erada followed Jasen's gaze. "Hello, Papa!" she said.

"Papa?" Jasen echoed faintly.

"Children!" the woman said. "I am extremely disappointed in you! Is this the way proper young lords and ladies behave? Stop this foolish nonsense at once and line up!"

The children did as they were told. "Aren't you ashamed of yourselves?" the woman continued. "Just look at you! Look at the state you're in! What could have possessed you? Who is responsible for this?"

The children all looked over to Jasen, who remained sitting in the mud. He had hoped the woman and the king would remain distracted enough that he could sneak away, but that now seemed unlikely. He stood up and kept his head down.

"And who are you, young man?" the woman said.

Before he could answer, the king said, "Lord Jasen? Is that you?"

Jasen wished that he could sink into the mud and disappear, but since that wasn't an option, he gave him a little bow. "Yes, Your Majesty."

"What are you doing here?" the king asked.

"...playing mudball?"

The king laughed. The sour-looking woman glanced back and forth between the two of them uncertainly. The king looked to his daughter. "Did you all get plenty of exercise?"

"Oh yes, Papa, and we had so much fun, too!"

The king turned his attention back to the woman. "Well,

Madame Certia, it seems your new program is a success, yes?"

"I suppose so, Your Majesty, but how are they to return to their lessons in such a state?"

"Perhaps lessons can be put off for one afternoon," the king said. He addressed the children. "Although you should be more mindful of your play in the future."

The children bowed and curtsied while murmuring their agreement, but they were all exchanging excited looks. The reward of canceled lessons didn't seem like a good motivator for behaving better in the future, but Jasen wasn't about to protest.

"Yes, Your Majesty," Madame Certia mumbled. She clapped her hands. "Straighten up, children! You may not have lessons this afternoon, but you will still conduct yourselves with proper decorum! Follow me—straight line, if you please!"

The children followed Madame Certia off the field, which left Jasen standing alone in the muddy field. The king bowed slightly to him and offered his arm.

"I'm going to get you all muddy," Jasen said.

The king smiled. "I do not mind."

They followed Madame Certia and the children off of the field and down the main path. Jasen held the king's arm stiffly at first, not sure exactly how he should be acting. He didn't even dare look at him, keeping his gaze fixed instead on the ground.

"And how did you manage to escape Lady Isalei today?" the king asked.

Jasen sneaked a peek at his face. He was smiling at him, his kind blue eyes dancing with amusement. Jasen couldn't help but smile back. "Oh, I'm very ill today. Too ill to get out of bed, in fact."

"I am sorry to hear it."

Jasen had a sobering thought. "Someone will probably spot me if we walk along the main path."

"That is most likely so," he said. "Perhaps we should not enter by the main path." He stopped. "Wait here for a moment."

The king went ahead, catching up with Madame Certia. While he spoke to her, Erada peeked at him from the line and waved, a big grin on her face. He waved back. A few moments later, the king returned to Jasen's side. "Now then," he said, offering his arm again. "Which path shall we take?"

They ended up winding back around towards the orchards. "I was supposed to be more refined the next time I saw you," Jasen said as they walked.

"I am glad to find you unchanged."

Jasen almost didn't continue, but it wasn't as if he had much to lose. "I was thinking that you didn't want to see me."

The king stopped. "Why would you think that? Surely Lady Isalei told you I wanted to meet with you again."

"She did, once, but said nothing after that," Jasen said. He paused before continuing. "And then I heard you were meeting with others…"

The king took a deep breath through his nose and let it out slowly. "Lady Isalei is a wise woman. I rely on her advice for the finer points of courtly manners, and none are more knowledgeable than she in matters concerning marriage matches. However, she and I are having a… disagreement at the moment. As a compromise, I agreed to entertain other consorts before you, for appearance's sake. There is much that is delicate about this situation, as I am sure you understand." The king took his hand. "But she was to tell you of my strong desire to meet with you again. It seems she did not properly convey that sentiment."

Jasen hadn't been fully aware of the tension he'd carried in his heart until the moment when it was released. He felt so light that he might float away. "No," he said with a small smile. "She didn't."

The king returned his smile and tucked Jasen's hand back into his arm. They resumed their walk, taking their time as they strolled through the trees. "Was my silence what prompted your, ah, 'illness?'" the king asked.

"Maybe a little," Jasen admitted. "It's also been a bit of a shock being here. Things in Grumhul are much different."

"I remember," the king said. "I have only visited once, when I took a tour of all the Allied Realms when I was crowned king. I enjoyed my stay there more than any other. I am very fond of your Queen Urga, but like you, she is restless in the Draelands, especially during Court."

"My mother and Queen Urga were good friends," Jasen said. "I have a hard time imagining her here, too. Especially in the middle of hog-breeding season."

The king laughed. "Yes, she always said she preferred the hogs of Grumhul to the ones of Court. While I disagree on that account, I do admire how plain-spoken she is."

"Really?"

"Why does that surprise you?"

"Well, I didn't think that anything Grummish was much admired outside of Grumhul."

"Perhaps by some, but I am not among them. I wish there was more of Grumhul in the Draelands."

Jasen nudged him with his shoulder. "I could always teach you how to play mudball."

The king laughed. "I am a bit too old for mudball, I think."

"You're never too old for mudball. Even my dad plays sometimes. Besides, you aren't that old, are you? Maybe ten years older than I am?"

The king was silent for a moment. "How old are you?"

"Twenty."

"I had been a king for three years by your age," he said. "I was a husband the next year, and a father the year after that. I was a widower at twenty-eight." His gaze was now fixed off in the distance. "I feel older than my years."

"I'm sorry," Jasen said.

The king patted his hand and turned back to him, his expression light again. "Do not apologize. I could use the reminder that I am not an old man."

"Glad I could help."

They continued on for a while until they reached the wildflowers. The king's face lit up. "I have not visited this garden for a long time. I used to spend some time every day here when I was younger."

"I think it's my favorite," Jasen said.

"Mine as well. I had to fight with the gardener, Awen, to get her to agree to a plot of wildflowers. She's a disciplined woman and not particularly fond of disorder."

Jasen cocked his head. "You specially requested this? Why?"

"It reminds me of my mother's homeland of Rakon. There are many beautiful fields just like this. It is my opinion that Nature is the most skilled gardener of all." He gestured in the direction of the other gardens. "But of course, I also admire the skills of our human cultivators. Awen has a dragon-blessed gift for plants. Her work is impressive."

"But you like the wildflowers better."

The king smiled. "I do."

As they strolled through the garden, Jasen took a moment to appreciate the sun on his face and the fresh air all around him. The enjoyment only lasted a few moments. He would be back at his lessons soon, bound up in the suffocation of it all again.

"Is there something wrong?" the king asked.

"No," Jasen said, and then, "Well, yes. I'm not relishing going back."

"Why is that?"

"I'm not used to being so monitored. They make you feel like a child. And there's so much that I'm expected to do, and I can't make sense of any of it. There are so many rules."

"And you do not do well with rules."

"I'm not used to having them! Or at least, the ones in Grumhul make sense: Don't go off in the swamp alone. Avoid spitting directly in people's faces, even if you don't like them. Try not to drag your sleeve in your soup. All sensible. But here, there's a thousand things you must do, and each and every one of those tiny things holds equal weight, even though there isn't any reason behind it that anyone can explain to me. And then there's the uncomfortable clothing, and history and politics and music and dance and it's all foreign to me, and the others laugh at me and I don't know how to deal with it—any of it! I don't!" He realized, with mortification, that his voice had become loud and high, and he was not so much breathing as panting.

The king considered him. "Perhaps we should sit down for a moment."

They sat down on a grassy slope. Jasen had calmed himself by that point, but now he was overcome with embarrassment. He rested his elbows on his knees and held his head in his hands. "And now I feel like an idiot. You just finished telling me about the enormous pressures you've been under since you were three years younger than I am, and here I am complaining about having to learn the waltz and how to make boring conversation. I'm sorry."

"Yes, but my responsibilities were always meaningful to me. It must be maddening to feel so much weight over that which does not seem to have value." The king paused. "Have you studied history?"

"Not really. I've never studied much of anything."

"But you are no doubt familiar with the Time Before Dragons?"

"Of course—I'm not *that* ignorant."

"It was a dark time before King Athard united the humans with the dragons. All of the kingdoms of Monolia were in perpetual war—"

"But then King Athard brought the dragons, who defeated the armies of the wicked kings and queens and united the realms in perpetual peace," Jasen finished for him. "Yes, I know. I was kind of hoping for a break from lessons, you know."

The king held his hands up in appeasement. "Then I shall make my point quickly. King Athard brought the realms together, it's true—but an alliance between ten realms is not a feat that is accomplished in one gesture. The realms disbanded their armies, but Athard couldn't make them get along. Our cultures all have their idiosyncrasies. That is why he began holding Court. The manners you learn now were put into place so that the different cultures could feel on the same footing. Once there was an agreement of a 'proper' way to behave, it became much easier for citizens of each realm to speak to one another."

Jasen blinked. "I hadn't thought of it that way."

"It is a problem I have contemplated for many years," the king said with a smile.

Their eyes met for a moment. Jasen looked away, tucking a strand of hair behind his ear. "I don't know what I should call you—'Your Majesty'?"

"Perhaps in the company of others," he said. "But it would sadden me greatly if you called me that in private. My family simply calls me Rilvor. I would like for you to call me that as well."

"All right, Rilvor."

They gazed into each other's eyes. It was at this point

with other men that Jasen might initiate a kiss, but so much about this situation was beyond him.

Jasen stood up. "We should get back. They might start to miss me."

Rilvor stood as well. "You should not concern yourself too much with Lady Isalei's displeasure. I can always speak with her."

"I would rather you didn't. Our first meeting in the draemir made me a combination of a laughing stock and a subject of envy. It would be easier on me if no one found out about this." Jasen slapped a hand to his forehead. "Except, of course, Madame Certia and the children already know. Damn."

"Madame Certia will say nothing. And sadly, there are many nobles who barely speak to their children." He paused. "I had not considered the problems I might be causing for you. I apologize."

"It isn't your fault." He thought about it for a moment. "I think a more formal meeting between us would alleviate some of the resentment. It would seem less like I'm using stunts to get your attention."

"I think that Lady Isalei will have no choice but to agree to such excellent logic."

They eventually made their way out of the gardens, where the king bade him a quick good-bye, lest they attract too much attention. Jasen timed his return to the East Wing to coincide with the time most of the other consorts would be in lessons; he was able to slip back up to his room without anyone noticing. He bundled up his dirty clothes and shoved them under his bed and then changed back into his night shirt. He rang the servant's bell to request a bath.

As he waited for the bath, part of him felt dizzy with giddiness, but another part of him sunk even further into despair. He had almost managed to convince himself that he was indifferent to the king's affections, but the more he talked to him, the more he became aware that wasn't true. He liked him. He more than liked him. He wanted him in a way that he'd never felt before. Attraction was one thing—he was accustomed to that. But this wasn't a gossamer-thin strand of physical desire that broke apart the moment that desire was satisfied. There was more to it. It elated him. He wanted to explore it.

But why, oh why, did Rilvor have to be the king?

To Jasen's relief, his adventure in the garden seemed to escape notice, and the next day life continued as usual. The next afternoon was archery practice, which was an activity Jasen actually enjoyed. The tutor had them work in pairs. Since Risyda was an expert and Jasen was good enough to not require much instruction, the tutor left them to themselves.

"So how was your day off?" Risyda asked as they settled at their target.

Jasen didn't know how much he wanted to say when others could overhear. "Interesting," he decided on.

"That's a mysterious answer."

"Later," Jasen promised.

Polina and two of her toadies—Lord Banither and Lady Lalan—approached, choosing the target beside them. They began to speak a little more loudly than was strictly necessary.

"Oh Princess, will you tell me all the details of your visit with the king again?" Banither said. His eyes flickered over to Jasen and Risyda.

Polina giggled. "I've already told you a dozen times, it seems! Surely it must bore you."

"Oh no! It is too thrilling!" Lady Lalan exclaimed. "We hang upon your every word!"

"All right, then!" She droned on about how she met with him yesterday morning and about the immediate connection they had felt. On and on she went as they all practiced their shots. Jasen tried to keep a straight face, but when Polina got to the part where her meeting with the king had supposedly gone on well into the afternoon, he couldn't help but laugh a little.

"What?" Risyda said.

"She's lying," he said. "There's no way she could have seen him in the afternoon."

"How can you be so sure?"

Jasen dropped his voice. "Because I was with him," he said, unable to keep a grin off of his face.

Risyda let out a delighted laugh. Polina stopped talking and looked over at them, eyes narrowed. Risyda waved to her. "Good morning, Polly!" she said.

"Good morning, Lady Risyda," she replied after a moment's hesitation. She glanced back and forth between Jasen and Risyda's cheerful expressions. "I was just telling Lord Banither and Lady Lalan about my meeting with the king yesterday."

"We heard you," Risyda said.

"Oh."

"Well?" Risyda said. "Aren't you going to finish your story? I am dying to know exactly how many times he called you beautiful."

"I was done with my story," she sniffed. She notched an arrow and shot. It barely hit the target.

"Missing the mark, as usual," Risyda said.

Polina's face flushed. She grabbed another arrow, notched it, and concentrated. This time, she hit a bull's-eye. She looked back to Risyda in triumph, her face still red. "There. What do you think about that?"

"I think that you should try to shoot straight more often," Risyda said. "You might actually accomplish something."

"Like what? Win an archery competition, like you?" Polina spat. "What a small, stupid goal. And what a stupid sport this is." She threw her bow on the ground, gathered her skirts, and stormed off. Her minions scrambled off behind her.

"Why do you two hate each other so much?" Jasen asked when she was gone.

Risyda shrugged. "I don't hate her. We used to be friends when we were children. Then one year, she decided I wasn't her friend anymore. She said I didn't take our mission to find a spouse seriously enough. I mean, she was right—it was probably better that she ended the friendship when she did."

For a moment, she seemed incredibly sad. Jasen wasn't sure what to say, but then Risyda was back to herself again, giving him a sly smile. "So! I don't think I can settle for later. Tell me everything."

Now that Polina and Banither had left, they had a cushion of a target on each side of them. Jasen didn't think anyone would overhear, as long as he kept his voice low. "Well, it all started with a game of mudball..."

~

AFTER ARCHERY, Risyda left for her language lessons while Jasen went to practice dance. The weather had returned to its normal warmness for this time of year, and going straight from the archery to dance left Jasen feeling overheated and short of breath. His damnable corset was only making things worse. After luncheon, he headed out for a secluded spot behind the East Wing. He went there whenever he had a moment to grab a few moments of solitude.

On his way there, he ran into Larely. "Oh, thank heavens," Jasen said when he spotted him. "I need you."

"You need me?" Larely echoed. "For what?"

Jasen grabbed his arm and pulled him behind a tree. He took a quick look around to make sure no one else was there and shed his jacket. He turned around, bracing himself against the tree. "Undo my breeches," he said.

Larely sputtered. "What?"

"Quickly, before someone sees us!"

It took a moment, but Jasen soon felt Larely's hands on him, undoing the laces. Once he had them open, Jasen shimmied the breeches around his hips. "Now unlace my corset—not all the way, because I'm not going to have time to take it off completely. Just loosen the laces a little."

There was another moment of hesitation, but Larely complied. Jasen took a long, deep breath of relief. He turned around. "Thank you, I feel much—"

But he didn't have the chance to finish that sentence, because Larely's lips were suddenly pressed against his own. He put his hands on Larely's chest and pushed him away. "What are you doing?" he asked angrily.

Larely looked as confused as Jasen felt. "I was kissing you?"

"Why?"

Larely's face was already flushed, but it grew an even deeper shade of red. "You said you needed me, and then you pulled me back here and asked me to undress you!"

"I didn't mean it like that!"

"Well, what was I supposed to think?"

Jasen had to admit that Larely's reading of the situation was not unreasonable. "But I thought that you and Risyda were...intimate."

Larely furrowed his brow. "Why would you think that?"

"She kissed you the other night."

"What, when I brought the wine? She was just teasing me —you know how she is!"

"Why did you blush?"

"I blush at everything—I have very fair skin! And you would, too, if Risyda kissed you— it's embarrassing, like being kissed by your sister. She knows I like men." Larely rubbed the back of his neck. "And I thought I made that clear to you as well."

"I thought that you were just a naturally flirtatious person. I wasn't sure it was directed at me in particular."

"Well, now you know," Larely said shortly. "I take it that this means you aren't interested."

"But you know that the king is courting me."

"I thought you said that you didn't want to marry the king."

"It's complicated," Jasen mumbled.

"Not that complicated," Larely said. "Of course you would marry a king if you got the chance. That's why you're here, isn't it? It was stupid of me to think that a noble like you would stoop so low."

Jasen's cheeks heated. "That isn't fair."

"Nothing ever is, *my lord*," Larely said with a bow. "I won't bother you any further." He made to leave.

Which meant leaving Jasen with his clothes undone. As if this whole situation weren't awkward enough. "Wait!"

Larely turned back. There was a tiny bit of hope in his eyes. "I need your help getting dressed again," Jasen said tightly.

Larely stalked over to him and did up his corset and breeches. When he was finished, Jasen turned around. Larely's face was still beet red. He seemed so embarrassed that Jasen felt a twinge of sympathy. "Larely, I—"

"Don't," Larely interrupted. He bowed stiffly. "Good day, my lord." This time, he left for good.

Jasen slid down to the ground and put his hands over his face. He felt like screaming. How was he going to explain this to Risyda? He gave his face a vigorous rub. It was probably time for him to go inside—the last thing he needed today was to make more trouble.

CHAPTER 6

*J*asen didn't say anything to Risyda about what happened with Larely. In fact, he avoided her entirely that night, claiming a headache. The next morning, Lady Isalei called him to her parlor. Jasen was so nervous that he felt like he might vomit—had she found out about his rendezvous with the king? He didn't think he'd be able to lie to her if she asked. His hands shook as he poured them both tea.

"I heard that you were quite ill the other day," Lady Isalei said. "Have you recovered?"

"Yes," he said, his voice quivering.

"Are you quite sure? You seem a bit unsteady."

"I suppose I am still recovering a bit," he said, happy to have an excuse for his jitters.

Lady Isalei took a sip of her tea. "The king wants to meet with you tomorrow."

Jasen's heart soared. "Tomorrow?"

"Of course, if you still aren't feeling well—"

"No, I'm fully recovered!" he said, and then realized that he had just contradicted himself. "I mean—I will be fully

86

recovered by tomorrow. I just need another night's rest, I'm sure."

"Good. He was very insistent on seeing you as soon as possible."

Jasen suppressed the big, goofy grin that wanted to break out on his face. "I am anxious to see him as well," he said with as much refinement as he could manage.

"Then it's settled. A footman will take you to king tomorrow around mid-morning."

"Thank you, my lady."

As soon as he left the parlor, he did a little dance of joy. An official meeting with the king! But the joy quickly faded as he ruminated on the "official" part of it. Every other meeting between them had been just the two of them. Was this to be a formal affair? Would things between them be different? He supposed he would have to wait and see. Still, it wasn't enough to dampen his enthusiasm.

Risyda was thrilled at the news, but Jasen made her promise not to tell anyone. It didn't matter—by dinner time, everyone had heard the news. Polina made especially sour faces at him during dinner and loudly explained to her cohorts how much she admired the king's dedication to fairness, seeing as he made time for even people from "the lesser realms."

Polina's bitterness wasn't enough to spoil his mood, but he still felt uneasy about his encounter with Larely the previous day. Larely approached him as he was about to retire for the evening. Risyda had already gone upstairs. "Hello," he said. He seemed sheepish.

"Hello," Jasen said back.

"I'm an ass," Larely said. "A great big giant ass, and I'm sorry for yesterday."

"You don't have to apologize."

"Of course I do. I said some very unfair things." He paused. "I hear you're off to see the king tomorrow."

"Yes."

"Is it what you want?"

"Yes," Jasen said. "It really is."

"Then I'm glad for you." He handed him a bottle. "Here— an apology gift from me. It's Yarlian wine— a very fine vintage from my father's vineyard."

Jasen accepted the bottle. "Thank you," he said. "Why don't you come up to Risyda's and have a glass with us?"

"Not tonight," Larely said. "Some other time, maybe."

"Oh. All right, then."

Larely smiled at him, although it was a little strained. "Good night."

"Good night."

Jasen headed up to Risyda's, the wine bottle feeling heavy in his hand. He couldn't help but feel he'd lost a friend. Maybe that would change later. He decided against telling Risyda. They had a lot of other things to discuss, after all. His stomach did a little flip just thinking about what was in store. Tomorrow seemed both too far away and too soon.

JASEN AWOKE EARLY the next morning to prepare. A breakfast was sent up to him, but he was too nervous to eat. Even the unflappable Rotheld seemed fussy rather than efficiently meticulous. Since it was a morning appointment, Rotheld recommended less formal attire, which Jasen agreed to eagerly. The outfit they settled on was a deep blue, with only a little lace trimming and a modestly flared frock coat. They argued over the shoes; Jasen won and wore a pair with only a slightly raised heel.

Finally, a valet arrived to escort Jasen to the king's private apartments. He hadn't been in the palace proper yet. When they stepped into the front hall, it was all Jasen could do not to gape. The high ceiling was covered with the most beautiful murals Jasen had ever seen. They depicted the Drae, which were the central figures of their religion—the beings that were half-human, half-dragon, who had both the magical abilities of dragons and the reason of men. They were too powerful and too reckless, however, and the gods split them apart into separate creatures, and it had been that way ever since. The stories had always seemed distant to Jasen, particularly since there were no dragons in Grumhul, but the murals were so clear and so lovely that he felt the truth of it for the first time.

They wound their way up some stairs and through some halls until at last they reached the king's apartments. The valet bowed and left. Jasen hesitated. Should he knock, or was he just expected to enter? While he was deciding what to do, his gaze rested on a full length portrait of a beautiful blonde woman, standing in front of one of the more spectacular fountains of the Bedrose Gardens. In one hand, she held an orb of water. Jasen realized that it must be the late Queen Consort Quendra—she had been powerfully blessed with water magic. Her eyes were blue and serene. It was a bit disconcerting to be confronted by her image right before he met with her husband. Jasen wondered what she would think of him. Would she approve? He closed his eyes briefly and swallowed, collecting himself. He decided to enter without knocking—the king was expecting him, after all.

The receiving room was dazzling to behold. There was gold everywhere, etched into the walls in swirling patterns and gilding the frames of the many paintings hung there. Even the furniture seemed more like works of art than things to be sat upon. Jasen wasn't sure he could even find the courage to speak in such a place—even the rugs seemed better than him. To his surprise, the room was empty, but there was another door at the other end of the room, which was slightly ajar. He heard voices just beyond—the king and someone else's.

Curious, Jasen crept closer and peered in through the crack. He wasn't that surprised to see Minister Adwig there.

"—must admit that Princess Polina is a perfect match. She is royalty, first and foremost, and her family has been blessed by the dragons. And she is beautiful, is she not? Her manners are without peer—"

"I appreciate your advice, as always," the king interrupted, although he didn't especially sound as if that were true.

"Then why are you meeting with this Lord Jasen?" The minister's voice dropped. "I would not want to interfere with Your Majesty's pleasure, of course, but is it quite necessary to make an official courtship of the young man?"

His pleasure? Jasen's heart sank. Was that all the king wanted from him?

Jasen must have made a sound, because they both stopped talking and turned to the door. The king's face lit up. "Lord Jasen! Please, come in."

Jasen stepped through the door. He bowed deeply to both of them. "Good morning, Your Majesty," he said as formally as possible.

"You remember Minister Adwig," the king said. "Although I don't think you were properly introduced. I am sure he is honored to make your acquaintance."

"But of course," the minister said in a voice that didn't match the scowl on his face. He bowed to Jasen. "How pleasant to meet you."

"The minister was just leaving," the king continued.

Adwig forced a smile and bowed to the king. "I hope you have an enjoyable morning, Your Majesty." With that, he left, shutting the door just a little too loudly behind him.

The king moved to Jasen side as soon as the minister was gone. "You have excellent timing," he said. "You've saved me from a tedious conversation."

"Your Majesty does me a great honor," he mumbled.

The king took Jasen's hand. "Please, no more of that. You're to call me Rilvor, remember?"

Jasen's heart sank further. Of course he didn't want to be formal with Jasen. That was why they were meeting practically in his bedchambers. A pleasure, nothing more. He supposed the thought should relieve him—after all, wasn't becoming the king consort something he wanted to avoid? But he couldn't be with Rilvor if he was to marry someone else. It would break his heart.

The king frowned. "What is the matter? You have grown pale. Lady Isalei said you were unwell earlier—do you feel unwell still?"

"I do," Jasen said. "Maybe I should leave." Better to stop this before it went any further—no matter how much he cared for Rilvor, he wouldn't consent to being a pleasurable distraction from his real duties.

The king sighed. "The children will be so disappointed."

"The children?" Jasen said with surprise.

"Yes. I had hoped that we could all enjoy some time together."

Jasen didn't know what to say. Spending time with the king's children didn't seem like something he would do if Jasen was only a mere dalliance to him.

At that moment, four children and a nurse entered the room. Jasen recognized Ados and Erada. The other two had to be his youngest daughters. One was a sweet-looking girl of five with blonde curls. The other was about two years old, who was the only child who shared her father's dark hair. She was in the nurse's arm and was sucking her thumb thoughtfully.

Erada beamed and ran up to him. "Hello, Jay!" she said, but then stopped. "I mean, Lord Jasen." She curtsied.

"It's nice to see you again," Jasen said, grinning back at her. He looked over at Ados. "Both of you." And it really was. The dread that had crept into his heart was rapidly fading.

The nurse handed the little one to Rilvor, who also took the other girl by the hand. "I wanted you to meet my other daughters. This is Denas," he said, indicating the five-year-old. "Denas, say hello to Lord Jasen."

Denas hid behind her father's legs, but managed a very soft, "Hello."

Jasen bowed deeply. "I am pleased to make your acquaintance, my princess," Jasen said with great seriousness. When she peeked out at him, he stuck his tongue out at her. She giggled.

"And this is Ayera," he said, holding the little one closer to Jasen.

"Hello to you, too," he said. She slapped him in the face and squealed.

"Believe it or not, that means she likes you," Rilvor said.

"We're going to see a puppet show!" Erada said.

"If you are feeling well enough." Rilvor hesitated. "I know it is not a traditional audience between a consort and the king, but it has been some time since I have been able to spend time with the children. I hope you are not offended. If you would prefer something more formal, we can meet this afternoon—"

"No, this is perfect," Jasen said with a grin. "And I'm feeling much better now. There's nothing I would rather be doing."

The king returned his smile. "I am happy to hear it."

Soon afterward, the puppet players arrived. The players put on a show about the great King Athurd, the first Lord of the Drae, and his unification of the Allied Realms. The show was intended to amuse children while offering some light history, but Jasen was embarrassed that he himself was finding it educational. Grumhul was always the odd kingdom out when it came to the Allied Realms, so they weren't as steeped in the lore as the other kingdoms were. Combining that with Jasen's abysmal education meant he was a great deal fuzzier on the history than he cared to admit.

The puppeteers started with a comically frenzied battle between a dozen knights and kings and queens, although the real Wars Without End were not so jolly. The ten kingdoms that now made up the Allied Realms had nearly destroyed themselves with their constant battling. As the puppets fought, an impressive puppet dragon swooped upon them, representing how the dragons of old, who were mindless and wild, would often attack humankind. Great kings and queens would occasionally tame one and thus gain dominance over their neighbors, but dragons were unpredictable and often turned against their masters. Dragon slaying was therefore a wildly spread sport—a thought so blasphemous now that it made Jasen queasy to even think of it. Truly, it was a wretched time for all involved.

The combatants and the dragons disappeared from the stage, replaced by a puppet figure of Gilda, the Blessed Mother, with baby Athard in her arms. She came across the dragon egg that would one day be Zimura, the first dragon with reason. Gilda placed the egg in and the baby in a cradle. The narrator of the show intoned that the egg would not hatch for fifteen years, but in the meantime, some extraordinary things began to happen to the village of Heabrook, where Gilda and Athard lived as humble peasants. Crops never failed. Plagues that ravaged nearby villages left Heabrook untouched. Wolves, robbers, and raiders alike seemed unable to disturb the peace in their land.

The baby puppet was replaced by a boy puppet—the young Athard with flaming red hair. By the time he was ten, Athard was curing injuries and disease, playing with wild animals, and making prophecies. The puppeteers had fun depicting the bumbling of the local lords in their attempts to possess this miraculous boy, but Athard stayed put in Heabrook, which remained immune to all attack.

With great fanfare, the puppeteers depicted the glorious hatching of Zimura and the subsequent ascension of Athard as the first Lord of the Drae, with godlike powers over all of the elements. Athard took his baby dragon and went on his grand tour of the realms, seeing for the first time the wickedness of the world. The kings and queens all scrambled to capture him, but he was untouchable.

He spent ten years traveling the lands, performing miracles and righting wrongs, until at last Zimura was fully grown. The mood of the play shifted to something darker as they depicted the Battle of Oxham, when the realms united to destroy Athard at last. This was a mistake, as Zimura fried their armies to a crisp. She and Athard retreated then to the lands beyond the Ashfell Mountains. When he returned a year later, he brought with him an army of dragons, who were wild beasts no longer. Through Athard and Zimura's connection, they now had the reason of men.

The puppeteers depicted Athard's conquest as a happy one, although Jasen was sure it was not particularly pleasant for the wicked kings and queens. Once the rubble had settled, Athard elevated only the most righteous people to rule the realms. He and the dragons began blessing the worthy of all classes with magical abilities, thus ensuring that the ruling class were no longer the only ones with power. A happy ending. But as a Grumhulian, he felt a bit of ambivalence—Athard brought peace to the realms, but it was a peace that had been forced. That didn't sit well with the Grummish.

The finale of the show was grand, with all of the magnificent puppet dragons on full display, moving with amazing grace and spectacle. All in all, the show had been enjoyable. Erada had bounced with excitement the whole time, pulling on Jasen's sleeve and often exclaiming with glee at a particularly impressive part. Ados was more dignified, but by the end he was as enraptured as his sister. The nurse had stayed to help with the little ones, who naturally paid less attention to the entertainment, but Rilvor tended to his younger children as much as the nurse did. It resulted in a lot of interruptions, but Jasen didn't mind. He even held Ayera in his lap for part of show. She pulled at hair and neatly done cravat, messing them both up. Jasen couldn't bring himself to care, although he was sure Rotheld would be disapproving.

Afterward, Rilvor sent the children off with their nurse so that he and Jasen could have a private luncheon, which the servants had laid out for them.

"Did you enjoy the show?" Rilvor asked as they sat down.

"Oh yes, very much," Jasen said as he selected some of the delicious-looking fruit from the spread in front of them. "I've never seen such a marvelous use of puppets. But the history is—" He stopped before he could finish the thought. Lady Isalei's tutors encouraged their pupils to engage in light debate, but criticism of the very foundation of the Allied Realms was about as light as a boulder.

Rilvor raised his eyebrow. "But?"

"Oh, it's nothing. Just a silly thought."

"Your expression just now did not look silly."

"Believe me, it is. I don't exactly have a keen analytical mind. I'd only embarrass myself."

Rilvor frowned. "It disheartens me to hear you speak so poorly of yourself. I do not share your assessment." He put a hand on Jasen's. "I would very much like to hear your thought, if you would indulge me."

Jasen's heart gave a little flutter. "Well—it's wonderful that Athard stopped the wars and brought the realms together, but it isn't like anyone had a choice in the matter. And that's still true, isn't it? The only reason that the realms stay united is out of fear of Reckonings." A Reckoning was when the dragons determined that nobles were taking advantage of their people and kicked them out of power. In the first two centuries of the Allied Realms, Reckonings involved the guilty families getting burned to death. Reckonings were less common and less violent now, but they still happened. No one knew the exact triggers of a Reckoning—it was solely the discretion of the dragons. Even the Lord of the Drae could not stop a Reckoning. "It's disturbing that the dragons have such power, and humans get no say in it."

Rilvor smiled a little. "That is an opinion shared by your queen. It is a valid point, and most definitely not a 'silly' thought." Rilvor buttered a roll and took a bite before he spoke again. "It is unfortunate that humans have proved themselves incapable of controlling their darker natures."

"But that isn't true. Grumhul has no dragons—we never have." At the time of Athard's reign, Good King Stan of Grumhul was judged to be the only worthy king, for he had never waged war nor oppressed his people. They were left to govern themselves, which they did for two hundred years before they agreed to join the other Allied Realms. "And we do just fine. Our kingdom isn't exactly prosperous, but everyone gets taken care of. Our monarchs and our nobles don't oppress. Everyone gets a say in the laws, and no one is exempt. Corrupt monarchs are thrown out. If we can govern ourselves without the threat of dragons toasting us, I don't see why other realms couldn't do it as well."

"I agree."

Jasen blinked rapidly. "You do?" he asked in disbelief.

"Yes. Inviting the common folk to have their say is a worthy idea. Why do you sound so surprised?"

"Well— I mean—" Jasen sputtered for another few moments before throwing his hands up in exasperation. "You're Lord of the Drae! You're the connection between humans and the dragons! That is the whole point for your existence! Why on earth would you question their involvement in human affairs?"

Rilvor raised an eyebrow. "I'd like to think that my life has some meaning aside from my link to the dragons."

Jasen felt his face flush. "Oh no, I didn't mean to suggest otherwise! Please forgive me—I'm such an idiot—"

But Rilvor did not look offended. If anything, he seemed amused. "I will forgive you on the condition that you stop insulting yourself."

Jasen opened his mouth to disagree, but shut it again quickly. He reached for his glass, swallowing down the rest of his self-incriminations with the last of his wine. "All right," he said with a weak smile. "I'll try."

"Good." Rilvor refilled Jasen's wine glass as well as his own. "As to your question—I did not say that I think humans and dragons ought to be separated again. The benefits of our connection are obvious for both of our species. However, there is much nuance about human societies that the dragons miss. It is said that dragons can see into the hearts of humans and separate the good from the wicked…" He trailed off.

"But you don't think that's true?" Jasen asked when he didn't continue.

"I think it is true in a limited sense. Dragons do not understand human complexities, I fear, just as we do not understand them."

"But you're linked with the dragons. You can communicate with them."

"Yes and no. Dragons' minds are linked to each other, and I am party to that link. But I don't understand their thoughts directly. I can get impressions of their intentions, their emotional states, just as draeds and draedesses can. My connection to them is even stronger, but we can't *speak* with them. Direct communication—talking the way you and I are now—is beyond the scope of our powers."

"But they tell you their names, don't they?"

"That is about the extent of it. In truth, I think they only choose names for the benefit of humans. I'm not sure they even have a language as we understand it."

"But King Athard did. That's what all the stories say."

"It has been five hundred years. Stories grow old, just as we do, and they aren't always accurate." Rilvor looked pensive, as if his gaze were directed inward instead of to the world around him. But it was only for a moment. He smiled. "But mysteries are beautiful, are they not? Think of how drab the world would be if there were no mysteries left."

Jasen raised his glass. "To mysteries."

"To mysteries." He clinked his glass against Jasen's.

The subject appeared to be closed, but Jasen couldn't help but ask one last question. "Are you really thinking about adapting Grummish policies?"

Rilvor shrugged. "It is only a thought. I doubt it would go over well with my ministers or the nobles—or even, indeed, the common folk."

"Or maybe it would. You can't know until you try."

"If only politics were that simple. There is no trying—a leader must decide, and then carry through." He rubbed his temple. "But that is enough talk of politics. I wish to turn my attention to more important matters."

"Like what?"

"You, naturally."

Jasen tried to will himself not to blush. He wasn't sure it

worked. "Before we stop talking politics, can I ask you something?"

"Of course."

"I couldn't help but overhear your discussion with Minister Adwig earlier. It seems like he doesn't exactly approve of me."

Rilvor sighed. "I had hoped you had missed that particular conversation. No wonder you were so pale. Please do not worry about Minister Adwig. He has some strong opinions as to whom I should marry—but those are his opinions, not mine. And *I* approve of you. That is all that truly matters."

Jasen's lips quirked upward. "That's good to hear."

They spent the rest of the time in lighter conversation. Their time together was over all too quickly, but Rilvor had kingly duties to attend to. Rilvor accompanied Jasen to the door. "I would walk you back to your room," he said apologetically. "But I'm afraid I would be mobbed."

Jasen grimaced at the thought. "Yes, that's probably true." He looked down at his shoe bashfully. "Will I see you again soon?"

"If I had my way, I would see you tomorrow, and the next day, and the day after that. But I am a king, and my time is not my own."

Jasen's good mood soured a little at the reminder of Rilvor's royal status. "I understand." He paused. "Will you be seeing other consorts?"

"Most likely."

Jasen turned away, hoping to conceal his flush of jealousy, but Rilvor put a hand on his cheek and gazed into his eyes. "My ministers are more likely to accept my choice if I have satisfied them that I have explored all of my options. I hope I do not need to explain that the thought displeases me as much as it does you."

"Of course not," Jasen said, but in truth, it did feel good to hear him say it.

Rilvor brought Jasen's hand to his lips and kissed it. "Until next time."

There was no one to accompany Jasen back to his room; he wasn't sure if that was an oversight or if they finally trusted him to find his own way around. He felt dazed as he drifted across the palace, like he was floating on air. Or perhaps as if he were riding on the back of a dragon.

He came crashing back to earth when he round the corner and ran straight into Minister Adwig. The man's eyes swept over him. "Good afternoon, Lord Jasen." His tone was respectful, but there was a smirk on his face. "I trust you had an enjoyable morning with the king."

Jasen's instinct was to get away quickly, but he made himself hold his ground. He lifted his chin and met his gaze. "Yes, it was very enjoyable."

Adwig's smirk grew smugger. "Indeed. You may want to have your valet redo your cravat and hair before you return to your lessons—I am sure Lady Isalei would not approve of you looking quite so...disheveled."

Jasen blinked at him for a moment until he understood what he was getting at. No doubt he thought Jasen had hastily dressed after the king had taken the "pleasure" that Adwig had so graciously insisted he would not interfere with. His face grew hot, but he did his best to keep a hold of his temper. "Thank you for letting me know. I was having too much fun with the little princess to notice."

Adwig's brow furrowed. "The princess?"

"Yes—Princess Ayera. She sat in my lap during the puppet show. Didn't the king tell you what he had planned for me this morning? We had a lovely time—it was so nice getting to know his children."

Awig scowled. "How delightful."

Jasen tried to hold back his grin of victory. "It was."

"I suppose this is *all* very delightful for you," Adwig continued. "Your lovely rooms in this palace, all of your fine clothing—such a change from your previous circumstances, is it not?"

It was so shockingly rude that Jasen wasn't sure what to say. "I-I suppose so."

The minister smirked. "I am sure you have lessons to attend, so I won't keep you any further." He bowed. "Good morning."

Jasen gave an awkward bow in return. "Good morning."

Jasen let out a breath as soon as the minister was out of sight. The pleasure of his time with the king had faded and all of his insecurities came rushing back. But why should he be intimidated? Rilvor seemed as if he didn't put much stock in Adwig's opinion. It still hurt that the man thought so little of him. He tried to put it out of his mind as he made his way back to the East Wing. If Rilvor didn't care, then he wouldn't care, either.

At least that's what he told himself.

CHAPTER 7

*J*t was another two weeks before he heard from
Rilvor again. In the meantime, Rilvor met with
Lady Merey, a beautiful and charming young woman from
Genyon with red hair not dissimilar from his own. Jasen
bore the news quite maturely. He only got a little bit drunk
the night he heard about it, and when he overheard her
telling her friends what a marvelous time she had with the
king and how gallant and handsome he was, Jasen gritted his
teeth and politely excused himself from the room instead of
screaming.

It was easier to bear when Rilvor met with Lalan, since it
caused a pretty entertaining tiff between her and Polina.
Polina lorded over her minions with more benevolence than
bullying, but a meeting with the king was an insubordination
that she could not endure. Of course, Lalan didn't have any
say in the matter, but that was no excuse, according to
Polina. Lalan, for once, stood up for herself, which led to
increasingly snide remarks between the two. Over the course
of a few days, it escalated into an actual physical confronta-
tion after etiquette lessons, in which Polina snatched the wig

off of Lalan's head. The teacher, the elderly Lord Consort Fricio, tried to separate them, which resulted in *his* wig also being knocked off. Lord Drancis, who was a consort in training from Camory who had been sponsored by Fricio, decided to throw himself into the fray. One by one, the refined young lords and ladies got caught up in the brawl—no punches were thrown, but there was a great deal of fan-slapping and clothes-tearing.

In the end, four guards had to be called to break it up, after which everyone in the class was confined to their quarters for the rest of the day. That was fine with Jasen—it meant a break from classes, and it had given him the best laugh he'd had in a long time. It was even worth sitting through the stern lecture they all received from Lady Isalei, who threatened to deny all future engagements with the king until after the Suitor's Ball. Polina and Lalan both gave an extremely tearful apology. Jasen suspected they were croc-odile tears, but later that night in the Swan Parlor, Polina and Lalan secluded themselves in the corner of the room and wept as they held each other and made declarations of undying friendship. For some reason, that put Risyda in an extremely sour mood, but Jasen thought it was sort of sweet.

Jasen was a little concerned that Lady Isalei would follow through on her threat, but a few days after the brawl, a discrete white card arrived with Jasen's breakfast, requesting his company on a horseback ride through the draemir.

"Horseback riding, Rotheld!" Jasen said, waving the card at him. "I bet I don't have to wear a corset just to ride a horse. And I'll get boots, won't I?"

Jasen could have sworn he saw the corner of Rotheld's mouth twitch into a brief grin, but it was gone too quickly for him to be sure. "You are correct, my lord."

Jasen beamed.

He finished his breakfast and allowed himself to be

dressed with a minimal amount of complaining. His good spirits, however, didn't last very long. When he entered the parlor where he took his usual remedial etiquette lessons, he was surprised to see Minister Adwig waiting for him.

Adwig bowed. "Good morning, Lord Jasen. Are you quite well? You look pale."

"No, sir," Jasen stammered. "I mean, yes, I am well."

"I am glad to hear it. I understand that you are to go riding with the king—it would not do for you to be ill."

A feeling of unease stirred in Jasen's stomach. "Forgive me, sir, but I'm supposed to meet with my tutor now."

"You are excused from your private tutelage today."

"Why?"

"I have spoken with Lady Isalei, and she agrees that you would benefit from a riding lesson."

"I know how to ride a horse," Jasen said curtly. "I don't see how this is necessary."

"You know how to ride in the Grummish style, no doubt. The riding style differs here. We wouldn't want you embarrassing yourself in front of the king."

Jasen's face flushed. "Forgive me, but you are not my instructor. I would like to speak to Lady Isalei."

"Lady Isalei has other business to attend to at the moment." Adwig produced an envelope from inside of his coat and handed it to Jasen. "But she did leave you this message."

Jasen opened the envelope and scanned its contents. Sure enough, it read exactly as the minister had said it would.

"I could have had a servant send it," the minister continued. "But I thought it might be nice for us to get a little better acquainted."

Jasen had nothing to say to that, but Adwig didn't seem as if he expected a reply. He bowed. "And now I will leave you to prepare yourself. I hope you have a pleasant outing."

Jasen just stood there for a moment after the minister left the room, but soon shook himself out of it. It was clear that the minister wanted to rattle his confidence, but he wouldn't let him. With new determination, he headed back to his room and summoned Rotheld to help him change. After he was ready, he made his way to the stables.

When he arrived, there was only one person in the stable that he could see. It was a petite young man, brushing a white horse that had clearly just been out for a run.

"Excuse me," Jasen said, approaching the figure. "Can you tell me where to find the stable master?"

The figure turned, and Jasen couldn't help but let out a gasp of surprise. It wasn't a young man after all—it was Princess Polina. "Oh! I thought you were a boy."

She seemed just as surprised to see him, but recovered quickly. "What are you doing here?"

"I could ask you the same thing."

"I ride every morning," she said.

"Dressed like that?"

"Yes," she snapped. "I couldn't very well ride in my usual gowns, could I?"

"I suppose not," Jasen stammered. He couldn't stop staring at her—she looked so different without her enormous hair and elaborate dresses. He realized for the first time how tiny she was. Without her shoes, she was only as tall as his shoulder. "I just didn't think that you would want to be seen in such…well, dressed like a boy."

She flushed. "I am not dressed like a boy. It is perfectly acceptable for a proper young lady to wear suitable riding attire. It isn't as if I'm running around without a jacket, like some ill-mannered people do." She turned back to her horse. "Besides, there isn't anyone here to see me." She scowled. "Or at least there isn't usually."

"I'm sorry," Jasen said. "I didn't mean to disturb you." He

wanted to ask her why she was grooming her own horse, but decided it might not be prudent.

"So what are you doing here?" she said. "I thought your people lacked the refinement for the equestrian arts."

"I know how to ride a horse," he said, exasperated.

"You know how to sit on them and move from place to place," she said. "It isn't the same."

Jasen felt himself flush with anger. "Perhaps you're right. That is why I'm here, actually—to learn some of your customs. Lady Isalei wanted me to be prepared for my ride with the king tomorrow."

She dropped her brush and whirled around, her mouth opened in a perfect *oh* of outrage. "Another audience already?"

Jasen couldn't help but smirk a little. "Yes."

Their conversation was interrupted by the arrival of a large man with a fearsome black beard, who was accompanied by a young stable boy—Jasen guessed he was the stable master. "And how was your ride this morning, Princess?" he said with a fond smile.

"Enjoyable as always," Polina said. "Thank you, Darcer." The stable boy stepped in to lead her horse away.

The man addressed Jasen. "I assume you are Lord Jasen?" He sounded notably less fond than he had when addressing Polina. "Minister Adwig has told me that you require some lessons. Is that so?"

Jasen didn't like the way he was looking at him. "Yes."

"I will be happy to assist you in a moment." He turned back to Polina. "Is there anything else I can do for you this morning?"

"No, thank you, Darcer. It's become rather crowded." With that, she left.

Once Polina was gone, Darcer approached him again. "Let's get a mount for you and we can begin," he said. "Boy!"

he called to the stable boy, who promptly appeared. "Prepare Barbaras."

"Barbaras?" the boy asked. "Are you certain?"

"Yes, I'm certain!" he bellowed. The boy went scrambling back into the stalls. A few moments later, he came out leading a monstrous red stallion. The horse held his head high and seemed to look down his nose at Jasen.

"I'm not sure this is the horse I want," Jasen said.

"Nonsense," Darcer said. "You're an *experienced* rider, aren't you? And Barbaras is one of our more striking stallions. One of the king's favorites. I think you'd look quite good on him, with your red hair and all. And that is what's important here, isn't it. Looking good for the king." The last was said with just a trace of a sneer.

Jasen didn't like his attitude, but what could he do about it? "I suppose so," he said. Jasen approached the beast. The horse met his gaze and exhaled noisily. He was definitely judging him. Jasen swallowed.

"Does my lord require help mounting?" Darcer asked.

"Of course not," Jasen snapped. He grabbed the reins and got onto the beast successfully.

Unfortunately, that was the most successful part of the ride. Once they were out in the yard, things went downhill. The saddle was much smaller than Jasen was used to, and the reins felt different as well. Darcer kept shouting directions at him about his posture, the way he held the reins, the position of his legs—apparently, everything he did was wrong. And Barbaras certainly wasn't willing to make things easier for him. The horse clearly couldn't believe he'd been saddled by such a rube—or at least, that's the way it seemed to Jasen. He had to fight with him every step of the way.

At last, Darcer declared the lesson over. They went back to the stable, where Jasen shakily dismounted. At least he'd managed not to fall off. Darcer was giving him a smug look

—no doubt Minister Adwig had put him up to it. The trouble was that it had worked; his confidence was completely shattered.

He had trouble concentrating the rest of the day. He made mistake after mistake, even in areas that he thought he had mastered. He'd been so excited about seeing Rilvor again, but now he was dreading it. Even though he knew he was playing right into Minister Adwig's plans, that knowledge didn't help any. After all, it turned out he was right. Jasen didn't know what he was doing—with the riding, or with anything else, for that matter.

❧

THE NEXT MORNING, Rotheld fussed over him as usual; the riding clothes were certainly more comfortable, but it still involved a lot of primping. There was to be no corset, thankfully, and boots instead of shoes. His brown frock coat was much shorter than usual, and his breeches were not quite so tight. He would carry no fan, obviously, but his hands were not left unadorned— he wore tan leather riding gloves. They had a brief argument about his hair—Jasen thought that it should be simple, since they were going riding, but Rotheld strongly felt that the simplicity of his outfit ought to be complimented by a more ornamental hairstyle. They compromised on an ornate top hat. It had to be pinned in his hair with great precision, ensuring that it didn't budge. Jasen thought it looked ridiculous, and it pulled at his hair uncomfortably. But he supposed it was a fair trade for the lack of a corset.

He made his way to the stables. Rilvor had just arrived. He was wearing a red riding suit that perfectly complements his features. His long, black hair was tied back, much as Jasen's was, except he wasn't wearing a hat. He was standing by his own mount—a silver horse, sleek and lovely. They made quite a striking picture together.

Rilvor caught his eye. "Good morning."

"Good morning," Jasen replied. Already he could feel himself sweating with nervousness.

Rilvor considered him carefully. "I hope you enjoy riding. It just occurred to me that I never asked."

"Oh, I like it fine." He kept his gaze down at his gloves as he pulled at the fingers. "Although I'm afraid I don't really know all of the customs of riding the Draelands. Darcer was kind enough to give me some instruction, but it turns out I'm not very good at it. In Grumhul, we're more pig people than horse people. Not that we ride on pigs! I don't think that's possible, except for maybe the Queen's pet pig, who actually is quite large. She always let the children take rides on him. I used to ride him when I was a child—not her current pig, obviously, since it was a while ago, and I think her new pig is a girl. Anyway, I was pretty good at it, too, but of course there are no rules for riding pigs—you just sort of hold on and hope for the best—"

A touch of a finger at his chin stopped his babbling. Rilvor lifted his face until their gazes met. "I am sure you are a fine rider," Rilvor said.

Rilvor dropped his finger, but not his gaze. His eyes were such a nice blue, so gentle and yet piercing at the same time. Jasen felt his face flush. The moment was interrupted when Darcer entered from the stalls with Barbaras in tow.

Rilvor frowned. "Were you riding Barbaras yesterday?" he asked Jasen.

"Yes," he said. "Darcer said he was one of your favorites."

Rilvor turned to the stable master. "I enjoy Barbaras, but he is much too spirited for a less experienced rider. You ought to have known better, Darcer."

Darcer looked at the ground. "Yes, Your Majesty."

Rilvor thought for a moment. "Bring me Shae."

Darcer bowed and led Barbaras away. "Shae will be more suited to you," Rilvor said once the stable master was gone. "You need a steadier mount."

Darcer returned a short time later with a dapper mare. Immediately Jasen felt better about his chances of not making a fool of himself. Both he and Rilvor mounted their steeds, and soon they were off, heading towards the draemir.

They ambled along at a leisurely pace. Shae proved to be a much better match for Jasen, responding easily to his commands. They rode in silence for a little while. It wasn't uncomfortable, exactly, but it didn't seem right that they should be out together and not talking about anything. The only topic that came to Jasen's mind was the weather, which was unacceptably banal.

Jasen rode slightly behind Rilvor, a position that gave him the opportunity to examine him without Rilvor noticing that he was staring. Rilvor sat straight in his saddle, his command over his horse effortless. He was the embodiment of regal. His handsome face was neither severe nor open, but falling somewhere in between. It was comforting to be in his presence—to cede control to someone so clearly capable of taking care of everything. It wasn't any mystery why he was a popular king.

But that was the only thing that *wasn't* a mystery about him. In spite of the ease of their last meeting, Jasen couldn't think of a thing to say. Their conversation over lunch had been enjoyable, but it was only after it was all over that Jasen realized that the whole time they'd been talking about Jasen. All of their meetings had gone that way; any of Jasen's attempts to find out more about Rilvor had been so deftly reflected that he hadn't even realized that it had been happening.

Jasen had attempted to sniff out some personal details,

but there didn't seem to be much to learn. Polina claimed to know all of his personal preferences, down to his favorite vegetable, but guarded those secrets jealously, as if she expected wearing the correct flower in her hair and exclaiming her love for spinach would somehow forge a bond between them. Jasen knew better. Those sorts of details didn't say much of anything about who a person really was.

So what did he know about Rilvor? He was a good king, everyone agreed. He was adept at soothing tensions between the Allied Realms. He appeared both impartial and deeply caring at the same time, leaving all offended parties feeling as if their grievances had been heard, which was often all that was needed to diffuse a situation.

Rilvor was also known to be a devoted father, which Jasen had witnessed for himself. But his deep love for his children led to questions that no one seemed willing to answer: what had the relationship been like between the king and his queen consort? Everyone said they had made a good couple. She was known as being kind and virtuous. No one had ever talked about any rift between them, and Rilvor had been heart-broken when she died. But there were the rumors —that their marriage was strained, and that's what had caused her illness. They were only rumors, of course. But it still gave Jasen pause.

And then there was the matter of his tragic ascension to the throne. By all accounts, Rilvor should have never been king. He was the fourth son, with two older sisters and a brother ahead of him in line for the crown. But a devastating plague had wiped out his mother and all of his siblings, and his father died from grief a short time later, unable to bear the burden of being Lord of the Drae without his love. Love had much higher stakes when it involved the Lord of the Drae—it could literally be a matter of life and death.

Jasen was curious about all of this, but it didn't exactly

SERA TREVOR

make for the sort of conversation for a light outing. What was he supposed to say? *Did you love your wife? How about that dead family of yours? Could marrying you kill me?* He was better off sticking with the weather.

He urged Shae forward a little to ride more fully beside Rilvor. "It's a nice day," he said, feeling like an idiot.

"Yes," Rilvor agreed.

"A little muggy, maybe," Jasen continued. "It would be nice if there was a breeze."

Rilvor nonchalantly waved his hand. A gentle breeze wafted over them. "Is that better?"

Jasen laughed. "Yes, actually." It was the first time Rilvor had used his magic in front of Jasen. He wondered what the extent of his powers were. As Lord of the Drae, his magic was naturally stronger than everyone else's, but the specific magical abilities of the Lords and Ladies of the Drae varied. Some were extremely gifted with one blessing, while others were able to access more blessings but with less power. From what he'd heard, Rilvor fell in the latter category. "What was your original blessing?" Jasen asked.

In response, Rilvor waved his hand again. Nothing happened for several minutes, but then a small red bird flew up to the king and landed on his shoulder. Another one followed, landing this time on Jasen's saddle. Still other birds of all different kinds flocked overhead. Squirrels and chipmunks came down from their trees and scampered along side of the horses. Even a few deer emerged shyly from the forest, following them at a distance.

Jasen gawked at their animal coterie. His little bird friend cocked its head, as if curious as to why he found the situation at all unusual. "So," he said when he'd found his voice. "Animal affinity, I take it?"

Rilvor merely smiled.

"Is this how you keep all the nobles in line?"

Rilvor laughed. "It does not work on humans, as far as I know. My job would be much easier." He waved his hand again, and gradually the animals left them. Jasen's bird tweeted a farewell and flew off.

"I spent a great deal of my boyhood on my own in the wilds of Rakon," Rilvor commented. "I found animals more agreeable companions."

Jasen cocked his head. "I would think that your royal duties would have kept you too busy."

"I was a fourth son," he said. "No one expected that I would ascend the throne."

"Is that why you were raised in Rakon instead of the Draelands?"

"I do not know," he said. "I was never told."

"That seems cold," Jasen said before he could stop himself. He cursed himself inwardly for his bluntness. "I mean—I'm sure your parents had their reasons," he added rather weakly.

Rilvor didn't respond right away. Jasen was worried that he'd mortally offended him, but then he said, "In truth, I did not mind. I much preferred the wilderness of my mother's home country to the Court in the Draelands. There's a strong tradition of ascetic draeds in Rakon—many of them lived in the draemirs that surrounded our castle. I spent much time in nature, learning from them." He paused again. "I have suspected that my mother might have been dragon blessed with prophecy and knew a terrible fate would befall our family. I believe she sent me away to keep me safe."

"If that were true, why didn't she ever say anything?"

"Prophecy is more of a curse than a blessing. It is often vague, and there is no changing what is foreseen. Living life under the threat of doom is an empty existence. She may have thought it best not to inflict that upon us." He shrugged. "Or perhaps that is just the wild speculations of a lonely child."

"I was on my own a lot, too," Jasen said. "My mother died when I was twelve. Although I wasn't alone, exactly—I spent most of my time with the villagers. My father was from, er, humble origins, so he never forbade it. And we were so isolated from what passes for courtly life in Grumhul, anyway."

"And how did it come to pass that your father wed your mother?"

"Well—he sort of gambled his way into it."

Rilvor raised an eyebrow. "And how did he manage that?"

"He and my mother were courting in secret before her father found out. Since my mother was the firstborn child and the heir to his estate, my grandfather didn't have the right to dictate who she would take as her consort. But he was the one who still controlled the purse strings, and he refused to let my mother pay the consort price to my father's family. My grandfather figured that was the only reason my dad was wooing my mother, anyway, and would give up once he realized no money would be forthcoming. But my parents actually were in love, so my dad went to the gambling tables and won more than enough to pay his own consort price, to prove that his intentions were true. The story got around that my grandfather was too cheap to pay for his daughter's consort, so he relented out of embarrassment and gave them his blessing." Jasen paused. "I can never decide if that story is romantic or not."

Rilvor laughed. "I would say so."

"The less romantic side of it is that it only intensified his faith in gambling. That's the only reason I'm here—he won my place at Court with a bet."

"Then I will always pray for your father's good fortune."

Jasen flushed a little.

They rode on in silence for a little while, with Jasen trailing Rilvor by a few paces. Rilvor sat straight in his saddle, his form perfect—the very essence of regality. Jasen tried to reconcile the king in front of him with the small, wild boy he must have been, the forgotten fourth son of a dynasty that thought it would never need him, keeping company with the wild ascetic draeds of Rakon. Who would he be now if his family had survived? Or even more interesting, what would he be like if he wasn't royal at all?

Jasen nudged his horse to quicken her pace until they were at pace with Rilvor. "What would you do if you weren't king?" Jasen asked.

"I suppose I would have become a draed," he said. "That was what was expected of me."

"But what if you didn't have any duties? What if something happened where you didn't have to be the king anymore? What would you do?"

Rilvor raised an eyebrow. "That is not possible. I am the Lord of the Drae—that isn't a position that one can abdicate."

"But let's just say you could," Jasen said. "Would you?"

"I think it would be difficult for a former king and somehow magically displaced Lord of the Drae to make a living to support his children," Rilvor said with a quirk of his lips.

"What if you didn't have them to support?"

"My life would be quite empty without my children."

Jasen made a sound of frustration. "Are you being thick on purpose? I'm trying to ask you what you would do without any responsibility."

"No responsibility," Rilvor echoed. He thought about it for a moment. "So in your scenario, I command no lands, and I cannot have a profession?"

"No."

"And I cannot have my children?"

Jasen shook his head. "Sorry, but no."

"Could I have you?"

Jasen's face flushed. He looked down at his hands as he tried to think of a response. As he was thinking, he passed under a low-hanging branch, which got caught in one of the ribbons on his ridiculous hat. He yelped as he yanked on the reins to bring his horse to a halt.

Rilvor stopped his horse as well. "What is it? What's happened?" he said.

"It's this damned hat—it got caught in a branch." Jasen struggled to untangle himself. "Who would put so many ribbons on a hat?" he fumed. "What possible purpose could they serve?"

"Can't you just take it off?"

"I can try, but it's pinned in place." Jasen pulled out a few of the pins and then tried to yank the hat off. It barely budged. Worse than that, he could feel his hair getting tangled around the remaining pins, making him more stuck than ever. Jasen nearly screamed in frustration. "I think Rotheld must have used some sort of dark sorcery to stick this damned thing on!"

Rilvor dismounted and approached Jasen's horse. He waved his hand; Jasen felt the hat break free of the branch.

"Thank you," Jasen mumbled, still feeling ridiculous. He attempted again to extract the hat from his head to no avail.

"Come down here and let me help," Rilvor said.

Jasen dismounted and stood beside Rilvor. Rilvor didn't use any magic this time as he carefully removed the pins from the hat and Jasen's hair. They were so close that Jasen could feel the heat of Rilvor's body.

Jasen tried to stand still, but the intimacy of the situation and his own lingering embarrassment made it difficult. "I told Rotheld that it was a ridiculous hat to wear for a ride," Jasen said. "He can be so stubborn, though. It's like he can't stand for me to be completely comfortable. I escaped the corset this time, so naturally I had to suffer in some other—"

He broke off as Rilvor pulled the hat free and handed it to Jasen. Jasen's hair, now in tangles, fell around his shoulders. "You can tell Rotheld that I prefer you unadorned," Rilvor said, his voice now deep and soft. "If I had my way, I would have you always be as I saw you the first time in the draemir, in the simplest garments, free of ornament and formality."

Jasen could feel his face turn even redder as he clutched his newly-freed hat to his chest. It seemed as if he hadn't stopped blushing since they had begun their ride, which was absolutely ridiculous. Jasen wasn't exactly inexperienced. So why was it so different with Rilvor? Why did he feel like a blushing virgin every time he looked at him?

Rilvor brushed his fingers through Jasen's hair. "You ask me what I would do if I were free. I would take you to Rakon with me, back to the wilderness where I spent my childhood. I would show you the woods that sheltered me when I needed escape from the dreary castle that was supposed to be my home. I would introduce you to my true family—to the animals and the birds, to the blooming wildflowers and cold, sweet brooks, and of course, the dragons. I would show you the meadows I ran through, the trees I slept under. And then we would make our home there, apart from the pressures of the world."

Rilvor leaned in so close that Jasen could feel his breath on his face; it smelled sweet, like honey. Jasen's heart sped up. He felt both thrilled and terrified, because he realized at last what was different. Rilvor didn't want a quick roll in the hay—he wanted *him*. But why? What made him so special?

Rilvor ran his hand over Jasen's hair again, his fingers combing through the tangles. "You are so lovely," he murmured.

And just like that, the spell was broken. *Lovely.* Of course. That was it.

Jasen turned his head away and took a small step backward. Rilvor removed his hand from Jasen's hair and frowned. "I've upset you somehow," he said.

"No, not at all," Jasen mumbled unconvincingly.

"Was it because I said you were lovely?" Rilvor asked. "Do you not believe that I speak truly?"

"Oh, no," Jasen said. "No, I know that I'm attractive. Extremely attractive. You might even say that it's my most interesting quality." He put his hat on and turned back to his horse. "We should probably get going."

Rilvor stopped him with a hand on his arm and gently turned Jasen around to face him. "Not until you tell me how I offended you." His voice was soft, but firm. Jasen could tell that they weren't going anywhere until he gave him a satisfactory answer.

"It's just—" Jasen couldn't quite think of how to put it. "My father is enormously fat."

Rilvor blinked. "I must confess that I cannot see the relevance of your father's weight on the current situation."

"He was very fit as a young man. Dashing, handsome. He was a complete nitwit and remains so, but he was so good-looking that nearly everyone wanted him. And then he reached thirty years of age and became about as wide as he is tall. So if lovely is what you want, please keep in mind that there is a good chance that I will not be so lovely ten years from now."

"I see," Rilvor said after a moment. "In my family, we have the opposite problem. We become skeletal as we age. We begin to stoop as well. As the years pass, I may resemble a vulture more than a man. I should think that it would be good for my health to have someone who would make sure I ate. I would value that much more than loveliness."

Jasen lips twitched up in a brief grin. "We'd be quite the pair: the Vulture and the Hog."

Rilvor nodded. "I am sure many a snide comment would be made about us behind our backs."

Jasen's grin widened. "Oh, I'm used to that. It wouldn't bother me in the least."

"I know," Rilvor said. "One of the many things that I cherish in you."

Jasen was back to blushing again. He mounted his horse so that Rilvor wouldn't see his pink face.

Once they were both back on their horses, Rilvor asked, "Am I forgiven?"

Jasen glanced down at him casually. "For what?"

That seemed to be good enough for Rilvor.

The rest of the ride was nice enough, although their conversation fell into more casual pleasantries than real conversation. That was fine with Jasen—his mind was so abuzz with what they had already discussed that he was surprised he was capable of any conversation at all.

They returned to the stable and dismounted. After their horses were put away, Rilvor dismissed the grooms so that they could have one more moment of privacy. "I fear this is the last time I will be able to see you before the Suitor's Ball," he said. "Indeed, it may be quite some time before we can meet again privately."

"I understand," Jasen said, trying to keep the disappointment out of his voice. "Kingly duties and all that. I suppose you'll have to go back to ignoring me."

Rilvor raised an eyebrow. "Ignoring you? Is that what you think I've been doing?"

"Well—yes."

"I have already expressed to you how unhappy that I am about the circumstances," Rilvor said tightly.

The well-mannered consort inside of Jasen was shrieking that one simply must not pick a fight with the king of all people, but hadn't Rilvor just said he preferred Jasen to be himself? "I understand your duties, but I'm not going to pretend it doesn't hurt my feelings to watch you court other people. I know you don't *want* to ignore me, but as you said, propriety demands that you entertain other consorts and not communicate with me for days on end—in other words, that you ignore me."

Rilvor's gaze dropped. "That isn't entirely fair."

"No," Jasen agreed. "It isn't."

Rilvor's lips were pressed together. His normally gentle gaze had become a bit stormy. "Perhaps the fact that these young ladies hearts are doomed to be dashed will ease your jealousy."

Jasen crossed his arms and glared right back at him. "That isn't fair, either. Part of the reason I hate this is because it hurts so many people. Courtship shouldn't be a game with winners or losers."

Rilvor rubbed his face. "On that, we agree. And yet, we must play. Even a king is a pawn at court."

Rilvor looked so miserable that Jasen couldn't help but feel guilty. "Well, I prefer mudball to chess," he said with a small smile. "It's much more honest, and you get to tackle your opponents."

Rilvor returned his smile. "From what I understand, one can also employ that strategy in the game of courtly love, as your compatriots did the other day."

Jasen laughed. "So you heard about that?"

"Naturally. You did not happen to have a role in that, did you?"

"Of course not!" Jasen said with faux indigence. "I said I *preferred* mudball, but I'm perfectly capable of playing chess if the situation calls for it. I just don't like it." Jasen bit his lip. "I'm also not very good at it."

Rilvor took Jasen's hand in his own. "On the contrary," he said, his voice deep in a way that made Jasen uncomfortably aware of the tightness of his breeches. "Your moves are well made."

He began to bring Jasen's hand to his lips. Jasen didn't pull his hand away, but he also wouldn't let Rilvor lift it. "All kidding aside, I want you to know that this *isn't* a game to me," he said while looking directly into his eyes. "I understand that we must keep up appearances, but when it's just the two of us, it needs to be honest."

"I would not have it any other way." Without breaking eye contact, Rilvor lifted Jasen's hand again. This time, Jasen let him. His lips pressed against the fabric of Jasen's glove. It was one of the most intimate kisses Jasen had ever experienced, and Rilvor's lips hadn't even touched his skin.

It might have turned into something more, but the appearance of a valet at the stable door spoiled the moment. "Minister Adwig wishes to speak to you, sire."

Rilvor sighed. "Duty calls." He gave Jasen's hand one more brief kiss before releasing it.

Jasen gave a faint nod. The blood had rushed from his head to elsewhere, leaving him a little dizzy, and his legs felt weak. "When will we see each other again?"

"At the Suitor's Ball, most likely. I may not be able to dedicate myself solely to you, but that it not the same as 'ignoring' you. You will have as much of my attention as I am able to give. That is, if you will give me the pleasure of a dance or two."

Jasen swallowed. The thought of every set of eyes in the ballroom on him dancing with the king set his heart fluttering, but he wasn't sure whether it was from excitement or panic. "I had already assumed I'd see *the king* at the ball. What I meant to ask was when I would see *Rilvor* again."

Rilvor laughed. "At the soonest opportunity, I swear it." He paused. "And while propriety restrains my actions, there is no reason why we cannot communicate privately. If you ever wish to speak to me, write me a note. I will write to you as well. Would that make you feel better about the situation?"

Jasen smiled a little. "It would, actually."

"Then you shall hear from me soon." He gave Jasen's hand another kiss, and then he was gone.

JASEN FLOATED BACK to the East Wing. He took a look at one of the grand clocks in the hallways—it was just about time for luncheon, but most consorts were still at their lessons. He knew he ought to go back to his room and get changed, but the thought of confronting the stairs while his legs still felt wobbly was too daunting. He decided he'd sit in the Swan Parlor for a few minutes to collect himself.

It should have been empty, but it wasn't. Of all people, Polina sat there alone, working at her cross-stitch. It shouldn't have surprised him too much; Polina was deemed so advanced that she had much fewer classes than the others.

She looked up at Jasen and smirked. "Lord Jasen—your hair looks a fright! What happened? Were you thrown from your horse?"

Jasen removed his hat, which was probably crooked seeing as his hair was still knotted from his fight with the hat. "Oh, no—my hat got caught on a branch."

"So you ran into a tree? Oh dear, that must have been embarrassing."

Jasen ought to have left it alone—as Rilvor had said, hearts would be broken once this terrible 'game' had ended, and of all the consorts, it seemed that the princess's heart stood to take the most damage. He'd meant what he said to Rilvor—he didn't relish the thought of people getting hurt. The noble thing to do would be ignore her.

But Polina was a smug little would-be saboteur, and Risyda would never let him live it down if he passed up an opportunity to annoy her. "You're right," he said, collapsing on the sofa beside her. "I was hopeless at riding. How did I ever think I could ever measure up to the refinement of the Court?" He threw his hat down with exaggerated dejection.

To Jasen's surprise, Polina's facial expression shifted. "Don't feel too badly," she said, her voice sounding almost kind. For a moment, Jasen actually thought that Polina was going to be a decent human being for once, but she continued. "You can't help that you're Grummish, or that your upbringing was so lacking. As my auntie always says, it is the height of cruelty to allow the mediocre into finer society. It can only lead to embarrassment for everyone involved." She gave his leg a little pat. "But don't worry. I'm sure you'll be able to land a lesser noble who can appreciate your rustic charms."

Jasen just stared at her for a minute. "What a *kind* thing to say. Would you mind if I asked you a favor?"

Polina set aside her sewing. "Not at all," she said with a condescending smile.

"Would you help me redo my hair? I don't feel like making the trek up to my room before luncheon. Rilvor did his best to help me straighten it, but as we didn't have a brush, he had to use his fingers."

Her smile abruptly transformed back into her usual scowl. She snatched up her sewing again. "Well, I don't have a brush either," she snapped. "I don't think anyone at luncheon would notice, since you always look such a mess. And just so you know, it is beyond gauche to refer to His Royal Majesty by his first name. Even little children know better than that."

"But that's what he's asked me to call him." Jasen put his hand on his chin as if in thought. "Etiquette is so confusing. I would think that a king's wish would take precedent over the finer points of manners, but maybe I'm wrong. What do you think?"

Polina stood up. "I think that you're a liar, and that His Majesty will soon see you for the fraud you are!" She gathered her skirts and huffed out of the room.

Jasen couldn't help but grin. He couldn't wait to tell Risyda. As he stood up, he noticed Polina had forgotten her sewing. It was a scene of a horse, galloping through a wood. For some reason, it put a dent in his glee over Polina's snit. Maybe he wouldn't tell Risyda after all. After all, they had plenty of other things to discuss.

CHAPTER 8

*J*asen was floating in the water.

He wasn't sure where he was—it was a lake of some sort, fresh water, unusually warm. It was night-time, but the moon was full, its light unnaturally bright. He gazed at it for awhile as he floated on his back, not sure what to do. After a few moments, he righted himself. His feet did not find any purchase, but he was able to tread water. He looked around, but there was nothing in any direction—only water, so calm it was almost like a mirror.

That calm didn't last for long. The water rippled, as if something were coming to the surface. All of a sudden, Jasen found himself lifted out of the water, his legs straddling something huge. He began to flail in panic, but two arms closed around him from behind, holding him still. He tried to turn to see who those arms belonged to, but he couldn't manage it. Huge wings spread out on either side of them. They were riding a dragon. Its scales reflected a deep blue.

Soon they were flying through the sky. He tried again to twist to see the face of his companion, but again failed. All he glimpsed was long hair, so fair that it was silver in the bright moonlight. Since he *couldn't make out a face, he looked down at the hands that were holding him. They were slender, feminine. A woman, then. He opened his mouth to ask her who she was, but found that he couldn't speak.*

They continued to fly through the sky, leaving the water behind. They passed over a palace—Strengsend, surely, although they moved so quickly that he didn't have time to contemplate it. They flew over the steep peaks of mountains and to the other side...

A forest spread out under them, but it was no ordinary forest. The trees were ten times the size of the trees they had left behind, and they weren't the color of ordinary trees. They were every color of the rainbow. The dragon kept flying until they reached a clearing. And in that clearing were at least a dozen dragons.

Jasen's stomach dropped as they descending, landing in the midst of the clearing. He startled as the rider behind him spoke.

"Go on, now," she said. "Don't be afraid."

But Jasen was afraid. A dragon on its own was overwhelming. A group of them was almost unbearable. It wasn't fear, exactly, but an awe so powerful that it might as well be fear. He screwed up his courage and slid down. His feet touched the ground, but he was so shaky that he stumbled. He felt arms around him again, helping him to his feet.

"It will be all right," the rider said in his ear. He turned around to get a look at her at last, but she had vanished. The dragon he had ridden on had joined the others. There was no going back.

Shakily, he moved forward until he stood in the middle of them. All of their eyes fixed on him, like enormous jewels. He wondered if he was supposed to say something. He hoped not, because he felt as if he had forgotten how to speak.

The dragons began to move, circling him. One stepped forward —Jasen's heart leapt when he realized it was Tasenred. He felt his voice come back to him, but before he could say anything, Tasenred opened his enormous mouth and let out a ball of fire. Jasen cried out as the flames engulfed him—

—and Jasen gasped as he sat up in bed, his heart racing as he heaved in huge, panicked breaths. It took him several moments to compose himself. It had all been a dream—or a nightmare. He wasn't sure which.

Sunlight was already streaming through the window, shining on his face. It was unusual for him to wake up this late. He wondered where Rotheld was before he remembered that it was "dressing down" day—the day before the Suitor's Ball, when they welcomed the nobles arriving to find themselves a spouse. All of the consorts were given the day "off"— they could dress as they pleased and do whatever they wanted, even things that were usually forbidden. *Especially* things that were forbidden, according to Risyda. Jasen had been looking forward to it, but his dream had spoiled his mood.

He got out of bed and splashed some water on his face. Even though Rotheld also had the day off, he had thoughtfully left some clothes for Jasen: a plain shirt and jacket, plus comfortable trousers and best of all, sensible shoes and no corset. After he dressed, he shaved and brushed his hair, and that was the extent of his *toilette* for the day. Jasen felt his mood improve a little.

He made his way to the banquet hall, where breakfast was still underway. A buffet had been set up, but for once there were no servants to wait on them. Jasen grabbed a plate and served himself.

"There you are. I thought I was going to have to come get you."

Jasen jumped at Risyda's sudden appearance, nearly dropping his plate. "Don't sneak up on me like that!"

Risyda raised an eyebrow. "You seem awfully jumpy this morning. Everything all right?"

Jasen considered telling her about his dream, but he didn't want to dwell on it. "I'm fine. I just need to eat."

Risyda had already finished her breakfast, but she sat down beside him anyway. It was odd to see her in such plain clothing. She wasn't even wearing a dress—instead, she wore the same sort of feminine trousers that Polina had been dressed in when he had met her in the stable. Her normally elaborate hair was tied into a loose ponytail. It was a good look for her. "Here," she said, grabbing a bottle from the table. "Have some champagne."

Jasen accepted the glass but only sipped it. Judging from the giddiness of the other consorts, many of them were already a little tipsy.

"So what do you want to do today?" Risyda said. "I thought we could go to the gardens and you could teach me mudball—it sounds wonderfully messy…"

Jasen made a non-committal noise, only half listening to her as he surveyed the room. It was so strange to see everyone unadorned and acting like they were peasants at a festival instead of their usual stuffy selves. Jasen almost felt as if he were still dreaming.

He was startled out of his thoughts when Risyda snapped her fingers in front of his face. "Are you listening to me?"

"What? I mean, yes, of course. Mudball. Sounds good."

Risyda cocked her head. "Are you sure you're feeling all right?"

"I'm fine," he said, trying to sound like he meant it. "I just didn't sleep very well, and I have a headache."

Risyda shrugged. "If you say so. So, finish up already and let's get outside! It's a beautiful day."

Jasen was usually the first one to bolt out of the castle when given the chance, but he still felt shaky from his dream. Besides, there was something he wanted to do, and he needed to do it alone. "Go ahead without me," he said. "I need a couple of hours to get rid of this headache. I'll meet you for lunch, and we can do mudball in the afternoon."

Risyda punched him in the shoulder. "Fine. But if you abandon me all day, I will never forgive you."

Jasen gave her a weak smile as he rubbed his arm where she'd hit him. He knew she meant it playfully, but it still hurt. "I won't. I'll pick up a picnic basket and meet you around noon—I promise."

"You'd better." With that, she left him.

Jasen finished up his breakfast. As he cleared his dishes, he caught Polina out of the corner of his eye. She was drinking champagne directly from the bottle. He decided he'd do his best to stay clear of her; he was fairly certain she was a mean drunk.

He made his way out of the East Wing and to the palace proper. There were still guards hanging around their usual posts, but the informal tone of the day seemed to be rubbing off on them as well. He was able to sneak past them and up to the hall outside the king's chambers. Rilvor did not have the luxury of abandoning his duties and was most likely at his daily meeting with his ministers. The fact that there were no guards directly in front of the door seemed to confirm his conclusion, but he still waited in the shadows for a little while. When he was fairly certain he was alone, he stepped into the light, positioning himself in front of the portrait of the queen consort.

He wasn't sure what he was looking for, but he felt that he had to see the portrait again. He was sure it was she whom he dreamed about, but was it just his mind playing tricks on him? Surely she hadn't returned from beyond the grave to infiltrate his dreams. He looked into her eyes—of course, he saw nothing helpful there. It was only a painting of her, not the woman herself. He was being ridiculous.

He turned to leave—and almost tripped over Erada, who was standing behind him. "Hi, Jay!" she said with a toothy smile.

"Ah, hello," he said, trying to compose himself for the second time that morning. Risyda was right—he *was* jumpy. "Shouldn't you be at lessons?"

"No, silly. We have the day off too, you know." She did a little twirl, causing her plain skirt to swish around her. "See?"

Jasen laughed a little. "Yes, I do. Sorry. I'm not myself this morning."

She nodded sagely. "Me neither. That's the whole point, isn't it?" Then she grinned again. "So what are you doing here? Papa isn't around."

"Nothing," he said, but his eyes darted to the portrait in spite of himself.

"You came to look at my mother's picture?"

There was no denying it. "I suppose I did."

He braced himself for her to ask him why, but she didn't. They stood together for a moment, gazing at the portrait. Her little face was difficult to read—what was she thinking? Had he made her sad? Jasen had been twelve when his mother had died, but poor little Erada had only been six. He couldn't even imagine the devastation she must have felt. "I lost my mother, too," he said.

"Really? How did she die?"

"She choked on a piece of meat." It was a thoroughly unglamorous end for his mother, who had always longed to bring some romanticism to dreary, practical Grumhul. It made her fate seem even more unfair.

"My mama was sick for a long time. I think it would have been better if it had happened fast."

It was such a shockingly morbid sentiment coming from a child that Jasen wasn't quite sure what to say. "I think it would have been best if she hadn't died at all."

"Everyone dies, though." Her tone was so matter-of-fact that it broke Jasen's heart a little. "But it's all right. Mama says that our lives are like drops of rain—separate for a little while, but then we all go back to the great River of Life, where we're one again."

"That's right," Jasen said, although he wasn't sure he believed it. The Grummish were much less religious than the other realms, wearing their skepticism as a badge of honor. However, he certainly wasn't going to bring that up with a little girl—but was that for her sake or his own? Jasen had the startling realization that he would be this child's stepfather if he and Rilvor were married. It wasn't that he hadn't known that before—he'd just hadn't felt it so viscerally up until this point.

While he was trying to puzzle out the best thing to say, Erada took his hand in hers and smiled up at him. "I'm glad you're here."

He squeezed her hand. "I am, too."

"And don't worry—she likes you," she said, gesturing to the painting.

Jasen went very still. "You mean, she *would have* liked me," he corrected.

"No, she likes you. She told me so."

Jasen was at a loss for words for several moments. "Erada —sweetheart—I'm not sure how that can be true."

"She comes to me in my dreams sometimes. She visited me a few nights ago."

Again, Jasen wasn't sure what to say. "When I lost my mother, I would dream of her sometimes, too," he said carefully. "It could feel real, but I think that it was just my memories of her."

"But my mother was dragon-blessed," Erada said, just as carefully, as if *she* were the adult in this situation and was trying to explain something very basic to a small child.

"But she was blessed with the power of water, wasn't she?"

"Yes—and water is the essence of Life. Like the River of

Life. So she can move through it." She cocked her head. "Why don't you believe me? She came to you, too, didn't she?"

A chill ran down Jasen's spine. "I-I don't know. I had a dream, but I wasn't sure if it was about her."

"Did she say anything to you?"

"I don't remember," he lied. "Does your father know about your dreams?"

Erada bit her lip. "Mama said it would make him sad. She's tried to go to him, but she can't make her way in. She thinks he doesn't want to see her."

"Why wouldn't he?"

"I don't know. Grown-ups are confusing."

Jasen laughed a little. "Yes, we are."

"She says Papa has a broken heart. But now you're here, and you can fix it, right?"

Tears stung in Jasen's eyes. "Oh, Erada." He dropped to his knees so that they were level and hugged her. But he didn't answer her question.

Erada returned the hug. After a moment, she pulled back. "So are you going to play mudball today? That's what Lady Risyda told me, and she said I could come if I wanted to."

"Yes. After lunch."

"Hooray!" She kissed him on the cheek. "I'll see you later!" She skipped off down the hall.

Jasen wiped the tears from his eyes before getting back on his feet. He looked up at the portrait of the queen consort again. She had told him not to be afraid.

It was advice he wasn't sure he could take.

As promised, Jasen picked up one of the picnic baskets that had been prepared for the consorts and went off to find Risyda. He found her at the same field where he'd played mudball with the children weeks ago. Erada and many children were also there—they had already started their own game. Surprisingly, there were also about two dozen consorts. They all gave a little cheer when they saw him.

Jasen was bemused at the reaction and the size of the crowd. With the exception of Polina and her gang, no one was exactly mean to him, but most people kept their distance, as if afraid that his uncouth manners and general ineptitude might be catching. Risyda was a bit more popular —the fact that she found Court laughable ruffled a few feathers of the stuffier consorts who took things seriously, but her easy-going manner and sense of humor endeared her to as many people as she put off. But even so, he was surprised she was able to convince so many of them to play.

One of the lords approached him. It took a moment for Jasen to recognize him as Banither, Polina's toady. He normally wore a wig, but today his head was bare, exposing shortly-cropped, spiky black hair. He looked a little like a porcupine. "Please allow me to relieve you of your burden," he said, taking the picnic basket from Jasen's arm.

"Er—thanks. Are you here to play, too?"

"Oh yes," he said with enthusiasm. "I am aware that my normal demeanor is perhaps overly refined, but I am also quite adept at fencing. I have no trouble with athletic endeavors—indeed, I am quite eager to receive your instruction in this 'mudball.' It sounds very amusing!"

Jasen just stared at him.

Banither cleared his throat. "I'll go put this aside then, shall I?" He whisked the picnic basket away, setting it down under a nearby tree beside several more identical baskets.

Risyda kicked the ball over to Jasen. "So the kids have taught us a little, but they say that you're the real master. Care to demonstrate?"

Everyone was staring at him. Showing off for the kids

had had been fun, but having all this adult expectation pointed directly at him made him want to turn heel and run all the way back to Grumhul.

Of course, that wasn't an option at the moment. He put his foot on the ball. "Well, children aren't hard to impress," he began, figuring he should keep expectations as low as possible. He popped the ball up with one foot and juggled it between his knees before sending it soaring into the air and then caught it on his back, just as he had done for the children weeks before.

There was silence for a moment, and then the consorts erupted into applause—cheers, even. They seemed even more delighted than the children had been, which struck Jasen as odd. Surely these worldly consorts had seen better entertainment than someone kicking a ball around. Still, the positive attention felt good. He ran the ball down his arm and back to the ground.

"Oh, bravo!" said Banither, who was clapping the loudest. "How extraordinary! How athletic! I implore you to teach me!"

Jasen gave him a long look, still half- suspecting that he was mocking him, but he seemed sincere. "Why don't we start at the beginning?"

Risyda had acquired several balls, so Jasen split the consorts into smaller groups to practice basic volleys. Risyda, unsurprisingly, was a natural. And Banither took to it quickly as well—it seemed he hadn't been lying about his athletic skills. While they were practicing, Jasen marked out the goals, with some help of Erada and the other children, who had stopped their game to come watch the adults.

Once Jasen was satisfied that everyone had the basic techniques down, he split them into teams. Soon, the game was in full swing. It seemed like all of the pent up frustrations of life at Court were expelled on the field. After the game, they all tucked into their picnic baskets with relish. There was no place for fine manners here—everyone ate with their hands, tearing their meat apart with their teeth like wild dogs and gobbling up the fruit with no regards to the juices running down their chins. By the end of the day, everyone was pleasantly spent—exhausted, but still giddy. There was a lot of raucous laughter as they made their way back to the palace. The consorts who hadn't joined them laughed at their dirtiness, but it was all good-natured. Jasen's earlier gloom had diminished—although thoughts of the queen consort and her strange message still lingered in his mind, he shoved them firmly back. There would be time to puzzle that out later. For now, he didn't want to think about it.

Everyone went back to their rooms to clean up and get changed for dinner—it may have been dressing down day, but they were still required to keep up some decorum, and dining while caked in mud was definitely out of the question. Once Jasen was presentable, he went to Risyda's room to meet her before they went down for dinner. She had the hookah out, which she offered to Jasen.

"Mudball is fantastic," she said as Jasen took a puff. "I haven't had that much fun in ages. We all should physically try to destroy each other more often—it's a lot more honest than all the usual back-biting."

Jasen laughed as he exhaled, which set off a coughing fit. "It was a good time," he agreed. "I was surprised that so many people joined in."

"I'm not. I think you should prepare yourself for your new popularity."

Jasen blinked at her. "What are you talking about? I'm the laughing stock of Court."

"You *were* the laughing stock of Court. Now you're the star."

Jasen bafflement only increased. "But—how?"

"Well, Lady Wulfa heard from her lady's maid, Athel, who heard from Othwin, one of the king's guards, who heard from Bely, a chambermaid who works in the king's quarters, who overheard an argument between Minister Adwig and the king. Apparently, he doesn't want to entertain any consort but you from now on."

Jasen's heart swelled. "Really?"

"Yes. But it seems Adwig won the argument, so don't expect to get him all to yourself just yet."

Jasen took another puff as he absorbed that information. "But if that's true, shouldn't everyone be trying even harder to pull me down?"

"Why would they? The battle is clearly over. With the suitors arriving tomorrow, the consorts will be turning their attention to prey they actually have a chance at snaring. And what better way to prove you'd be a social boon to a potential spouse than by showing you are an intimate friend of the future king consort?"

Jasen flashed back to the rapturous applause he had received on the mudball field. It all made sense now. "That's so cynical."

Risyda laughed. "That's Court for you. Be prepared to have at least a dozen new best friends by tomorrow."

Jasen blanched. "I don't want a dozen new best friends." A picture flashed through his mind: he could see himself at Court, surrounded by fawning nobles, all expecting him to be the perfect consort. The terror of that thought brought his dream about the queen consort roaring back into his mind. His stomach twisted. He actually felt he might be sick.

There must have been something in Jasen's tone that made Risyda realize the extent of his distress. Her expression softened. "Hey," she said, taking his hand gently. "Are you really that nervous? Is that why you were acting so strangely this morning?"

Jasen considered telling her about the dream, but he didn't really want to talk about it. Instead, he simply nodded.

She pulled him into a hug. "I suppose you imagine you're going to have to go it alone, you great big idiot," she said as she pulled away. "I'm not about to abandon you to the wolves of court! I will be right there with you. I've done this twice already, remember? And despite what Lady Isalei would have you think, this isn't a test—for you especially, since you already found your husband." She grinned at him. "If you feel overwhelmed, come stand by me, and I will make you appear dazzling. All you'll have to do is smile. All right?"

Jasen tried a smile but wasn't quite sure he managed it.

Risyda handed him the hookah. "Have another puff, and then let's go to dinner."

Jasen took that puff—and another two on top of that—until his anxiety was sufficiently dampened. They made their way to the dining hall.

Sure enough, at dinner, a minor fight broke out when Lady Treburess slipped into the chair beside Jasen right as Lord Banither was about to take it himself. Risyda smoothed everything over. Just as she had promised, she handled most of the conversation, bouncing it around as skillfully as Jasen would a mudball. This surprised him—Risyda always made fun of the frivolous conversations they were expected to have, but she was really good at it when she tried. It was as if she were a candle that had at last been lit, and now she shone, her flame dancing merrily.

In fact, it seemed as if all of the consorts had their flames alight. Their collected mood had shifted again, from the messy playfulness of the day to a more calculated good humor, trying out their best quips and most coquettish ploys on each other. It was almost fun, in a strange way.

But there were two people not having a good time at all. Polina sat at the end of the table with Lalan. Polina clutched a wine bottle to her chest, taking long swigs from it as she watched the rest of them. Jasen couldn't hear what they were talking about over the din of the conversation of the rest of the room, but Lalan's expression was imploring while Polina's was dark. She stared directly at Jasen. Their gazes met. Jasen tried to smile at her—he almost called out to ask her to join them, but she rose before he could say anything, clutching her bottle to her chest as she staggered from the room. Lalan trailed off after her.

"It's not our problem," Risdya said under her breath.

Jasen turned his attention back to her. "What?"

"Polina. She's not our concern," she continued, quiet enough that the others wouldn't hear her. "Trust me—she gets like this every year, and there's no reasoning with her. Try not to engage with her at all from here on out. If she wants to sink herself, that's her own business." She eased back into the conversation around them before Jasen could reply.

At last, dinner ended, and the consorts dispersed—some to the parlors to continue their merriment, others to their rooms to prepare for the next day. Risyda invited Jasen back to her room, but he demurred. The bad feeling he'd started the day with was creeping back up on him. He just wanted to lie down.

He arrived at his room and went to open the door. Much to his surprise, the door opened before he could even touch the knob. A woman stumbled into him, nearly knocking them both over. The intruder tried to leave, but Jasen caught her by the arm. "Polina?"

Polina tried to shake herself out of his grip. "Let me go!"

"Not until you tell me what you were doing in my room!"

With a burst of strength, Polina freed herself, but she didn't run away. She stood there for a moment, glaring at him as she swayed back and forth. "I was looking for you," she said finally.

"Why?"

"Because I have things to say to you! Do you know how long I have trained for Court? *Do you?*"

Jasen shook his head.

"I have been in refinement school since I was eight years old. Eight! And I have worked hard. I know all the rules. I know all the dances. I can play the flute as beautifully as a bird's song. My needlepoint is without peer. I am well-read, able to converse on any subject. I work hard to make myself lovely to look at. My sense of fashion is impeccable." She blinked her eyes rapidly. "None of that comes easily to me. I spend every moment of every day *working* for this. And then you come in here and do everything wrong, but somehow, everything falls straight into your lap. How is that fair?" She wiped one eye with the heel of her hand.

Jasen reached out to touch her arm. "Don't cry."

She jerked away from him. "But you haven't won yet," she sneered. "Oh no, you have *not*. The king will grow bored with your innocent country boy act, and then he'll come to his senses and realize that he needs someone who is his equal. And that certainly isn't you!" She gave him a triumphant look, and with that, she marched away.

Or at least she tried to, but she tripped and fell flat on her face. Jasen got to his knees beside her. "Are you all right?"

"I'm fine! Get away from me!" But she started to sniffle.

"I'm not trying to beat you," Jasen said. "None of this is a game. You have to stop thinking of it like that."

She laughed through her tears. "If you think that, then you really are a simpleton." She dried her eyes on her sleeve and got to her feet, waving away Jasen's attempt to help her. She staggered off down the hallway.

Jasen waited until she disappeared around the corner

before entering his room. What had Polina been doing in there? He glanced around. Because Rotheld hadn't been on duty today, it was not as tidy as it usually was—Jasen hadn't straightened up his things before he left. It was therefore difficult to tell for sure if anything had been disturbed. Nevertheless, it didn't seem as though much was out of place. Besides, he couldn't imagine Polina stealing anything from him, even if she was intoxicated. So why had she been in there? To spy on him?

If that had been her ambition, then she would have left frustrated. There wasn't anything in his room that would have given her any information. But again, everything seemed in order—if she had been digging through his things, she hadn't left any sign of it. Jasen decided the best explanation was the simplest—she was drunk and came looking for a fight.

Jasen shrugged out of his clothes and went to the bath tub. After giving it a few taps, it filled with warm water. He climbed in. The warm water soothed his body but didn't do much to soothe his mind.

He finished up his bath and got ready for bed. It was early yet, but the day's events wore on him. Besides, he would need all of his energy for the coming day. He expected it to be a challenging one.

CHAPTER 9

*J*asen woke up just before dawn, with Rotheld arriving shortly after. He brought a small meal for Jasen, but Jasen was too nervous to eat. They didn't say much as Rotheld got Jasen ready—they had already extensively discussed his wardrobe for this day. For his morning outfit, he would wear a beige frock coat with delicate flowers embroidered on the skirt. He also wore a blue boutonniere to signal that his interest lay with men entirely. Those who favored women wore red flowers, and those who had interest in both wore purple. The purpose of the first outfit of the day was to entice, not dazzle—that effect was saved for the ball. Rotheld handed him a pale blue parasol— the consorts would be expected to spend much of the morning waiting for all of the suitors to arrive and thus required protection from the heat. Jasen thought that maybe wearing lighter clothes would be more useful, but he had long since passed trying to apply logic to fashion.

When Rotheld determined his appearance passed muster, Jasen made his way to Risyda's room. Her lady's maid was still working on her hair when Jasen entered, weaving violets into her dark curls, which hung loose over her shoulders. Like Jasen's frock coat, her dress was also embroidered with flowers, although it was a soft yellow instead. Her purple corsage stood out against such muted colors. She also wore a gold necklace with a sunflower pendant.

If only her expression were as sunny as her outfit. She barely managed a smile when she saw Jasen in the doorway. Her maid curtsied and left them. "What's the matter?" Jasen asked when she was gone. "You look so dour."

She patted her hair as she gazed at her reflection, her expression still grim. "I'm just not particularly excited about getting up on the auction block."

Jasen was pretty sure she wasn't serious, but he still felt himself go a little pale. "There's an auction block?"

At that, she laughed. She stood up and gave him a kiss on the cheek. "Only a metaphorical one. I'm sorry. Don't let my sourness make you nervous. Today will go well, I'm sure of it." She took a step back to examine him. "You look marvelous."

"You do, too."

She waved a hand dismissively. "I'm passable, certainly. But I doubt anyone is going to notice me if I'm standing next to you."

She'd meant it as a compliment, but it only served to make him feel more nervous. "Won't they all be in for a shock when they realize this is an elaborate disguise and that I'm only a backward country boy after all?"

"So what if they do? You've already won over the only two people who matter."

"Who?"

She gave him a cheeky grin. "The king and myself, of course." She linked her right arm with Jasen's and grabbed her parasol with her left. "Now come on. There's no sense in dawdling."

They made their way downstairs, where all of the consorts were gathering. He saw Polina and her entourage. She was dressed a light green, which matched her current complexion. She looked like she was going to be sick and was leaning heavily on Lalan and Banithar.

When all of the consorts arrived, they began migrating toward the main palace. Lady Isalei and the other mentors led the way. As soon as they went outside, all of the consorts opened their parasols, like a field of wildflowers blooming all at once. The sun was shining brightly, but it was still early enough that the heat of the day wasn't bearing down on them. The consorts were strutting with courtly grace, but they couldn't help but talk excitedly with one another. The mix of all those hopeful conversations sounded like the hum of a hive of very well-mannered bees.

With everyone dressed so gaily and in such a good mood, Jasen's nervousness eased. He still wasn't looking forward to the suitors' arrival, but it was hard to feel gloomy. He glanced at Risyda, who smiled at him. It seemed as if her sour mood had melted a bit as well.

They arrived at the front gates of the main palace and arranged themselves along the path to the great doors. A coterie of guards was there to meet them, all in formal uniform meant more for spectacle than practicality. Jasen caught sight of Larely, who winked at him. Jasen grinned back. Further along down the path were a group of servants, also in fancy attire. One footman was particularly fancy—he would be receiving the lords and ladies and formally announcing them. Servants handed out baskets of flower petals to all of the consorts—they were supposed to throw them at the feet of the arriving suitors.

"How are we supposed to hold onto our parasols and throw these petals at the same time?" Jason asked Risyda.

"Awkwardly."

It was another half an hour before the first suitor of the day arrived. The consorts gave a cheer as his carriage pulled up to the path. One of the footmen opened the carriage door, and a moment later a lord emerged. He didn't look much older than the consorts, but he was significantly heavier than most and had a very red face. The footman handed a scroll to the fancy royal footman.

The footman cleared his throat. "Presenting Willix, Duke of Symes in the kingdom of Banmor."

The Duke of Symes made an awkward bow to the consorts and made his way down the walkway. Most of the consorts held their little baskets in the same hand with which they held their parasols, leaving their free hand to strew the petals. However, some of them with more elaborate parasols had to put them down. Jasen noticed that Polina wasn't even trying. She was holding on to her parasol with both hands and holding very still, as if any attempt at movement would cause her to fall over. He couldn't help but feel a little sorry for her.

After the duke had passed them by, Risyda leaned over to whisper to Jasen. "He came into his title last year. By all accounts he should be a prime prize—he's a duke, after all— but Banmor is so barren and boring, and the poor duke is so sweaty and awkward, that no one accepted his proposal, and I know for a fact he made at least three. Poor fellow—I think he'd make a nice enough husband, but I can't say I blame the ones who turned him down. I danced with him once and his hands were so sweaty that he left my dress damp. Imagine what bedding him would be like."

Jasen blinked at her. "Do you know that much about all of the suitors?"

"Of course. Well, the ones who were here last year, at any rate, although I have been keeping my ears pricked for information about our new arrivals. The gossip is the only thing that makes this whole charade bearable!"

Jasen laughed a little, but he felt his nervousness return. The gossip had been bad enough when it was just the consorts, but with the arrival of the suitors, everyone would be on high alert for scandals. He knew he was already a popular subject for conversation—he'd just have to make sure he did as little as possible to stoke that interest any higher.

After the duke's entrance, the suitors began to arrive in a steady stream. Most of them had made the journey from their home kingdoms some time ago and had been staying with one of the noble families of the Draelands before taking up lodgings just outside of the city. There was a mix of returning suitors and ones fresh to the Court.

Watching all of the suitors parade in front of them was interesting for a little while, but after about an hour, Jasen got bored, even with Risyda's entertaining commentary. He could tell he wasn't the only one. The day had begun to heat up, but the strain of holding up their parasols began to get tiresome, so many of them folded them up and were thus unprotected. Several took out their fans, and Jasen cursed himself for not bringing his the one time it would have been useful. Even though the servants continued to refill their flower petal baskets with new petals, they all seemed as wilted as the consorts who threw them.

Another hour passed, and just when Jasen thought he was about to drop from the heat and the tedium, he was invigorated—although he would have much preferred the boredom to the shock he got. A familiar carriage had arrived, although he couldn't quite place it at first. It all became clear when the door opened and the lord inside stepped out.

"Presenting Bertio, Lord of Cheny in the kingdom of Genyon."

And sure enough, it was him. A little older and a great deal fancier, but the same Bertio he remembered from all those years ago. Well, four years ago, at any rate.

When he got over the shock, he snapped open his parasol and held it in front of him like a shield. Risyda gave him a quizzical look. "What's wrong?" she said, a little louder than Jasen thought necessary.

He shushed her. "I know him," he said in a terse whisper.

Risyda raised an eyebrow. "Is he an enemy of yours?"

"Worse. He's my ex-lover."

Risyda's eyes widened. "That's not good."

Jasen stayed hidden under the parasol until he heard Bertio's footsteps fade. He took a quick peek to make sure he was gone, but of course at that exact moment, Bertio turned around. Their gazes met for the briefest moment before Jasen ducked behind his parasol again.

"What's he doing?" Jasen asked Risyda. "Is he still looking this way?"

"No, he's moving forward again."

"Do you think he saw me?"

"What was there to see? You only peeked for a second!"

Jasen twisted a finger around a lock of his hair. "I tend to stand out," he said rather grimly. He glanced at the other consorts, who were staring at him and Risyda. Banither in particular seemed to take particular interest. "Let's talk about it later," he said even more quietly. Risyda nodded in agreement.

The rest of the procession was a blur. At last at around noon, they were all given leave to go. The consorts ambled back to the East Wing, as worn out as any mudball player might be after a game. And to think they still had the ball this evening.

Their usual luncheon was not held in order to give the consorts time to rest and recuperate. Instead, trays of food awaited each of them in their room. Rotheld helped Jasen out of his morning outfit and left quickly, for which Jasen was grateful. He needed a moment to think. He sponged himself off before putting on the mercifully comfortable leisure outfit that Rotheld had left for him—a shirt made of light linen and some loose pantaloons, as well as a robe. Jasen was pretty sure he wasn't supposed to leave his room wearing such casual clothing, but he didn't really care. After wolfing down his food, he headed for Risyda's room.

She opened the door before he could even knock and pulled him inside. She was dressed the same as him, with her hair loose over her shoulders. "Tell me everything," she said. "And quickly. My maid is going to be back soon to do my hair—it's going to take the rest of the afternoon."

"He was my first lover. We met when his family came to visit Queen Urga for the annual Hog Festival. We were both sixteen and very bored. So we made our own entertainment."

"Did things end badly?"

"No, he just left for home and we never saw each other again. I have seen his parents and his brother on occasion, but that's just the thing—he shouldn't be here! His brother is the heir. When his parents decided to pass along the title, it went to him." Although traditions differed from kingdom to kingdom, most noble families in the Allied Realms had a path of succession in which the title holding nobility, when they reached a certain age, could pass along their titles to the younger generation and enter retirement, if they wished. "And his brother is married! The only way he could have gotten the title is if both his brother and his wife were dead, and I certainly would have gotten word if that had happened. Unless it was very recent—but if that's the case, he should be in mourning, not looking for a spouse!" Jasen collapse dramatically onto Risyda's sofa. "I'm supposed to be a virgin! If he says anything, I'm finished."

Risyda sat down beside him. "It's less than ideal, but I don't think it's quite the disaster you think it is. If there isn't any bad blood between you, why would he make trouble for you?"

"He might not do it on purpose."

"So talk to him. Tell him you'd appreciate his discretion. I'm sure he'll understand."

The panic in Jasen's chest eased. Maybe she was right. Bertio was a decent person—at least, he was when they were sixteen. While they had had fun together, it had become clear by the second week that Bertio's favorite subjects of conversation were himself and money, so he wasn't exactly heartbroken to see him leave. But he wasn't a bad person. Surely four years hadn't changed him too much.

Jasen made his way back to his room. He was about to lie down to take a nap when there was a knock on the door. Jasen winced—who could it be? He opened the door and was greeted by a servant carrying a note. Jasen thanked him and took the note to his room. His heart raced as he sat down at his vanity—had Bertio discovered him already? But then he noticed with relief that the wax seal was Rilvor's. His racing heart skipped into more of a flutter. He quickly broke the seal and began to read.

My dearest Jasen,

I have no doubt that this morning was a strain for you, but please spare a thought for your poor Rilvor, who must be king almost without pause for the next month. As you read this, I am no doubt listening to many important people sing my praises, which I am sure is satisfying for many people, but alas, I find myself to be a tedious subject of conversation. But I believe our guests will be pleased with themselves, for their flattery will seem to have made me happy. They do not know that my smile is for you, imagining you as you read this—in bed, perhaps? Am I too forward to imagine you there? Forgive me if I am.

As I must be king tonight, I will perhaps not have as much time to devote to you as I wish. In fact, I am quite sure of it, as I long to devote all of my time to you, to the exclusion of all others. Alas, that is not a luxury I can afford. Please forgive the king for his divided attention, and remember that I remain always, in my heart—

Your Rilvor.

Jasen didn't have to look in the mirror to know his face had turned bright red. In fact, his face wasn't the only area blood was rushing to. He contemplated getting into bed and embodying Rilvor's vision, but he was interrupted by another knock on the door.

He was greeted by another servant, this one holding a pair of shoes. He bowed. "Your shoes, my lord."

Jasen blinked at him. "My shoes?"

The servant furrowed his brow. "Yes, my lord. These are yours, aren't they?"

Jasen examined them. They were indeed his—in fact, they were the pair he had planned to wear to the ball. "Yes, there are mine, but what are you doing with them?"

"I was told you had sent them to be polished. Have I made a mistake, my lord? It wasn't me who took them!"

He hadn't, but the poor servant looked miserable, as if he were afraid Jasen would start shouting at him. Perhaps Rotheld had done it. "It's fine," Jasen said, accepting the shoes. "Thank you. They look very shiny."

The servant gave him a relieved bow and left. Jasen put the shoes away and lay down for a nap, although it wasn't for as long as he would have liked. All too soon, Rotheld arrived, and they began the tedious process of getting dressed. It was the most challenging outfit Jasen had yet to wear. His clothes were a mixture of gold and deep emerald green, studded with jewels and so tight that he didn't know how he was expected to walk, much less dance. Jasen had managed to convince Rotheld to let him wear his hair down ever since he told him that the king preferred it that way, but Rotheld was determined to make even that uncomfortable, weaving sparkling ribbons through it so that there were flashes of gold whenever he moved his head. On his fingers, he wore rings that were probably each worth more than his estate in Grumhul.

Still, for as much that Jasen complained, he couldn't deny that the effect was impressive. He looked every inch the consummate consort. Staring at his reflection, he could almost believe that he was worthy of a king. He slipped into his shoes last—the jewels twinkled like stars. He hadn't wore this pair before, since they were rather showy. While he had gotten much better with his balance, these seemed especially tricky.

He made his way downstairs to join the mass of consorts waiting to make their way to the ballroom. While the energy in the morning had been giddy, everyone seemed a bit more sober now. After all, this was what they had been working towards for months—in fact, for years, in most of their cases. Of course, the somber mood could also be due to the uncomfortable outfits. It was hard to be giddy when half your concentration was on staying upright.

They moved toward the palace ballroom en masse, with Lady Isalei leading them. The sun had set, but the dragon lights shone especially bright, making them all glitter and shine. Jasen had to admit that it felt special. At long last, he felt like he belonged.

The ballroom was dazzling. They had all been several times to practice dancing and Jasen had always been impressed with its grandeur, but it was nothing in comparison to how it was now. The decorations were dragon themed, gorgeous and polished and impossibly grand. There was a stage erected in the front of the room, on which sat the throne. Rilvor would not make his entrance until later. Jasen felt a little bit of his new found confidence wane, especially since they were now all under the gaze of the suitors, who had already arrived and were milling about. They all stopped speaking with the consorts entered.

The herald arrived to announce the consorts each by name, just as he had announced the suitors earlier in the day. Jasen had known about this, of course—they had practiced it many times, and he hadn't been especially nervous about it. But the situation had changed—he realized there would be no hiding from Bertio. He bit his lip so hard that it almost drew blood. Risyda was right—he should just talk to him. Not that he had much of a choice, anyway.

After the introductions were over, the musicians began to play, and the suitors and consorts at last began to mingle. Jasen stuck by Risyda, who was especially tall tonight with her big shoes and enormous hair.

"You can't hide behind me all night," she pointed out as she grabbed two glasses of champagne from a passing servant. She handed one to Jasen. "Drink this. It will help. Then go find him and get it over with."

Jasen did as he was told and immediately regretted it as his nervous stomach rebelled. "But what can I say with everyone here? What if someone overhears—"

They were interrupted when a stunning blonde woman approached them. "Lady Risyda," she said. Her voice was deep and rich—everything about her was rich, really. She was dripping with jewels. "I was hoping you would be here again this year."

And then something extraordinary happened. Risyda blushed. "Good evening, Lady Wesor," she said in a voice that Jasen had never heard before. She actually sounded...shy. "May I present to you Lord Jasen."

Lady Wesor took his hand and kissed it. "It's a pleasure to

meet you. You are all anyone could talk about this afternoon."

Jasen had no idea what to say to that, so he drank some more champagne. Lady Wesor turned to Risyda once more. "I was wondering if you would do me the pleasure of giving me your first dance? Or are you going to make me chase you all night again?"

Risyda took a moment to reply. "Yes, of course," she said. She took Lady Wesor's hand and they were off to the dance floor. Risyda shot Jasen an apologetic look over her shoulder.

And so Jasen was left defenseless. Jasen scanned the room. Sure enough, he was attracting attention already, although no one approached him yet. He felt something like a deer amongst wolves who were still forming the best plan of attack.

He retreated to the refreshment table and took another glass of champagne. The queasy feeling continued, but it made a little of the panic recede. He looked to the throne, willing the king to arrive. Not that it mattered, he reminded himself sourly. As sweet as Rilvor's note had been, he'd all but said that Jasen would be on his own for much of the night.

No sooner than he had finished his second glass of champagne, he was approached by a rotund gentleman in a powdered wig. Jasen recognized him as the sweaty duke from Banmor. Before Jasen quite knew what was happening, the man took his hand and kissed it. "Forgive me for being presumptuous, but I was overwhelmed by your beauty and had no choice but to present myself to you. I am the Duke of Symes. Would it be unforgivably impertinent if I asked for the honor of a dance?"

"I'm afraid you'll have to wait," a familiar voice interrupted, and Jasen was abruptly confronted with the very man he had been attempting to avoid. Bertio put a hand on Jasen's shoulder. "I'm afraid Lord Jasen has already promised his first dance to me. We're old friends, you see." He gave the duke a charming smile.

"My apologies," the duke said to Bertio before turning back to Jasen. "I wouldn't imagine asking you to break a promise, but I do hope you think of me later this evening."

Jasen gave him a vague nod. When he had left, Jasen faced Bertio with reluctance. He was even more dashing than he was when they had first met. His wavy brown hair was cut roguishly short, and brown eyes were as pretty as Jasen remembered. "Hello, Bertio. Or Lord Cheny now, I suppose."

"Yes, but I will always be Bertio to you, I hope." He presented his hand to Jasen. "Shall we?"

Jasen took it. What else could he do?

Once they reached the dance floor, Jasen felt a surge of gratitude for all of the lessons he had so hated. His body moved with the music almost automatically. It was too bad the conversation was not as easy. They danced in silence for a minute or so before Bertio broke the silence. "'Oh Bertio, how good it is to see you!' " he said in a fairly good imitation of Jasen's voice. "Good to see you too, Jasen," he continued, switching back to his own voice. "It's been ages. Did you get those letters I sent you? 'Oh yes, I'm so sorry for not replying, but you know how it is in hog breeding season.'" He grinned. "You can jump in any time. Having to do both ends of the conversation is rather tiring.

Jasen couldn't help but smile. Bertio was pompous, but he could also be fun. "Sorry. I'm just surprised to see you."

"And I you. What are you doing here?"

"I could ask you the same thing. Did your brother die?" As soon as the words left his mouth, Jasen cringed. That wasn't a very sensitive way to put it.

But Bertio just laughed. "To the point, as usual. No, he's

alive." There was something in his tone of voice that made Jasen think he wasn't altogether pleased with that fact.

"Then how are you Lord Cheny?"

The barest hint of a grimace passed over Bertio's face. "It's a long story. And how are *you* a consort?"

"Also a long story. You go first."

Bertio sighed. "My brother was called by a dragon."

Jasen cocked his head. "What do you mean? Surely he hasn't abandoned his wife to become a draed?"

"No, nothing like that. She was called too, it seems."

"Called to do what?"

"To renounce his title, give away all his money, and live in communion with nature. It has something to do with how there is a great reckoning coming, and the nobles must be prepared to be judged for their indulgent way, and so on." Bertio rolled his eyes. "I don't believe a word of it. I think he was simply tired of trying to live up to Mother's standards, but if she was so concerned about keeping up appearances, then she shouldn't have let Father pass along the title. Now it's up to me, which is why I'm here to find a consort."

Jasen frowned. If his brother had given away all their money, how could Bertio afford to be here? He decided it would be rude to ask, so he said nothing.

"And now it's your turn. I thought the vetting process for consorts was rather extensive, and we both know you aren't exactly qualified."

Bertio's voice had been low, but Jasen couldn't help but look around and see if anyone had heard him.

Bertio leaned in close to his ear. "Don't look so nervous," he said in an amused whisper. "I can be discreet, if you remember."

Jasen leaned away. He didn't want think about the things that they'd done together which required the discretion in the first place. "If you must know, my father won a place for me in a bet."

Bertio laughed. "That seems about right. It seems he hasn't changed."

"Unfortunately, no."

The song ended. "It was nice catching up," Jasen said after they had bowed to one another. He turned to leave, but Bertio caught him by the hand.

"Surely you aren't so eager to dance with the Duke of Symes?" he said. "Dance with me again. You owe it to me after you ignored all my letters."

"You didn't send that many," Jasen said with a scowl. "And I did reply."

"Only once."

Jasen considered him. He had thought that the way they had drifted apart had been mutual, but had he been wrong? "All right," Jasen conceded. "One more dance."

The music started up again. "So," Bertio began, "I hear that you might be our next king consort."

Jasen wasn't sure what to say. "You would have to ask the king. It's his decision."

"But does it seem to be the direction things are headed?"

"I really can't say."

"Can't, or won't?"

"Both. Gossip is already spreading like wildfire. I don't want to add more fuel to it."

"Oh, come on. You can tell me. We are old friends, after all." He had a strange glint in his eye that Jasen didn't like.

"Really, Bertio, I can't. I'm sorry."

The glint in his eye hardened. "I'm discreet, remember? Just tell me." His voice now had an edge to it.

The situation was making Jasen uncomfortable. He tried to pull away, but Bertio's grip on his hand grew tighter. Jasen stopped dancing and yanked his hand away. "I said no."

Bertio began to scowl, but twisted his face into a more neutral position. "My apologies. I was merely curious." He reached his hand out again. "Shall we continue?"

"I don't think so." He bowed. "If you'll excuse me."

Jasen's abrupt departure from the dance floor did garner some attention. Jasen tried to ignore it. He didn't want to spend another moment with Bertio. He didn't like the way that he looked at him—as if he wanted something.

The song ended. He could see the Duke of Symes ambling toward him. He pretended not to see him and headed for the refreshment table, only to be confronted with two more nobles who were both looking at him expectantly. He stopped where he was and searched the room for Risyda and found her still in the arms of that lady—they were both laughing. Jasen felt betrayed. She was supposed to hate this as much as he did!

Just when he thought he was cornered, a trumpet blasted, and the herald appeared on the stage. The music and the dancers came to a stop. The herald cleared his throat. "Presenting His Royal Highness and Lord of the Drae, King Rilvor!"

Everyone applauded as Rilvor took the stage. The musicians began to play again—this time, the national anthem of the Draelands. He was resplendent in his royal regalia—he wore a red cape so long that two footman had to carry the train. A crown decorated with golden dragons adorned his head. In his hand, he held a scepter.

Rilvor waited until the anthem was finished, smiling and waving at the guests. When the music ended, he held up a hand to quiet the applause as well. "Welcome, everyone," he said. "It is always a pleasure to host this gathering—a time-honored tradition that has served to strengthen the ties between our realms by bringing noble families together. I am not one for long speeches, and I know you must be anxious to return to the hunt." That last line got a few chuckles. "But I would like to leave you all with a word of advice. The bonds that are made here should not only be between families and kingdoms." He scanned the crowd until he spotted Jasen. He smiled. "It should be between you and your spouse as well. Love is what truly unites us."

Everyone noticed where the king was looking. Jasen tried to appear smaller, but that was impossible, what with the enormous shoes he was wearing.

Everyone applauded again and the musicians began to play. The footman removed Rilvor's cape and he descended from the stage, making his way straight for Jasen. The crowd parted for him, and by the time he met Jasen, there was a large circle of suitors and consorts surrounding them, although at a respectable distance. Rilvor paid them no mind. He held out his hand.

"May I have this dance?"

Jasen took his hand. The two of them began to dance. Jasen could feel all of the eyes still on them, but somehow when he was in Rilvor's arms, it didn't seem to matter.

"I thought you were going to be too busy being the king tonight," Jasen said.

"And I will be, but surely my subjects would not be so cruel as to deny me one dance." He leaned in. "And besides, I want to make my intentions very clear. I do not wish for anyone to waste time courting either of us."

Jasen knew that the smile on his face must have been extremely goofy, but he couldn't bring himself to care. He wanted desperately to kiss him, but that really would be a scandal.

They glided around the dance floor. The other couples stopped gawking and began dancing as well. Not that Jasen was paying them much mind—it was impossible to think about anything other than the hand around his waist, and the look in Rilvor's blue eyes as they gazed at each other, lost in the moment—

But something went amiss. Jasen stumbled. He wouldn't think much of it—after all, his shoes really were uncomfortable—but then he stumbled again. Rilvor frowned at him. "Is everything all right?"

"Yes," Jasen said. "I'm sorry, I seem to be a bit clumsy—" But his words were abruptly cut off when he was lurched out of Rilvor's arms by some unseen force. He stumbled and spun across the room until he crashed into the refreshment table, sending everything scattering, including the punch bowl, which upended onto his head and soaked him.

The dancers came to a halt. There were several gasps, and even a few chuckles.

Rilvor raced to his side and dropped to his knees beside Jasen. "What happened? Are you all right?"

"I don't know," Jasen said. "I-I'm just clumsy, I suppose…" Everyone was watching them. Jasen felt a rush of shame so strong that it brought tears to his eyes. Who could possibly think that he was a suitable match for the king now?

But there was no embarrassment in Rilvor's expression— only concern. "Are you hurt?" He ran a hand down to his leg, and stopped when he reached his foot. A look of anger crossed his face, so intense that it took Jasen aback. He abruptly removed Jasen's shoes and flung them away as if they were poisonous vipers. He put his arms under Jasen's knees and shoulders and lifted him off the ground.

The crowd, which had begun to hum with murmurs, grew louder as Rilvor made his way to the exit. Lady Isalei approached them, moving rather spritely for a woman her age, catching up with him just as he reached the door. "Your Majesty, if Lord Jasen has been injured, I can send for a healer—"

"I will see to him myself," the king said tersely.

"Yes, Your Majesty, but the guests—"

"—can entertain themselves. They will probably be grateful for my absence, as they can gossip more freely." His voice was thick with bitterness. Jasen stared at him in wonderment. He had never seen Rilvor this angry—in fact, he hadn't been convinced that he was capable of it.

He could tell by Lady Isalei's expression that she was just as surprised. She curtsied. "Yes, Your Majesty."

The guards opened the door. Rilvor turned slightly so as not to bump Jasen's head, and so Jasen got one last glimpse of the crowd. His gaze happened to land on Polina, whose face had gone as white as her dress.

Rilvor kept a brisk pace, his gaze fixed in front of him, his mouth set in a thin line.

"I'm not injured, you know," Jasen said after awhile. "I can walk."

"Not until I examine you," he said.

"I know I'm on the smaller side, but surely I'm not *that* light. And if you throw out your back, where will that leave us?"

Rilvor's grim expression softened a bit. Carefully, he set Jasen down. "You will let me know if you have any pain?"

"The only thing I hurt was my pride. I promise."

"We cannot be sure of that."

"Why?"

"Because your shoes were cursed."

CHAPTER 10

*A*s soon as Rilvor said the words, Jasen understood what had happened. It was what Polina had been doing in his room—he hadn't thought that she took anything, but he had so many pairs of shoes that he hadn't noticed they were gone. She must have taken them and sent them to someone to curse, and then sent them back to him under the guise that they had been taken to be cleaned. "Oh."

Rilvor's expression hardened again. "You do not look surprised." He took Jasen's hand. "Come. Let us discuss this in privacy."

Rilvor led him to his chambers. He had Jasen sit down on the sofa as he ran his hands over his feet, concentrating. At last, he seemed satisfied. "I feel no more magic. The curse was not potent."

"Well, that's good news, although I think it would be impossible to make me even clumsier than I already am."

Rilvor rose from the floor to join Jasen on the sofa. "Do not speak lightly of this. This was a serious attack on you."

"Nothing that terrible happened. I was just embarrassed —something I would have probably done anyway."

"And what if the caster had sent you down a flight of stairs? This was a threat on your life!" That frightening expression was back on his face. "And you will tell me now who dared to do this. You do know, do you not?"

"I do," Jasen said quietly.

"Give me a name."

"And then what will happen?"

"They will be tried and convicted."

"And the punishment?" Jasen asked, his voice even quieter.

"Exile, if I am feeling generous."

Jasen bit his lip. Polina was terrible, but the thought of her being put through all of that made him feel queasy. "I'm sure she didn't mean to seriously injure me. She just wanted to embarrass me."

"So it is a lady I will be searching for."

"Let me talk to her. I'm sure it won't happen again."

"This person is a friend?" Rilvor asked, his voice rising in both surprise and fury. "Is it that tall one who is always with you? She dares to betray you, and you would protect her?"

"No! Not her. Someone else. I caught her in my room the other night—she must have taken the shoes then. She's petty and jealous, but I know she's also desperate. You don't know the kind of pressure the consorts are under. I don't think she deserves to have her entire life destroyed over a lapse in judgment borne out of desperation. She isn't a monster—she's confused. She deserves our pity, not our rage."

Rilvor looked as if he were going to argue, but he closed his eyes and took a deep breath instead. When he opened them again, the fire had left them. He lifted Jasen's hand to his mouth and kissed it. "Your heart is too pure for this den of vipers. Very well—but you must impress upon this young lady that it is only your mercy that is saving her from ruin. If something like this happens again, she will not be so lucky."

Jasen grimaced. He could imagine how well that was going to go over. He was soon distracted from any unpleasant thoughts when Rilvor ran his fingers through Jasen's hair before cupping his face in his hand. There was a different sort of fire in his eyes now—one that Jasen didn't mind at all. Rilvor leaned in for a kiss, but stopped at the last moment. He put his head on Jasen's shoulder instead.

"If I kiss you now, I will not want to stop," he said.

Jasen was about to ask him what was wrong with that, but then he remembered he was supposed to be a virgin, which led his mind back to Bertio, which then made him think of the crowd at the ball, and by the time his mind had made it through all of that, the mood was thoroughly spoiled. "Do we have to go back?"

Rilvor kissed his forehead. "You do not. I believe I should, alas. I will call someone to escort you to your room."

"I can find my own way."

"It is not you I am worried about. How can I know that the person who cursed you will not seek to hide her guilt with another attack on you?"

"She won't."

"Humor me."

Jasen sighed. "There's a guard by the name of Larely. Would you send him?"

"As you wish."

It wasn't long after Rilvor left that there was a knock on the door. Jasen opened it to find Larely standing there. "What in the name of the Drae is going on?" he said before Jasen could even say hello. "Are you all right? Why did the king throw your shoes?"

"Because they were cursed."

"*What?*"

"Can it wait until we get back to my room? I just want to get into some comfortable clothes."

When they got back to his room, they were surprised to find Risyda there, waiting outside his door. She pulled Jasen into a hug. "Thank goodness you're all right. You should hear the rumors going around already."

Jasen pulled back. "How did you get away?"

"Lady Isalei was too busy trying to restore order to notice me slip away." She opened the door to Jasen's room. "Let's get inside."

Once they were all in the room, Jasen told them the whole story. They were both quiet for a moment after he finished.

Risyda spoke first. "I'm going to kill her."

"Please don't."

"Then you should have told him it was Polina, because if he's not going to get the chance to officially put her on trial, then I'm afraid that you've left me no choice but to mete out my own justice."

"She was your friend once," Jasen said. "Don't you have at least a little sympathy for her?"

"I used to, but this is beyond the pale."

"Risyda's right," Larely said. "This was an attack. You should tell him who's responsible."

"I can't know for sure," Jasen said.

"I guarantee you I can get a confession out of her," Risyda said. Jasen could see smoke coming out of her fingertips—he wondered if that was on purpose.

"Please," he said. "Can we just sleep on it? I'm too exhausted to think straight. We can decide how to approach it tomorrow."

Risyda took a deep breath. "All right. But you can't just ignore this. She has to be held accountable. You don't know her like I do. Getting away with it is only going to make her bolder."

Jasen wasn't sure if he believed that, but he didn't feel like arguing anymore. Risyda pulled him in for another hug. "Poor Jasen. Get some rest."

After she released him, Larely patted him on the arm. "We'll get this sorted out."

As soon as they left, Rotheld appeared as if by magic. Jasen supposed it wasn't that surprising—no doubt the whole palace had heard of what happened. But Rotheld did not pepper him with questions, for which Jasen was grateful. He helped him out of his clothes and drew a bath, and then left him alone at last. Jasen did his best to relax, but he had a feeling that things were going to get worse before they got better.

~

It was still dark outside when Risyda came for Jasen, pounding at his door until he crawled blearily out of his bed, put on his dressing gown, and answered it.

"What is it?" he asked sleepily. She also only wore a dressing gown. She was holding her hand up beside her— gentle flames glowed at her fingertips, lighting the dark hallway. Jasen started to get worried. "Has something happened?"

"Not yet, but it's about to. Don't bother getting dressed. We need to get to Polina before everyone else is up."

"What do you mean 'get to her'? You aren't going to hurt her, are you?"

"Much as I am tempted, no. But like I said, she needs to know that she can't keep doing this. If you don't want the king involved, that means it's up to us."

Jasen bit his lip. This wasn't going to be fun. "All right. Let's go."

They moved through the hallways as quietly as possible, all too soon reaching Polina's door. Risyda pulled a key from a pocket in her gown. "Courtesy of Larely," she said as she slipped it into the lock. They went through the door and shut it behind them.

Polina, unsurprisingly, was still asleep. Risyda grabbed her by the arm and yanked her out of bed. She went crashing to the floor.

"Rise and shine, Princess," Risyda said, prodding her with her foot. This was already getting more intense than Jasen was comfortable with.

Polina looked up blearily at them from the floor. "What are you doing? Why are you here?"

"Take a guess."

"I-I'm sure I don't know," she said. She didn't look well—there were bags under her eyes, and her whole face was puffy.

"So who did you get to do it? How much did you have to pay? Curses don't come cheap, but I suppose that isn't a problem for you."

"I didn't—I didn't—" But she couldn't finish the sentence, instead bursting into tears.

"The king considers it an attack on Lord Jasen. He wants to see you dragged in front of a court and banished."

Polina cried harder. "Oh, no—please, no! I didn't want him to be hurt." She turned her teary gaze to Jasen. "Were you injured? You're all right, aren't you?"

Risyda cut in before Jasen could answer. "Stop acting like you care about anything other than your own miserable hide!"

But that wasn't true—Jasen did feel sorry for her. He put a hand on Risyda's shoulder. "I think maybe I should handle this," he said quietly.

Jasen was afraid for a moment that Risyda wasn't going to listen to him, but after a moment, she relented. "Fine."

Jasen turned to Polina. "Why don't you sit down on the sofa while I get you a handkerchief?"

She gave him a bewildered look. "A handkerchief?"

He smiled at her. "It will be hard to talk if you have the sniffles. Where do you keep them?"

"In my bedside table," she said, still sounding a little dazed. He didn't blame her—it had to be confusing going from being screamed at to having someone offer you a hanky. Jasen went to her bedside table and opened the drawer. Sure enough, there were some neatly folded handkerchiefs. He took one and brought it over to the sofa, handing it to Polina. She accepted it with a confused expression. "Thank you," she said hesitantly.

"You're welcome."

Jasen sat down beside Polina while Risyda remained standing, towering over them. "You are extremely lucky that Jasen is too kind for his own good. He's the only thing standing between you and the king's justice."

"You didn't tell him?" Polina asked. "Why?"

"Because I believe you," he said, giving Risyda a pointed look. She crossed her arms with a huff. "I don't think you truly meant to hurt me. I expect you only meant to embarrass me. But Polina, these stunts have to stop."

Polina laughed miserably into her handkerchief. "Oh, of course. The only one allowed to pull stunts around here is you."

Jasen sighed in exasperation. "I don't pull stunts!"

"Don't insult my intelligence. You've done nothing else since the moment you got here. Wandering half-naked into the draemir, sneaking off to play that ridiculous mudball game with his children, pretending you couldn't ride and crashing into a tree so that the king would have to rescue you..."

Jasen blinked—how had she known about the mudball? "None of those were 'stunts,' I promise you."

Polina sneered at him. "So you just accidentally ensnared him with your country boy charms. I find that hard to believe."

"I've told you before—this isn't a game to me, and it shouldn't be to you, either! You have many fine qualities—" Risyda let out a loud scoff at that, but Jasen ignored her. "I'm sure you could find love if you stopped treating this as a competition."

"But I have found love," she said, her lip quivering. "I love the king." And then she wept into her handkerchief again.

Jasen had no idea what to say. It had never crossed his mind that she had actual feelings for Rilvor. He'd always thought that she just wanted the biggest prize and figured the king was it. "You love him?"

She wiped her eyes. "Yes. I fell in love with him the last year. One day, I was on a walk through the gardens and I saw him there, sitting at a fountain, all alone. I could tell he had just been crying. Oh, he has such a tender heart, to still be weeping for his wife! And so I offered him my handkerchief, and he thanked me and invited me to sit down. And we talked for a while—I can hardly remember about what. He is so handsome, and so kind—not like all the lords and ladies who come through here, looking for a bride to buy. And he gave me my handkerchief back and told me that I had been a comfort to him." She smiled dreamily to herself. "I have kept that kerchief ever since. I sleep with it every night." Then she seemed to remember Jasen's presence, and her smile turned into a scowl. "Minister Adwig told me he was certain the king would choose me. And then you came along and spoiled everything!"

Jasen wasn't sure what to say. He believed that the

encounter had happened, but he highly doubted that it had meant as much to Rilvor as it had to her.

Before he could think of an answer, Risyda butted in. "And from that encounter you decided he must be desperately in love with you? He probably doesn't even remember it."

"I'm sure he does!"

"So I assume you talked about it when you had your audience with him."

Polina hesitated. "Not as such, but I'm sure he was thinking about it too! He was so kind to me—"

"He's kind to everyone. You aren't special. You mean nothing to him—and I don't think he means anything to you, either. You've always been ambitious, ever since we were girls. You want to marry a king. That's all that matters to you —you've made that very clear!"

Polina let out a nasty laugh. "I know it must be hard to imagine caring about something, since you care about nothing. You always thought you were so much better than everyone else, so above it all, even though you're only a merchant's daughter and should be grateful you were even allowed in!"

"Trust me, I'm not any happier about it than you are."

"Then why are you still here? If you hate it so much, then leave. No one's stopping you."

Risyda seemed taken aback. For once, she didn't have anything to say.

Polina scoffed. "I know why you don't want to leave. If you went back to your father's house, you would have no one to feel superior to."

Risyda's face had gone red. There was smoke coming out of her fingertips. "That isn't true!"

"So you don't think you're better than me?"

Surprisingly, Risyda's expression softened. "Not when

we were younger, when we skipped out of school to go playing in the forest, or when we played jokes on the tutors, or when we would sneak into each others' room at night and spend the whole time playing games and sharing secrets." She wiped at her eye with her sleeve. "But then you came back one year a complete stranger. Whatever happened to Polly?"

A few more tears rolled down Polina's cheeks. "I don't know. Maybe she's still playing with Rizzy somewhere. She seems to have gone missing, too."

Rizzy? Jasen thought, but he didn't have much time to contemplate it because now both of the girls were weeping and Jasen had no idea how to handle it. He ran over to the bedside table and got a handkerchief for Risyda, who accepted it. Jasen stood there helplessly as they both continued to cry.

Just when he was about to suggest a hug, Risyda wiped her nose and spoke again. "Are you going to stop this foolishness now?"

Polina shook her head. "Would you give up on true love?"

Risyda's expression hardened. Whatever tender moment they had shared was over now. "It's not true love."

"Don't tell me how I feel!"

Jasen put a hand on Risyda's arm. "We said our piece. We should go."

Risyda shrugged him off and went over to Polina, leaning in until their faces were inches apart. "If you ever think about trying something like that again, I will personally see to it that you lose everything. The king loves Jasen, not you." With that, she marched out of the room.

Jasen took one last look at the weeping Polina before he followed Risyda, shutting the door behind him. The hallway was now lit dimly by the first rays of the sunlight of the day coming in through the windows. Risyda was walking so fast

SERA TREVOR

that Jasen nearly had to jog to keep up with her long strides. "You have to tell the king," she said in a harsh whisper.

After seeing Polina so miserable, he was more reluctant than ever to put her through that. "I can't—I think it would kill her," Jasen whispered back. "She was your friend once—don't you have any pity for her?"

Risyda stopped abruptly and whirled around to face him. "Do you think it's merciful to let her continue on in her delusions?" she said as she struggled to keep her voice low. "The king will never love her, and she'll never accept it unless someone forces her to. And if we don't force her, then she will continue until she destroys both you and herself!"

"And how will it look when she's dragged off?" Jasen shot back. "It will look like I'm using my relationship with the king to get rid of people I don't like. Have you considered that?"

"Everyone saw what happened with the shoes."

"Did they? What if they thought I was faking it? I am sure that Polina is not alone in thinking that I pull 'stunts' for attention."

"Why do you care what they think?"

"Because if I become king consort, it will be my job!"

They both stopped talking as the weight of that statement sunk in. Jasen even felt a little lightheaded as the weight of the situation hit him.

"Has he proposed?" Risyda asked at last.

Jasen shook his head. "No. But he will." He leaned back against the wall and rubbed his face. "It's really happening, isn't it?"

Risyda gave him a small smile. "I'm afraid so, Your Majesty."

He smacked her in the arm, which made her laugh. They both froze when they heard noise coming from down the hall—the servants were probably up by now. "We should get back to our rooms," he said.

Risyda nodded. "But don't think this discussion is over. You have to take Polina seriously."

She was right, but he didn't feel like talking about it anymore at the moment. "Why don't we talk about it after breakfast? I could use a little kara weed."

It was too dim to see properly, but Jasen could have sworn that her cheeks colored. "I can't. I'm going riding."

Jasen stared at her. "What, with that lady you were dancing with?"

"I couldn't very well say no," she scowled. "It's supposedly the reason why I'm here, isn't it?"

"Did you want to say no?"

There was some more noise at the end of the hallway—the castle was definitely waking up. "Later," Risyda said.

There was more noise, so they quickly parted, going to their respective rooms. Once Jasen was safely inside, he crawled back into bed. Rotheld would no doubt be here shortly, but he didn't want to face the day yet. He knew that Risyda was right—but he knew that he was right as well. There had to be some solution that split the difference, but for the life of him, he didn't know what it could be.

CHAPTER 11

*T*he atmosphere was much changed, now that the suitors had arrived. The tedium of lessons was finally over—only to be replaced by the frenzy of courtship. The invitations came flooding in the morning after the ball. Almost everyone got at least one, with many receiving several. They all talked excitedly over breakfast, waving the papers at each other. Jasen, of course, hadn't received any, because who would dare court the king's favorite? But he was enjoying the excitement of the rest of them. He eavesdropped on Polina's group, who seemed to have done well for themselves. Banither held one invitation dramatically against his breast, declaring that its writer was his truest lady love already. Lalan had a large stack, which she kept patting as she giggled with delight. Polina appeared to receive several as well, which she had dutifully brought to breakfast. But she was pale, and her smile was thin. Jasen knew Risyda would be annoyed with him if he said so, but he did feel sorry for her, in spite of everything. He believed her when she said she was in love with Rilvor. He hoped she was at least entertaining alternate suitors, because this was the last year she would be admitted. Surely she had to realize that the king was a long shot and she needed to make back-up arrangements?

Jasen shook his head and returned his attention to the consorts sitting closer to him. When Jasen had entered the dining hall, a hush had fallen over the crowd, but that was something he was used to. But for once, everyone had more pressing, personal matters to hold their attention, and conversation had begun again quickly. Jasen fielded a few questions inquiring after his health. He offered his congratulations to the triumphant, and words of encouragement to those who were still waiting. It was pleasant enough, but what he really wanted was a conversation with a real friend. However, Risyda had yet to make an appearance. As the minutes ticked by, Jasen started to get concerned.

Breakfast finished, and still Risyda hadn't come, which made his worry worse. Jasen made his way to her room. He knocked on the door. "Risyda? Are you in there?"

The door opened a moment later. Risyda grabbed him by the arm and pulled him into the room, slamming the door shut behind him. To his surprise, she wasn't even dressed yet, wearing only a dressing gown, although her hair was arranged. For all of the scorn she heaped on the entire concept of the Court, she was never dressed any less than her best. It wasn't like her at all.

"Are you all right? What's the matter?"

She gestured over to her vanity. "See for yourself."

Jasen picked up a piece of paper lying by her mirror. He scanned it briefly. "It's an invitation from Lady Wesor." He looked up at her. "This is what has you so upset? Why?"

"Why? *Why?* How can you even ask me that?"

"It seemed like you were getting on with her quite well last night."

"But that's just the problem! I was!" She began to pace.

Jasen's brow was so furrowed that it was giving him a headache. "If you like her, then I don't understand the problem."

"The problem is right now, at this very moment, I must make a decision as to whether I want to spend my entire life with this woman." She gestured wildly. "This is insane—I barely even know her!"

"Isn't that the point of courting?"

"How well can anyone get to know someone over the course of a month? It's impossible!"

"You could always turn her down, you know."

She stopped pacing and looked straight at him. "But that's just the thing. I can't. Out of all of the suitors I've met, she's the only one I've ever even considered. I went on two outings with her last year before refusing to see her again—not because I didn't like her, but because I wasn't ready to get married. I'm still not ready. But this is my last year here. If I don't marry her, then it's back to my father's." She collapsed onto her sofa, her head buried in the crook of her arm. Was she…crying?

Jasen sat down beside her and put a hand gingerly on her back. He had no idea what to say. She was always the sensible one between the two of them, but now she was coming unraveled, and he had no idea how to ravel her up again. "Would you like some kara weed?"

She lifted her head out of her arm for a moment. Her eyes seemed a bit moist, but there weren't any tears on her cheeks. "That is an excellent idea."

Jasen got the pipe set up. After a few puffs, Risyda's posture relaxed. "I'm sorry," she said.

"Don't apologize. I'm usually the one in hysterics. It's only fair that you should get a turn."

She laughed bleakly. "What am I going to do? It's true that

I like Lady Wesor—but I don't love her. And I don't think a few horseback rides and walks around the garden are going to change that."

"No one can force you to get married."

"Maybe not. But what on earth have I been doing with my life if I don't? I always put off thinking about it, stalling for time. But my time is up now. I won't be welcomed back for Court." Risyda took another long drag. She puffed out the smoke in the shape of a heart, followed by another puff in the shape of an arrow. The arrow pierced the heart, causing both of the shapes to dissipate. "I pretend I don't care. I do think Court is ridiculous—but I also envy those who have a clear goal. They have a shot at finding happiness. But how can I be happy when I don't know what I want?"

They lapsed into silence, letting the haze of the kara weed drift over them. Jasen wished he had some wisdom to impart on her, but he barely knew what he was doing himself. "I don't think you should marry someone because you think you have no choice," he finally said.

"Then what should I do? My education centered around becoming a consort, so I can't go into a trade. Besides, my father would make sure no one would have me—and I'm not sure he would have me back, either. I'm an investment to him more than a daughter, and he is quick to cut investments that don't pay out."

"What about becoming a draedess? A dragon called you."

"That was a long time ago," she said quietly. "And I rejected it."

"I always got the impression that a dragon's calling was more open-ended than that. There are lots of stories about draeds and draedesses who rejected the call before embracing it."

"But I've done nothing with myself since then." Her voice

had gotten so soft that Jasen had to strain to hear her. "I've been selfish and lazy. Maybe I was worthy once—but not anymore."

And now she really was crying. Jasen didn't know what to say, so he pulled her into his arms and held her. When her sobs had quieted, he kissed her temple. "You've been a good friend to me. Surely that counts for something."

She laughed a little as she wiped her eyes. "I'm not sure if it counts in the grand scheme of things, but it means something to me."

Jasen opened his mouth to reply when there was an urgent knock on the door. Puzzled, they both got to their feet. When Risyda opened the door, Jasen was surprised to see that it was Banither, who was looking unusually disheveled and out of breath.

"What's going on?" Jasen asked.

"Lady Isalei has called an emergency meeting," he panted. "We're all to meet her in the Great Hall."

"Why?"

"There's been a Reckoning."

"A *Reckoning*?" Risyda gasped. "Where? Why?"

"Westrona, and how would I know? I expect we'll find out more soon enough." He dashed off to the next door before they could question them further.

Jasen and Risyda exchanged glances. He imagined his own expression was just as shocked as hers. A Reckoning meant that the dragons had decided that the ruling class of Westrona must be purged. "I didn't think Reckonings happened anymore."

"Neither did I. It's been over a century." Risyda cursed. "Help me get dressed."

Once Risyda was presentable, they made their way down the hall to the stairs, but they stopped in their tracks when they heard an agonized screech coming from around the corner.

"What was that?" Jasen asked.

"Only one way to find out." Risyda headed in the direction of the scream, with Jasen following close behind her.

The source of the commotion was not difficult to find. Polina and Lady Lalan stood in the hallway, along with Larely. Lalan was deathly pale, while Polina's face had turned red with fury.

"You can't take her!" Polina screamed at Larely, who seemed a bit shaken himself. "Whatever is happening with her family has nothing to do with her!"

"I'm very sorry, my lady, but we have orders from the king—"

"The king would *never* order such a thing!"

"But he has." Larely presented her with a scroll. "See for yourself."

Polina snatched the scroll from him and unfurled it. As she read, she sagged, like a wilting flower.

Lalan put a hand on her shoulder. "It's true—I've already read the order. I have no choice but to comply."

Polina shook her head and thrust the scroll back at Larely. "There must be some sort of mistake. The king would never be so unjust!" She threw her arms around her friend as they both wept.

Larely caught sight of Jasen and Risyda. *"Help!"* he mouthed silently.

Risyda took the scroll from Larely and read it. She passed it over to Jasen before approaching the two crying women. Jasen tried to read it, but he was as shocked as Polina and had trouble focusing. Would Rilvor really do something like this?

Risyda put her hand on Polina's shoulder, gently separating them. "The king won't let any harm come to her—he said so in the order. But the will of the dragons must be obeyed, even by the king. If they have called the ruling class to be judged, it's not for any of us to question it."

"It's not fair!" She sounded like a child.

"That isn't for us to decide. You need to let her go."

Lalan dabbed at her eyes with a handkerchief. "She's right. I must obey."

Larely spoke up again. "This way, my lady."

Lalan straightened herself and set her jaw, putting on a brave face, but after only a few steps, she swayed. Larely caught her, putting an arm around her waist to support her. "Here now, my lady, no harm will come to you. You're simply going home, is all."

They limped down the hall while Larely continued to murmur encouragements. Once they disappeared, Polina's sorrow morphed into fury again. She rounded on Jasen. "It's *you* who should be leaving, not her! You don't belong here!" Her gaze darted over to Risyda. "And neither do you!"

Before either of them could respond, Polina stormed back into her room, slamming the door shut behind her.

Neither Jasen nor Risyda said anything for a moment. "Do you think we should try to get her to come with us?" Jasen finally asked. "We're all supposed to be at the meeting."

"I'm fairly certain Lady Isalei would rather have her stay here in her current condition." She started off toward the stairs. "Come on, then. Let's find out what this is all about."

Lady Isalei had already begun to address the crowd when Jasen and Risyda arrived.

"—have every assurance that no harm will befall any of the consorts," she was saying. "The king himself will be flying to Westrona to sort this out. In the meantime, we will proceed as normal..."

Lady Isalei continued to speak, but Jasen stopped listening. *Will be flying* suggested that he hadn't left yet, which meant that Jasen might be able to catch him before he was gone.

"I'm going to the draemir," Jasen said quietly to Risyda.

"Are you sure that's wise?"

"No. But I'm going anyway. Cover for me?"

Risyda managed a weak smile. "Always."

With that, Jasen was gone.

JASEN RACED up to his room and managed to get himself out of his clothes. He dug out his peasant clothing from where he'd hidden it in his trunk and dressed as quickly as he could manage. After pulling on his boots and tucking his hair under his cap, he left his room and sneaked down to the ground floor. Fortunately for him, there was enough chaos that no one noticed him slipping out the servants' door, much as he had on his first day at the castle.

As soon as he was outside, he jogged toward the draemir. If Rilvor was flying to Westrona, that meant that he would be leaving from the draemir. Jasen had no idea if he would be alone or surrounded by officials, but he decided to risk it. He couldn't let Rilvor leave without speaking to him. He had to find out what was going on—he just hoped he wasn't too late.

Fortunately, it seemed as though Rilvor would be taking off on his flight without a gaggle of attendants, for Jasen found him standing in the draemir alone. Jasen breathed a sigh of relief. "Rilvor!"

The king turned around, a surprised look on his face. He was wearing the red robes of a draed, just as he had been the day they met. The Drae's cloak was draped across his shoulders, the jewel clasp sparkling in the sun. "Jasen? What are you doing here?"

Jasen didn't answer right away. Instead, he launched himself into Rilvor's arms. He hadn't planned on doing that —it just sort of happened. Rilvor was stiff for a moment, but soon relaxed into the embrace, if only for a moment. He pulled back to meet Jasen's gaze. "Is everything all right?"

"You tell me. Why have the dragons called a Reckoning? Are the nobles going to be burned to death?"

"Of course not! I would not let that happen."

"How can you be so sure?"

"I am the link between the humans and the dragons. They would not act without my consent."

"But they have. They started this Reckoning without you and already it's throwing everything into chaos! Why are they doing this?"

Rilvor sighed. "The queen of Westrona died two years ago with no direct heir, so there have been squabbles amongst the noble houses over whether or not the current queen has the right to the crown. Westrona is also rife with corruption and lawlessness. Dragons do not know nor care for the details of human law—they can only feel when the populace is on the brink of a violent conflict. It seems that brink has been reached." Rilvor smiled a little. "The Reckoning will save lives, not cost them. The only reason nobles were executed in the past was that was the only justice humanity knew, and the dragons took their cue from us. We are more enlightened now. The dragons will defer to my judgment, and I do not plan on having anyone burned."

Some of the panic began to subside, but Jasen still wasn't at ease. "You just expelled many consorts who had no part in whatever their family was up to. Why?"

"Because it is a Reckoning. If the dragons have determined that members of the ruling class has taken advantage of their positions, then all who count themselves among that class must be called to answer for it. You say that the consorts being sent home are innocent, but they enjoy many privileges as a result of their pedigree. If their families are abusing their power, then why should they continue to enjoy those privileges?"

Jasen pulled himself out of Rilvor's arms and turned away. "I don't know. I just know that it doesn't seem right."

Rilvor put his hand on Jasen's shoulder and turned him back around. "I am also disturbed by this turn of events, but this is my duty. That is why I must go to Westrona—to discover what has happened, and to make sure things are sorted out."

Jasen leaned into him again. "I don't want you to go," he said, his voice muffled against Rilvor's chest. He knew he sounded childish, but it was the truth, all the same.

"And I don't want to leave you. But it must be done. I will right this, I promise."

The sky darkened. They looked up—a dragon was heading toward them, growing larger and larger as it came closer. They moved back to make way for its landing. Jasen blinked up at the dragon in wonder. It was much larger than Tasenrad, its scales white and purple instead of the warm, red hues of Tasenrad.

Rilvor smiled at the dragon. "Hello, old friend. What have you gotten us into?"

The dragon snorted—a loud, hissing sound, as steam left its nostrils. Jasen wondered if he should be worried, but Rilvor was still smiling.

"Jasen, this is Woria—the Dragon Queen."

"The queen?" Jasen echoed. The dragon blinked slowly and then nodded its head, as if in greeting.

"It is not the best description," Rilvor continued. "Dragons do not have a hierarchy as humans do. But she is the one whose link to the humans is strongest, and the others follow her judgment."

Jasen wasn't sure what to say. She didn't seem frightening, exactly, but whereas Tasenrad had made him feel welcome, Woria had an air about her that was more restrained. He didn't think he could do much more than tremble and stammer in her presence. He shut his eyes to try to get a hold of himself.

Jasen felt a hand touch his chin. When he opened his eyes, he met Rilvor's gaze. "You have no reason to be frightened. No one will be harmed."

But Jasen didn't need assurances from Rilvor. Screwing up his courage, he moved toward Woria. He kept his gaze on the ground until he was right in front of her, so that he wouldn't lose his nerve. He sucked in a deep breath and met her gaze again. "Is that true? That no one will be harmed?"

Woria tilted her head and blinked her eyes again. More steam puffed out from her nose. At last, she made a deep, low sound—like a moan, or growl, so low and deep that Jasen felt it in his bones. He had no idea what to make of it, but he wasn't finished saying his piece. "People make mistakes. We aren't always our best selves, but for the most part, we try. Please keep that in mind when you're making your judgement." He bowed awkwardly and added, "If it pleases Your Majesty."

Woria let out another snort that sounded almost amused. Jasen's mind became strangely foggy. As he was trying to orient himself again, a word swirled in his mind. *Well-chosen*. He didn't know what that meant—it certainly wasn't his own thought.

He was startled out of his trance by the sound of Rilvor chuckling. Jasen was surprised to find him standing by his side. He blinked—when had that happened? "Dragons aren't ones to stand on ceremony. No need for formal addresses."

Jasen didn't respond right away—he still felt too mentally foggy. He put a hand to his temple.

The smile on Rivor's lips faded. "Does something trouble you?"

Should he tell him what had happened? Jasen decided against it—he wasn't sure what it had meant, and he had enough of dealing with mysteries for the day. "No," he said, managing a weak smile.

Woria let out another snort, which sounded impatient. Rilvor took Jasen into his arms one more time. "I must go now," he said.

"When will you be back?"

"I do not know. I hope to appoint some Westronans to deal with the aftermath, as it is their kingdom. And my ministers have made it very clear that they expect me back at Court as soon as possible." Rilvor ran a finger over Jasen's cheek. "I have unfinished business here."

Jasen felt heat in his cheeks. "Hurry back, then."

"I will." He leaned forward, and for a moment Jasen thought that he would kiss him. And he did kiss him—only it was on the forehead. Before Jasen could protest, the king left his embrace and went to the dragon's side. Woria leaned down and moved her wing to the side to allow Rilvor to mount her. Once Rilvor was firmly seated, the dragon ran down the draemir and lifted off, flying through the sky.

Jasen shielded his face from the sun with his hand and watched until the dragon was a speck on the horizon. He heaved a great sigh and rubbed his face. He supposed he should get back. He wondered if he was going to be in any trouble, but he couldn't summon up the energy to care. Besides, he felt as if Lady Isalei probably had bigger things to worry about at the moment.

He made his way to the edge of the draemir and was about to enter the castle ground proper when he saw a guard rushing toward him. It seemed he was in trouble, after all. There was no sense in running, so he stayed where he was, arms folded, ready to meet whatever demand the guard was sure to bark out at him. But as the guard drew closer, he saw that it was Larley—and he didn't seem as if he were there on official business.

"There you are—I've been looking for you," he said, panting a little. "Did you get to speak with the king?"

Jasen nodded.

"Did he happen to mention if the Reckoning is affecting merely noble families, or are commoners also affected?"

Jasen furrowed his brow. "Why do you ask?"

"No reason!" Larely said a bit too quickly. But in spite of his words, his wild-eyed look only grew wilder. "So just the nobles, then?"

"Are you worried about someone?"

"No! Of course not! My father is a legitimate busi-nessman!"

"Right," Jasen said slowly. "He runs a winery, doesn't he? I don't see why the dragons would have any interest in him."

Larely nodded to himself and ran a hand through his sweaty hair. "Yes, of course. Why would they? It's fine, I'm sure."

"Of course." It didn't take a genius to figure out that he wasn't being entirely truthful. Jasen looked around—they were standing in a rather conspicuous place. He took Larely by the hand. "Why don't you come with me so we can talk somewhere a little more private?"

Larely allowed himself to be led back into the draemir and into the trees. Once the castle was out of sight and he was sure they were truly alone, Jasen folded his arms and gave Larely a look. "Are you going to tell me what's really bothering you now?"

Larely opened his mouth as if to deny it again, but then his shoulders slumped. He leaned against a tree and stared at his feet. Jasen didn't press him any further, waiting for him to begin. "I wasn't telling the truth. My father isn't a legitimate businessman," he said eventually.

"So he doesn't run a winery?"

"No, he does. It's just the winery isn't his primary business."

"Then what is his primary business?"

For a moment, Jasen didn't think he would answer, but then he heaved a great sigh and spoke again. "Banditry, for a start. Or rather, not directly, but bandits come to them to convert their stolen goods into coins. He is the biggest name in the black market of the country. It isn't a secret, exactly— he pays his liege lord to ignore his activities."

Jasen blinked. It seemed as if the dragons had the right idea about the country, if nobles were accepting money from criminals.

Larely continued: "That's why I came to the Draelands —to get away from my family's 'business.' I never wanted any part of it, but everyone in Westrona knew what family I came from. There was basically no choice but for me to become a criminal as well. So I changed my name, managed somehow to get a position as a guard, of all things, and I haven't spoken a word to them in over five years."

"In five years?" Jasen knew all about having a complicated relationship with family, but he couldn't imagine not speaking to his father for that long of a time. "Do you think they're worried about you?"

"I don't know. I did give a rather impassioned speech about how disgusted I was with the whole business and vowed to never return, but they didn't take me very seriously." Larely rubbed his face. "I still don't agree with what they do, but at the same time, they are my family. If they're in trouble, I want to be there for them. But how can I return after making such a scene? Would they even welcome me?

And if I give up my job here, what will become of me? I don't know what to do."

Jasen didn't know what to say. It was indeed a difficult situation. "I think you should go to them," Jasen said at last. "Like you said, they are your family."

"But if I give up my job here, what will I do?"

"Say that you got word that a family member was ill."

"I'm not sure even a death would make the captain let me out without letting me go completely—especially not during Court season, and extra especially when there's a Reckoning panic."

"I'm the favorite of the king," Jasen said. "I'll tell him that it's my express wish for you to be guaranteed that your position will be there for you when you return."

"You would do that for me?"

"Of course I would. I still don't know how I feel about this whole future king consort business, but I might as well do something useful with my position."

Larely gave him a smile of relief. "Thank you." His expression switched back to more serious. "We should get you back. I don't think anyone's noticed your absence yet, but they're bound to. Mine as well, for that matter."

They walked back to the palace grounds together. Once there, they lingered around the corner from the servants' door to the East Wing, waiting for the coast to become clear.

"Do you think you can make it back in unnoticed?" Larely asked.

"I made it out all right, didn't I? For once, people have something to think about other than me. After I get dressed in my proper clothes, I'll go put a word in with the captain."

"I appreciate it." Larely's smile was a little sad now. "I suppose I should get packing."

Jasen started to feel sad himself. Larely was the first

person he'd met here. It would be strange not to have him around anymore. "You'll come to say good-bye, won't you?"

" 'Course I will!" He was trying to sound upbeat, but Jasen could hear the uncertainty in his voice.

Jasen put a hand on his shoulder. "I'm sure everything will work out."

"I hope you're right." Larely laughed a little. "Next time I see you, you'll probably be the king consort."

Jasen groaned. "I'd rather not think about it."

"But you have to," Larely said earnestly. "You're going to make a great king consort. Don't think of it as a trap. Think of the good you'll be able to do."

"Unless I spectacularly screw things up. That's a very real possibility, especially with you gone. Who is going to make sure Risyda and I stay out of trouble?"

Larely gave him a crooked grin. "I'm sure you'll manage."

Jasen pulled him into a quick hug. "Take care."

"You too."

Once Larely had left, Jasen listened at the servants' door, waiting for it to sound either empty enough that he could sneak in or busy enough that no one would notice. But he badly mistimed it, for when he opened the door, he ran straight into a kitchen maid. In fact, she fell out into the courtyard, almost as if she'd been leaning against the door.

"Sorry," he said, keeping his head down. He didn't wait for a reply as he slipped past her.

Fortunately, he had no more mishaps and made it back to his room without further incident. He took his time getting dressed again—he knew that Risyda was probably dying with impatience, but he needed a moment to clear his head. It seemed as if every time he thought he had a handle on what was going on, the carpet was pulled out from him yet again. Hopefully this would be his last big surprise, but somehow he doubted it.

He realized that his days of sneaking away were probably coming to an end. The reality of his future position was starting to sink in, but he felt—well, not at peace with it, but that it might be bearable. And he was starting to realize it had its benefits—Larely was right. There was a lot of good he could do.

CHAPTER 12

*C*ourt resumed as usual the next day, as if the Reckoning hadn't happened, although there was an undercurrent of unrest amongst both the consorts and the suitors, who had lost some of their number as well. Lady Isalei had held another meeting for the consorts, ordering them to keep up an attitude of cheerfulness and gaiety upon threat of disciplinary action, although even without that hanging over their heads, it seemed as if no one wanted to think much about it. Jasen supposed that there wasn't much use in worrying about it any more—it wasn't as if there were anything they could do other than wait.

Risyda ended up accepting the invitation from Lady Wesor. She had been reluctant to leave Jasen on his own, but there was little sense in them both sitting around with nothing to do. Jasen set himself up in the Swan Parlor with some of the other consorts who had yet to receive invitations. It was very strange not to be busy after all of the bustle of training. Jasen wasn't quite sure what to do with himself.

He had just selected a book of poetry to read when a

footman approached him, carrying an envelope on a cushion. Puzzled, Jasen accepted it and broke the seal.

Dearest Lord Jasen,

Would you do me the honor of accompanying me to Lake Vensea for luncheon and a friendly afternoon ride on the lake? It would be nice to catch up, as old friends. If you choose to honor me with your presence, you will find me at the front gates of the palace at noon.

Yours in friendship,

Bertio

It seemed innocent enough. There was nothing particularly scandalous about accepting invitations — indeed, it was expected that each of the consorts would entertain multiple suitors. Bertio also seemed keen on emphasizing that this was a meeting of friends. And Jasen really did need to talk to him, even if his attitude had seemed a little odd at the ball. Besides, it beat hanging around the Swan Parlor all day.

The footman offered Jasen a pen to write his reply. He scribbled out his acceptance and gave it back to the footman, who bowed and left. Jasen made his way back to his room to get changed. He liked outdoor activities—the outfits were much less fussy.

～

As PROMISED, Bertio was waiting for him at the appointed place, standing in front of a carriage. He smiled when he saw Jasen. "I am so glad you decided to join me."

"Of course. It will be nice to catch up."

"Indeed." He gestured toward the carriage as a footman opened the door. "Shall we?"

The carriage took off. Jasen racked his brain for some subject of conversation—he didn't want to jump right into a discussion about discretion. Consort training had provided him with dozens of subjects for small talk, but none of them seemed right with someone he already knew. "I haven't been to the lake yet," was what he finally came up with. "I hear it's nice."

"Yes," Bertio agreed. "Very nice." He gave him a wry smile. "Do you remember when we went swimming in Lake Belpool?"

Jasen couldn't help but smile back. "I remember. Your little sister stole our clothes—"

"And we had to nick some off the clothesline of a nearby cottage."

Jasen laughed. "I remember the look on that poor woman's face when we returned the clothes the next day. She must have thought we were mad."

"Maybe she thought *you* were mad, since you insisted on paying her even though we returned them!"

"I saw it as a rental! That's not mad at all. My mother didn't raise a thief."

They both laughed, more at ease now. "We did have fun, didn't we?" Bertio said.

"Yes, we did."

For a moment, Jasen was afraid that Bertio was going to ask him why he'd never replied to his letters, but he seemed content to let the matter rest.

"How is your sister?" Jasen asked. "She must be what— fifteen by now?

"Yes. Believe it or not, she's becoming quite the gracious young lady. Or at least, she's acting a lot more graceful than I would have at her age if I'd been forced into reduced circumstances."

Jasen shifted in his seat uncomfortably. "She could always come to Court when she's older."

"I suppose." Bertio's expression had dimmed, but he seemed to shake it off quickly. "And how's your father?"

"Drunk and fat."

Bertio laughed. "It's good to know some things never change."

They spent the rest of the trip to the lake catching up, just as Bertio had said he wanted to. Jasen found himself growing more and more relaxed. He may have decided that Bertio wasn't a serious romantic partner, but he did still like him. It was nice to remember the times that were less complicated. By the time they reached the lake, he was in a good mood.

The carriage dropped them off at the pier, where a number of rowboats were waiting for use. Jasen could see a few boats already out on the lake, the parosols of the consorts bright against the sky, like blooming flowers. Bertio got into the boat first and helped Jasen in. It was a funny sort of reversal, since Jasen had always been the sporty one between the two of them, having to coax Bertio into abandoning decorum for a little fun. But Jasen was expected to be prim, and so he was. He dutifully deployed his parasol as Bertio rowed them out onto the lake.

Jasen shut his eyes and enjoyed the cool spray of the water coming off the lake as the gentle wind made waves against the boat. It was a nice day, and the scenery was beautiful.

"Everyone was right," Bertio said. "This is lovely."

Jasen hummed in agreement. "It's nice to escape the palace. I've always loved to be outdoors."

"So I remember."

Jasen hesitated, not wanting to ruin the time they were having, but he really did need to broach the subject of their past. This was an excellent place to do it, too—although there were other boats on the lake, no one would be able to overhear their conversation. "I would have never guessed back then that I would ever be at Court in the Draelands."

"And yet here you are."

"Yes. But if I had known back then that this is where I was headed, I might have—made different choices."

"Surely you don't regret our time together."

"Of course not. It's just—well, I think that it would be best if we kept our past private, don't you think?"

"It would indeed be a shame if your situation was ruined because of past indiscretions."

"Exactly," Jasen said, feeling relieved.

"Do you know what's also a shame? That my brother's decisions have put me in the position that I must restore our family's reputation, and yet those same decisions have made it so I lack the funds to do so. Don't you agree that it's a shame?"

Jasen frowned a little. Something had changed in Bertio's tone. "Yes, of course. I'm sorry to hear that he put you in that position. But it surely can't be too bad if you made it to Court?"

"That's the thing. I had enough money to pay my way here, but I have little left over to offer a consort." Bertio shook his head. "A real shame, it is. I hope you never have to experience that sort of shame."

It took Jasen a moment to figure out what was happening. "Wait a minute—are you blackmailing me?"

Bertio's cheeks reddened a little. "I wouldn't put it like that, but as old friends, I think you're in the position to help me."

"But I'm not! That's the whole reason I went to Court in the first place—my father gambled away all of our money! I'm worse off than you!"

Bertio scoffed. "You're about to become the king consort. Everyone says so."

"But I'm not yet! What do you expect me to do? Steal something for you? I hardly imagine that would work out very well!"

"You could ask for some money. The king must know about your father's circumstances. You can say it's for him."

Jasen felt his face grow hot. He had been stunned at first, but now he was full of anger. "I'm not going to submit myself to blackmail! I won't lie to the king."

"But you are lying. He thinks you're a pure young consort, but we both know that that is not true. I know I wasn't your only lover, either."

Jasen shut his parasol with a snap. "How dare you!"

"You know I'm right," he said, his voice low. "Look, I don't mean to threaten, but I'm desperate. You know how my mother is. And think of my little sister—she doesn't want to be a consort. She received a dragon's blessing and has dreams of studying in the finest magic academies—dreams we can no longer afford."

Bertio was staring at him in a manner clearly meant to be intimidating, but Jasen just glared right back. "Don't you dare try to make it sound like you're being noble! Do you want to know why I never wrote you back? Because I knew that you were a weasel. You only care about yourself! You're conceited and snobbish, but I never thought you would stoop so low." Jasen crossed his arms. "Take me back."

"Not before you tell me if we have an agreement or not."

Jasen didn't know what to do. He didn't want to submit to blackmail—but did he have a choice? "I'll have to think about it."

Bertio gripped his hand. "I'm afraid I must insist. I have to know that my offer is secure before I start courting—they'll smell it on me otherwise."

Jasen yanked his hand back. "Get you hands off me! Maybe you should have thought about that before you came here. What were you going to do if I wasn't here to extort?"

Bertio didn't reply. Jasen studied his expression and came to a new conclusion. "You knew I was here, didn't you? And you knew that I was the favorite of the king. That was your plan all along."

"News like that travels fast," Bertio said. "No one can quite believe it—it's really quite scandalous. You may have tricked your way into Court, but you have a reputation, Jasen. I'm not going to be the first person from your past to come forward. You need to start thinking about how you're going to manage it."

"Starting with you," Jasen spat. "And how long will I be able to buy your silence?"

"Help me with establishing my marriage and I will never speak a word of it. That's all I ask."

"Forgive me if I am somewhat skeptical."

"I'm just doing what I have to do to secure my future. Anyone would do the same."

"I wouldn't."

"But you are. You've lied your way here. Don't pretend that you're better than me."

"And what if I tell you that the king wouldn't care about my past?"

"Maybe he wouldn't—but what about the ministers? They are going to want to assure that you are the best possible match—too much depends on it. Maybe the king himself wouldn't mind, but he has a kingdom to think about. Is his love for you strong enough that he would be willing to risk it?"

Jasen had no reply to that. He blinked rapidly, annoyed to find that tears were prickling up in his eyes. "Take me back—now."

"Tell me you'll help me."

"Never mind, I'll do it myself!" He made a grab for the oars, but Bertio got to them first.

"I'm not leaving this lake until you assure me that you'll get me the money!"

Jasen thwacked him on the hands with his parasol. Bertio cried out in pain and let go of the oars, allowing Jasen the opportunity to take a hold of them. But Bertio recovered quickly, shoving Jasen aside and he tried to take control again. Jasen shoved back—

—and then the boat tipped over, and they were dumped in the lake. Even though it was a sunny day, the cold water was still bracing. Jasen was only under water for a moment before he popped up, sputtering. Bertio surfaced a few seconds later.

"Are you all right?" Bertio asked, moving toward him.

"Stay away from me!" Jasen kicked off his shoes and took off his jacket, leaving them in the water (Rotheld was going to have a fit, but he didn't care at the moment) and swam for shore. Even without his shoes or his jacket, his clothes encumbered him, but he was a good swimmer. Better than Bertio, at any rate, who was hanging onto the side of the boat, calling after him. Jasen paid him no mind.

Several servants were gathered around the dock by the time Jasen got there—they must have seen them go over. A burly man helped Jasen out of the water. "My lord, are you all right?"

"I'm fine," Jasen said as he wrung out his hair.

"Where is the other gentleman?"

"With the boat," he said with a gesture. One rowboat had made its way over to Bertio, with the occupants helping fish him out of the water. But several other boats were making their way toward the dock as quickly as possible, no doubt eager to hear the latest catastrophe involving the king's favorite. Jasen gritted his teeth. Wonderful.

"We keep some dry clothing in the boat house," the servant said hesitantly. "Although it is not suitable for a man of your stature, naturally—I can send someone to the palace to fetch you more appropriate attire, if you wish."

"I'm sure whatever you have will be fine," Jasen said.

The servant led him to the boat house and quickly produced the clothes, which were too large for him. By the time he was dressed, several of the consorts and their suitors were gathered around the boat house, all waiting to see him.

Jasen sighed. "I don't suppose there's any way you can sneak me past them?" Jasen asked the servant.

"I don't think so, my lord. But I can make sure that your carriage is ready to go so you won't have to linger."

"Thank you."

The servant hesitated. "Do you wish to wait for your friend?"

"No. He can make his own way back to the palace."

The servant bowed. "As you wish, my lord." He left.

After a few minutes, the servant returned and escorted him outside. The ladies and gentlemen were all abuzz with chatter, which silenced when they saw Jasen. A few began inquiring after his health. He muttered some assurances that he was quite well, but refused to make eye contact. He couldn't manage to avoid Bertio, however, who lunged in front of him, blocking his path. He was still dripping wet.

"Where are you going?"

"Back to the palace. Where do you think?"

"Of course," he said. "But you must give me a moment to dry off. I've been told that the servants are procuring some clothes for me—"

"I'm sure that you can get a ride with someone else," Jasen said coolly. "I'm not waiting for you."

The chatter of the others had died down, with all of them leaning closer. They weren't even pretending not to listen.

Bertio must have noticed that, too, because he dropped his voice even lower. "Do you want to draw even more attention to us? Our little escapade is going to be the talk of Court already. People are going to be very curious why you're so angry with me."

Jasen pressed his lips together. What Bertio had left unsaid was that he himself would be a pariah if it were known that the king's favorite hated him, but what he said was still true. "Fine. But I'm not waiting around here a moment longer. Get in wet, or stay here. Your choice."

Bertio's expression clouded, but he soon composed himself. He raised his voice. "I must apologize again for how clumsy I am! I know that you were wearing your favorite jacket that's now been ruined. You have every right to be angry with me." He dropped down on one knee. "Please, I beg of you, forgive me?"

Jasen just blinked at him for a few moments. "You are forgiven," he said tightly. He didn't sound very convincing— he'd always been a terrible liar.

But it seemed to satisfy the busybodies. The chatter sounded less befuddled and more...gleeful, for the lack of a better term. Jasen was sure that it would make for some very satisfying gossip. He got into the coach without a backward glance. Bertio got in after him. The door was shut, and a few moments later, they were headed back to the palace.

"I think they believed it," Bertio said, although it sounded more as if he were talking to himself. "And when you think about it, it's more of a funny story than a scandalous one. If we play it right, this shouldn't affect either of our standings."

Jasen stared at him. "When did you start thinking of this? Was it the moment you hit the water?"

"No—my first thought was whether or not you were all right. When I saw you were perfectly uninjured, then yes, I did begin to consider what it would look like. Didn't you?"

"Don't pretend that you were worried about me. You were worried about whether or not you had drowned the king's favorite. I'm sure you would have preferred that I'd gone under—your gallant rescue of me would probably have been better for your reputation!"

Bertio glared at him. "Don't pretend you're better than this. This isn't Grumhold, and we aren't children anymore. If you aren't thinking about your reputation every moment of every day, then you are going to lose."

There it was again—the idea of the game. Jasen looked away. "This isn't a game to me."

"But it's a game for everyone else. You'd better start playing it."

"And my first move should be paying you off, I suppose."

"I'm only doing what I have to do—for the sake of my family." The puddle underneath him was growing wider by the moment.

Jasen folded his legs under him to avoid getting his bare feet wet. "Why didn't you come to me as a friend?"

That seemed to shock him—he actually flinched. It took him a few moments to collect himself. "Would you have agreed to help me?" he asked, his voice a little shaky.

"I suppose we'll never know," Jasen said sadly.

They sat in gloomy silence for the rest of the trip. When the carriage stopped, Bertio spoke again. "So I take it that you're refusing me?"

Jasen ran a hand over his face. "I didn't say that. I need some time to think. You owe me that much."

Bertio nodded grimly. "All right, then."

The door opened. Jasen got out first—although he tried to avoid the puddle, he couldn't help but get his feet wet. Once Jasen was out, Bertio followed. He also stepped in the water, but he slipped, falling face first out of the carriage and into the dirt. Jasen looked around to see who might have seen. Then he cursed himself that that was his first concern. There was no one else around, at any rate, except for the servants. No doubt they had gossip of their own. He started to consider what they might say, but firmly squashed that thought. It had been quite a tumble. He should help.

He took Bertio by the arm and helped him to his feet. "Are you all right?"

Bertio rubbed his head. "Yes. Thank you. We should—"

But Jasen didn't wait to hear the rest of it. He took off for the East Wing as quickly as he could without running. Bertio, thankfully, did not follow.

Jasen stayed in his room for the rest of afternoon. He told Rotheld he wasn't feeling well and had some dinner sent up to his room. Shortly after, there was a knock on the door. Jasen opened it and was unsurprised to see Risyda there.

"I heard what happened," she said. "But not what *really* happened, I imagine."

"Of course you've heard. There seems to be nothing useful for anyone in this damned Court to do but gossip!"

Risyda tilted her head. "Are you all right?"

Horribly, Jasen felt tears prick behind his eyes. "No, I'm not."

Jasen stepped aside to allow Risyda to enter the room. He poured them both a glass of wine—he didn't normally enjoy it, but he most certainly needed something to steady his nerves. Once she was settled, he told her the whole sordid tale.

When he was finished, Risyda drained the rest of her glass and poured herself another one. "Well, it's simple enough to solve," she said calmly. "I'll just kill him."

Jasen smiled a little. "What would I do if you were hauled off to the dungeon?"

"Oh, I wouldn't get caught. People spontaneously catch on fire all of the time, don't they?"

Jasen sighed. "What am I *actually* going to do?"

"It's your word against his. I think I know who the king will believe."

"So you think I should lie?"

Risyda seemed surprised. "Of course you should lie! I hate to say it, but he was right about one thing—you wouldn't have gotten into Court if the scouts had vetted you properly."

Jasen felt his face fall. "You're right—I don't belong here."

Risyda whacked him on the arm. "I didn't say that! I don't know if you've noticed, but almost everyone is lying in some way or another. Court couldn't exist without a careful balance of deceptions. Everyone has secrets."

Jasen slumped in his chair. "I say again, I don't belong here. I don't like secrets and lies."

"No one does, but it's—"

"If the rest of that sentence is 'how you play the game,' I'm going to scream."

Risyda poured him another glass of wine. "I know, I know —you hate that. Fortunately for you, I'm fine with playing games, and I don't mind playing dirty. Does Bertio have any evidence of your tryst? Any letters?"

"No. He sent me several, and I threw them out ages ago. I only responded once, and there was nothing in my reply that was at all improper."

"So it really is his word against yours. And you have yet another advantage—you know his secret. His family is broke —if you don't belong here, neither does he. I wonder what his marriage prospects will look like once everyone knows his family's true position? Gossip works both ways."

"So I should blackmail him back?"

"If you don't want to do it, I'd be happy to have a chat with him. In fact, I'm rather looking forward to it."

Jasen frowned. "As much as I hate what he's doing, I don't want to ruin his life."

Risyda rolled her eyes. "He's ruining his own life by coming after you. And as long as he stays quiet, we stay quiet. It's a stalemate rather than a win. I'm tempted to thoroughly ruin his reputation, but on the other hand, he'd be more motivated to keep quiet if he has something to lose. I'll still start some light rumors so that if we need to launch a more thorough campaign later, the ground will be laid."

"Please don't," Jasen muttered miserably.

Risyda gave him a surprised look. "He just threatened you! He declared war, not us."

"I know. But I won't be the one who escalates this. If we need to pursue a stalemate, fine, but that's all I agree to."

"If you say so. But the best defense is a good offense, in my opinion." She paused. "Can you think of any other past lovers who might come forward?"

Jasen felt even more miserable. "It seems like you and Bertio are on the same page. That's exactly what he pointed out."

"Well, are there?"

"I've had a few more lovers," Jasen admitted. "All right, more than a few, but only three other nobles. My other lovers were all commoners, so I don't imagine that I'm in danger from them."

"Why would you assume that?"

"Because they're not a part of all this horrid intrigue! And they're good people—I didn't sleep with just anyone! I considered each of them a friend."

"The promise of money has a way of changing people. Trust me, I've seen it before—my father is very wealthy, and people do all sorts of things for him. But I imagine your common-born lovers are in Grumhul, so I agree that they are probably the least of your worries. And I suppose we'll deal with any other potential blackmailers as they come." She stood up and smoothed out her gown. "I suppose I should go find Bertio."

"What, now?"

"No time like the present. In fact, I'd say that time is of the essence. Do you want to come with me?"

Jasen shook his head. "I don't have the stomach for all this intrigue."

Risyda leaned down and kissed his cheek. "Poor Jasen. You really are too good for this place. Don't fret—I will take care of everything."

She started to leave, but paused at the door. "Much as I hate to admit it, the lie that Bertio came up with as to why you were angry with him at the lake was a good cover. I think that you should get out and mingle with the other consorts. If you were just angry about a ruined jacket, there would be no reason for you to be hiding yourself away. If you stay holed up here, people might come up with rumors of their own."

The last thing that Jasen wanted to do was socialize, but Risyda made a good point. "All right," he said.

"We have this under control," she said firmly. "Don't look so hopeless."

Jasen tried to smile. From Risyda's expression, he wasn't altogether convincing, but it would have to be enough, damnit. After she left, he rang for Rotheld to come help dress him. After all, appearances were so important.

Once he was dressed, he made an appearance in the Swan Parlor. He picked out a book and pretended to read. Several consorts approached him and asked him about what happened. He told the story of Bertio's clumsiness and his annoyance. It actually got a laugh out of a lot of people. Banither dubbed him "Bertio the Bumbler," which got more laughter. Jasen realized that without intending it, he had dealt Bertio's reputation a blow. He knew that Risyda was correct that Berio had brought it upon himself, but he still felt sick about being a player in the game of Court.

Some time passed, and the consorts began excusing

themselves to retire to their rooms. Jasen retired as well and found Risyda waiting for him at his door.

"It's done," she said. "I can't imagine that he'll give you any more trouble." She grinned. "You should have seen the look on his face."

Jasen couldn't share her glee, but he did return her smile. "Thank you. I don't know what I'd do without you."

"Fortunately, you *do* have me, so stop worrying. It will be all right, you'll see."

But he wouldn't always have her. After Court was over, she would be gone—either successfully married or back to her father's. Jasen had had enough gloom for the day, so he didn't bring it up. He gave her a hug and wished her good night. Rotheld arrived soon after to help him undress. Jasen was so exhausted that in spite of the turmoil of the day, he dropped off to sleep as soon as his head hit the pillow.

CHAPTER 13

*A*fter the debacle with Bertio, Risyda decided that it would be best if Jasen was kept busy. She asked Lady Wesor to recommend honorable suitors to accompany Jasen on various outings. None of them were seriously courting him, of course, but they all seemed excited for the opportunity to make a good impression on the future king consort. Jasen tried his best to be charming and cheerful, even though he felt like neither of those things. He appreciated the extensive training that Lady Isalei had provided for him—it allowed him to go through the motions without too much effort. If any of the suitors noticed that his behavior was hollow, they didn't show it.

Bertio didn't appear to be having much luck. Jasen overheard two consorts laughing at invitations they had received from him, contemplating whether the risk to one's wardrobe was worth it. Risyda smugly predicted that he would leave Court early. Jasen wasn't sure how he felt about that.

In addition to Lady Wesor's friends, Jasen found himself spending a lot of time with his fellow consorts. It wasn't as if he had much choice—every time he tried to grab a moment to himself, he was found out and dragged into some amusement or other. He didn't mind, exactly. In fact, he had developed a certain fondness for some of them. He never felt quite comfortable calling them friends, though—he would never forget how they had made him feel when he first arrived.

He would also not forget how quick so many of them were to abandon Polina. Now that Lalan was gone, Polina was completely alone. All of her other "friends" had abandoned her. Jasen rarely saw her—it seemed she almost never left her room except for meals. When she did make an appearance, she sat alone in the corner of a parlor, working at her needlepoint absently. Jasen wondered if she was receiving any invitations. His question was answered one day when he saw a servant approach with an envelope. She just shook her head, refusing to even look at it. In spite of everything that had happened between them, Jasen wished he could do something to help her.

One night, Polina didn't come down for dinner at all. Worst of all, it seemed like Jasen was the only one who noticed.

"She's probably just not feeling well," Risyda said with a shrug when Jasen brought it up.

"She was your friend once. Aren't you even a little concerned about her?"

Risyda picked at her dinner. "Of course I am," she said eventually. "But what can I do?"

"Maybe we should go check on her."

Risyda snorted. "Do you really think a visit from either one of us would make her feel better? If anything, it would make it worse. If I were her, you and I would be the last people I'd want to confide in."

"I suppose so," Jasen said, but he wasn't so sure.

It was still on his mind after everyone had retired for the

evening. Maybe Risyda was right that he'd only make things worse, but he felt as if he had to do something. Jasen got out a quill and some paper. He sucked on the tip while he tried to think of what to say.

Dear Princess,

I noticed you weren't at dinner tonight and wanted to inquire after your health. You may feel like no one cares, but I do.

Risyda would probably slap me silly for saying this, but I understand why you did what you did. For what it's worth, I forgive you, and I wish you well.

Jasen

Once he was finished, he folded the paper but didn't seal it. He considered sending for a servant to deliver it to her, but since he had seen her refuse to even glance at letters presented to her, he felt as if a more direct approach would be better. He made his way to her room and slipped the paper under the door.

He returned to his room and read for an hour or so. Just as he was getting ready to get in bed, a paper slipped under his door. He picked it up.

Thank you, it said.

Jasen was surprised at how relieved he felt. He went to bed with his heart feeling significantly lighter.

The next morning, Jasen was pleased to see Polina at breakfast. He waved at her. She smiled and started to wave back, but then looked down, her expression grim again. It didn't take long to figure why.

"Why are you waving at her?" Risyda said, scowling.

"I sent her a note last night. I think we made up."

"*Made up?*" Risyda was red with rage. "You aren't friends who had a disagreement! She has done nothing but belittle you and sabotage you since the moment you arrived. Why does she deserve your forgiveness?"

"Forgiveness isn't something a person deserves or not,"

Jasen said. "She isn't a horrible person—just sad and misled. I'm sure Minister Adwig has been egging her on."

"You don't think Minister Adwig told her to curse your shoes?"

"I don't know, but at the very least, I think that he's been telling her that I'm the only obstacle standing in her way. I'm not excusing her, but I do understand why she acted the way she did. She's in love, and now her heart has been broken."

"So you feel sorry for her."

"Don't you?"

Risyda crossed her arms and huffed. "Feeling sorry for her isn't the same as forgiving her."

Jasen shrugged. "It makes me feel better to forgive her. That's enough of a reason, isn't it?"

"I suppose," Risyda said, but she didn't look convinced.

They were just finishing up when a valet approached Jasen with an envelope. Jasen tore it open without much thought, figuring that it was from yet another noble looking to curry favor with him, but he froze when he saw the signature: it was from Minister Adwig.

To the esteemed Lord Jasen,

I humbly request the honor of your presence to discuss a matter of some importance. As the matter is somewhat urgent, I would urge my lord to attend at the earliest convenience.

Your obedient servant,

Minister Adwig

"Who's it from?" Risyda asked.

"It's from Minister Adwig."

"What does he want?"

"He's asking for the honor of my presence to discuss an important matter."

Risyda snorted. "Perhaps he's finally come to terms with the fact that you're about to become king consort and wants to grovel."

"Maybe," he said faintly, but Minister Adwig did not seem like the grovelling type.

The valet cleared his throat. "If it is convenient for my lord, the minister suggests that you come with me."

"Yes, of course," he said. He wanted to get it over with.

Jasen followed the valet through the palace, all the way to the West Wing where the government officials had their cabinets. The valet knocked on one of the doors and was bade to enter.

The minster's cabinet was small and more subdued than the rest of the palace, although the dark wood paneling was still elegant. The man himself sat at a surprisingly humble desk toward the back of the room. He was writing something when Jasen entered, leaving Jasen to stand in wait awkwardly for several moments.

At last, he lay down his quill and stood. "My lord," he said with a bow. He gave a quick nod to the valet, who bowed and shut the door behind him. When they were alone, the minister gestured to a chair in front of his desk. "Please, have a seat."

The minister considered him for a long moment before he spoke again. "I'm sure it will not surprise you that the matter of the king's marriage has been on my mind. I imagine it's been on your mind as well."

Jasen swallowed. "It has."

Jasen wished he would just come out with whatever he had to say, but the minister seemed in no particular rush. "I had just started in a position at the palace when the king was born. I have served faithfully for thirty years, first under King Rilvor's parents, and then after their tragic deaths, under him. It was my privilege to assist King Rilvor in his ascent to the throne. It was a difficult transition, as I'm sure you can imagine, particularly since no one expected him to become king. The fact that he was barely more than a child at the time made it even more difficult. But despite all of the challenges that faced him, he has become a great king. It gives me great joy to serve under him."

It was difficult to imagine anyone as sour-looking as Minister Adwig taking great joy in anything, but he seemed sincere. "I'm sure the king appreciates your service."

The minister scoffed. "Certainly he does, but I know he also sees me as a troublesome old man. And it's true—I am a troublesome old man, particularly when it comes to the stability of the kingdom. I am willing to make myself a nuisance to protect my king. Which brings me to the subject of his marriage. I have received word from him that he will return to the Draelands in a few days' time. He has hinted that he has reached a decision as to his choice of spouse. Has he spoken to you about it?"

Jasen's heart fluttered. "Not so directly, no."

"But he has led you to believe that you will be his choice?"

There was little sense in denying it. "Yes."

The minister sniffed. "Are your feelings for the king genuine?"

Jasen couldn't find his voice, so he nodded.

"If that is true—if you truly care for the king—then you must refuse him."

Jasen blinked. "Refuse him? Why?"

"Let me be blunt—the Allied Realms are at a crisis point. Magic has been steadily declining since the king took the throne. The current situation in Westrona shows exactly how strained the relationship between the monarch and the dragons has become. Nerves are frayed in every kingdom. For the good of the realms, his next spouse must be from a family with both strong magical connections and unques-tionable pedigree. You have neither. Additionally, you are both male. That lacks the balance that the royal couple typi-cally embody."

Jasen had no argument—what he said was true. He felt ill.

"I know I sound harsh, but I am merely pointing out the reality of the situation. You have many virtues—your feelings for the king being among them. I am sympathetic to his feelings for you as well. Which is why I have a proposal for you. A compromise, if you will."

"What do you mean?"

"We can make a place for you at Court permanently. You could live with the dignity befitting a young lord of your stature, as the king's companion."

Jasen's cheeks flushed with equal parts anger and embarrassment. "You mean as his paramour."

The minister shrugged. "Whatever title would suit you best. It's true that it's a position that has fallen out of fashion, but there was no shame in serving the monarch in such a manner in the past."

Jasen wasn't a proud man, but the thought of being the king's glorified whore repulsed him. "And I suppose you'll choose a bride for him." He tried to keep his voice steady but wasn't quite successful. "Do you think whoever it is will agree to this arrangement?"

"I am certain of it. There is an abundance of pragmatic young women from eligible families at Court this year."

"And you think the king will agree?"

"As a matter of fact, I do not. Which is why you must convince him."

"And why would I do that?"

The minister sat back in his chair, considering Jasen coolly. "Forgive me, but I must be blunt once again. I have been keeping an eye on you for some time now."

Jasen choked back a gasp. "You've been *spying* on me?"

"I have been *vetting* you. The position of king consort is not one that can be left to something as flimsy as romantic feelings."

"And what conclusion have you come to?"

"That your feelings for the king are genuine, but you have no interest in a position of power."

The silence that followed was as heavy as a boulder. The minister steepled his fingers. "You are not a political opportunist, nor are you a parasite. That's to your credit. But what you are, Lord Jasen, is naive. You cannot love Rilvor the man without taking on the responsibility of Rilvor the king."

Jasen looked away. "I know that."

"And yet it seems as if you were prepared to accept the king's proposal, if he were to make it. Surely you must know that you are not suited for the position."

"I think that's for the king to decide."

"Not entirely. The council of ministers must approve his choice as well. You will not have their support. And besides, the king does not have all of the necessary information to make his decision, does he?"

Jasen's stomach dropped. "What do you mean?"

"I have spoken with Lord Bertio about your past affairs. I am puzzled that you were not more thoroughly vetted by our recruitment officials, but if what he says is true, you should not have been given a place in Court at all."

Jasen stuttered for several moments, trying to form a response. "Why would trust his word over mine?"

"Do you deny the accusations?"

Jasen opened his mouth, but nothing came out. He stared hopelessly down at his lap, fighting tears.

"And it seems that this sort of behavior is not confined to your past."

Jasen looked up at that, furrowing his brow in confusion. "What do you mean?"

"After Lord Bertio's made his accusations, I questioned some of the servants. Several of them observed you meeting clandestinely with another consort—"

"Lady Risyda?" Jasen interrupted. "But we're only friends! I have no interest in women—"

"—and a guard," the minister continued, talking over him. "Which is more troublesome. I have a witness to lewd behavior between the two of you—in the middle of the day, no less—"

Jasen racked his brain, trying to think what on earth he could be referring to. It finally occurred to him—that day Larely had kissed him. "That was a misunderstanding! If you really have a witness, you'll know that I pushed him away!"

"In that particular instance. Who is to say that there was not more between you when you had more privacy?"

"*I'm* to say!" Jasen shock was rapidly giving way to anger. "You said that you believed my feelings for the king are genuine! If you believe that, then surely you must know that I would never betray Rilvor like that!"

"Then why did you have the guard sent away?"

Jasen was plunged into confusion again. "Sent away? No! He left because of family business!"

"I have another servant who witnessed your good-bye. She said that it was less than proper."

"I hugged him because he's my friend! There was nothing improper about it!"

"Even if it were as innocent as you claim, a lord of true breeding would not be so familiar with servants—particularly not with the man in question. After I learned of the improper relationship between the two of you, I did some investigating. It seems that this Larely is from a notorious family of criminals—naturally he would have never been hired had we known." The minister picked up a quill and began to write. "I will write an order to find him and bring him back to Strengsend, so that I can question him further—"

"No!" Jasen cried.

"—and I believe that I should bring in Lady Risyda as well. Her use of illicit substances and complicity in your affair with this guard makes her presence in Court questionable, at the very best."

Jasen clamped his mouth shut, since all he seemed to be doing was making things worse for himself. But while he could stop himself from speaking, he couldn't stop the tears that sprang from his eyes. He wiped them away furiously with his handkerchief and took a deep breath, trying to steady himself. He would not fall apart in front of this man.

The minister set down his quill. "Of course, if you refuse the king's proposal, I won't have any need to investigate any of this."

So it was blackmail, then. "And what am I supposed to tell him?" Jasen's voice shook, but didn't crack.

"The truth—that you are unable to accept the responsibilities of the throne." The minister peered at him. "Do I have your word that you will not accept his proposal?"

Jasen twisted the handkerchief, unable to reply.

The minister's lips thinned. "The king won't be returning for several more days, so you will have some time to think. Once you have gotten over your shock, I am certain that you will see the wisdom of my words. The fate of the Allied Realms lies in your hands—do not let your own selfish desires endanger it."

He stood. Jasen got to his feet as well, albeit shakily. "Do you need assistance back to your room?"

Jasen shook his head. "I can find my own way." He had no desire to walk with any valet, now that he knew they were spying on him.

He made his way back to his room as swiftly as he could, doing his best to hold himself together. The moment he was safely inside his own room, he fell to the floor, weeping. The cruelest thing of all was that Adwig was right—he wasn't good enough. He couldn't believe he'd deluded himself into believing otherwise.

CHAPTER 14

*J*asen spent the rest of the morning hidden away. Risyda was on an outing with Lady Wessor and he didn't want to disturb her. Besides, he wasn't looking forward to telling her what had happened. He wasn't even sure he wanted to tell her at all. She was certain to urge him to fight, to get the king on his side and push back against Adwig...but that kind of bold action was something more suited to a person like Risyda. Jasen wasn't a fighter—he never had been.

His initial anger at Adwig's accusations had dissolved. He was right—there was no way that Jasen could accept a proposal of marriage from Rilvor, and he was a fool for having other thought otherwise. The only question now was whether or not he would accept Adwig's offer to become Rilvor's paramour. But the more he thought about it, the less viable it seemed. It wasn't just that it was an insult to his dignity—indeed, he had very little of that.

The real barrier was that he wasn't sure Rilvor would agree to it. Rilvor had shown, time and again, that his attraction to Jasen was more than physical. He loved him—of that

Jasen had no doubt. And because of his love, he would never accept Jasen being put in a position that degraded him.

But if Jasen couldn't be king consort, and if Rilvor wouldn't accept him as his paramour, where did that leave them?

A knock on the door startled him out of his contemplation. When he opened it, a valet presented him with an envelope. "I was told to wait for your answer, my lord," he said.

Wearily, Jasen opened it. He wondered how all of the nobles who had been courting his favor would feel once they learned all their efforts were for naught. But the note wasn't from a noble. It was from Lady Isalei. Jasen stomach churned. He wondered if Minister Adwig had let her in on his discoveries.

There was no sense in putting it off. He gathered himself as well as he could and followed the valet to Lady Isalei's parlor. There was no tea set out this time, and her expression was grave.

Jasen bowed. "Good afternoon, my lady."

"Good afternoon." She gestured to the sofa. "Please, have a seat."

Jasen did as she asked. She sat down not on the chair, but on the sofa beside him. She peered at him with concern in her eyes.

"I'm afraid I have some difficult news," she said.

Jasen swallowed and braced himself. "Yes?"

She handed him an envelope. "This came for you only just now. I think you best read it."

Jasen stared at the envelope in puzzlement. It wasn't the fine, creamy stationary that was used for invitations and other correspondence within the palace. This envelope was dirty, and had clearly traveled some distance. It must be from his father. Jasen tore it open.

O my son, it began.

Your old dad is in some trouble. I am most horribly, most dreadfully ill—my quill shakes as I write this to you—O how it pains me to intrude upon you, but I must see you again, as I lie on what could be my deathbed! It is most selfish of me—hate me not for my mortal weakness! A carriage awaits you to bring you to me —I am at an inn not far from the palace. Please hurry, my son!

Jasen's heart almost stopped—his father was *dying*? He read the note again. Why was his father at an inn outside the palace? Had he fallen ill while on the road? In a way, it was better, since he could get to him all the more quickly.

"You must go to him at once," Lady Isalei said. "The king will understand."

Jasen nodded vaguely. "Yes, of course."

She grasped his hand. "Do please write as soon as you learn of his condition. We have many excellent healers who can be of service. Hopefully this illness will pass quickly, and you can return to Court." She smiled. "And once things are settled between you and the king, I'm sure it would be no trouble to move your father in for a little while, until he recovers."

So Adwig hadn't spoken to her. At least he had been spared that awkward conversation. He smiled faintly. "Yes, of course." He stood. "I should prepare to leave, then."

Upon returning to his room, he was surprised to see Rotheld there waiting for him. He bowed when Jasen entered. "Lady Isalei has informed me of your immanent departure, my lord. I am sorry to hear of your father's illness."

"Thank you."

"I have take the liberty of packing your trunk," Rotheld continued. "And I have selected a traveling outfit for you."

The outfit in question was another of the outfits that had been lent to him for his time as a consort. "I can't wear that. It doesn't belong to me."

Rotheld frowned. "But surely you will be returning once your father has recovered."

"I don't know how long I'll be gone." He didn't add that he wasn't sure he'd be coming back. "I would prefer to wear something from my own wardrobe."

"Very well." Rotheld opened the trunk and retrieved the outfit that Jasen had been wearing when he first arrived. It looked so dull now in comparison with the fine clothes he'd grown accustomed to wearing. At least he wouldn't have to wear a corset.

Once he was changed, he wrote a quick note to Risyda, explaining his father's illness. She and Lady Wessor were on an outing and he couldn't wait to speak to her in person. He didn't add anything about his meeting with Adwig. He wasn't sure he would tell her at all—he didn't want her to know that his friendship with her had been used as blackmail. If she found that out, no doubt she would do something stupid that would imperil her match with Lady Wessor, and he didn't want that. He would talk to her only once everything had been settled with the king—whether Jasen became his paramour or returned to Grumhul for good. She'd be furious he made a decision without consulting her, but she'd forgive him in time.

He gave Rotheld the note to deliver and bade him farewell. It was difficult because he didn't know if he would see him again, but he couldn't let on that that was a possibility. Rotheld had helped him so much. He would miss him.

A valet arrived to carry Jasen's trunk to the carriage. Jasen had hoped to avoid as many of the other consorts as possible, but unsurprisingly, the news of his father's illness had already spread. He accepted the well wishes of several consorts as politely as possible while still hurrying along.

The carriage was waiting for him outside, as promised. He had hoped to see his servants Rodrad and Garyild again—

their familiar faces would have been a welcome sight—but the coachman was unfamiliar to him.

The coachman opened the door as the valet secured his trunk. Jasen took one last look at the palace. It had seemed like an impossible dream when he had first arrived. Maybe that's all it was, after all. He gathered himself and got inside. He didn't look back again.

THE COACHMAN TOLD Jasen that his father was staying at The Lucky Shrew, which was the same inn they had stayed at before making their final trek into the city months before. Other than that, the coachman could give him no further details. Different scenarios shuffled through Jasen's mind, each worse than the last. He thought back to the last time he'd spoken with his father. They hadn't parted on good terms, to say the least. Tears pricked Jasen's eyes—he would never forgive himself if the last words between them had been in anger. He and his father didn't have the best relationship, but he did love him, faults and all.

At last, they reached the inn. The coachman retrieved Jasen's trunk and brought it to the steps of the inn before heading back to the palace. Jasen left it for the moment, more concerned with reaching his father. He rushed in the door and approached the innkeep, who he remembered from their last stay. He was an older man with a belly to rival his father's. "I'm here for my father, the Earl of Hogas," Jasen said. "Am I too late?"

The innkeep furrowed his brow. "Too late? No, he's still here."

"What's his condition?"

"Condition? Well, I imagine he's still conscious, given that he just ordered some champagne."

Now it was Jasen's turn to be confused. "Champagne?" He frowned. If he was well enough to be ordering champagne, maybe things weren't too dire. He relaxed a little. "Can I see him?"

"Of course." He gestured to a barmaid. "Jonae, will you show the gentleman to his father's room?"

Jasen trailed up the stairs behind Jonae. She led him to a door. "Here you are, my lord," she said. "Let me know if there's anything else I can do for you."

"Could you send someone to retrieve my trunk? I left it at the door."

"Of course, my lord."

As soon as she left, Jasen took a deep breath and opened the door—

There was a loud pop, and then he was beaned in the forehead by a projectile of some sort. He cried out, more in surprise than in pain.

"Sorry, son!" his dad said cheerily. He was not lying in bed, wasting away—instead, he was sitting at a small table, a bottle of foaming champagne in his hands. "Guess the champagne got a little jostled on its way up here! Would you like some?"

Jasen rubbed his head as scanned the ground. He picked up the object that had hit him—it was a champagne cork. "You-you aren't sick?" he asked, his voice cracking.

"Healthy as an ox!" His dad belched cheerfully.

A wave of relief washed over Jasen, but the relief was immediately undercut by a surge of fury. "You *aren't sick*?"

The smile slid off his father's face. "I can explain—"

"Oh of course," Jasen spat out. "You always have explanations, don't you? What is it this time? Have you gambled so much that they won't let you leave until someone comes and pays your debts?"

"No, nothing like that!"

"Then what? What could possibly compel you to write to me telling me you were *dying*? Do you know how worried I was?"

"Well, then—you must be happy to see that I'm healthy!"

Jasen clenched his fists so tightly his arms shook. "You deceitful, drunken, despicable son of a whore!"

"Here, now—don't speak of your grandmother like that!"

Jasen let out a shriek and launched himself at his father. His dad yelped and leapt from his chair—he was surprisingly nimble for a man of his size. The room wasn't very large, though, so Jasen soon caught up to him. Just when Jasen was about to land the smack upside the head that his father so richly deserved, the door opened and a man entered the room.

"Is everything all right?" the man said.

Jasen froze. The man didn't look familiar. In fact, it was difficult to think much about his appearance at all—it was as if his mind simply wouldn't allow him to make sense of his features. But he knew his voice. "Rilvor?"

The man waved a hand over his face. All at once, his face snapped into focus, and Jasen could see that it was Rilvor. He must have been using magic to make himself unrecognizable. He was dressed in a manner more suited to a poor traveler than a king. Jasen blinked rapidly, not quite believing what he was seeing.

Jasen's dad scooted past him and slung an arm around Rilvor. Given that Rilvor was a good head taller than him, it was somewhat awkward. "Surprise!"

Surprise was right. Jasen looked back and forth between them. "What's going on?"

His dad puffed out his chest. "The king and I are old chums now! When he finished his business in Westrona, he popped by Grumhul to introduce himself. It was quite a sight, him coming in on his dragon!"

"I can imagine," Jasen said weakly. What he couldn't imagine was the process of him and Rilvor becoming "old chums." The whole situation was taking on an unreal quality —so much had changed since this morning.

His father plowed on. "So we got to talking about your whole situation, and the king was explaining the difficulties of getting some, ahem, time for yourselves." To Jasen's great horror, his father actually winked at Rilvor. "And so I came up with this brilliant plan! Everyone thinks the king is off consorting with the dragons, and everyone thinks you're off comforting your poor old dad, so that means the two of you can do whatever you want for a few days! Brilliant, eh?"

Jasen had to admit that it was clever. It was also horrible —he hadn't had time to decide what he was going to do about Adwig's proposal. The only good thing about Rilvor being away was that he'd have time to think, but now that had been snatched away. What was he supposed to do? He sank down into the chair his father had vacated and put his head in his hand.

Rilvor crossed the room and knelt beside him. "Is everything all right?" he asked, taking Jasen's hand in his. His eyes were so sweet and sincere. It hurt to look at him, so Jasen steadied his gaze on the floor.

His dad seemed to have finally caught on that Jasen was less than delighted. He cleared his throat. "I suppose I went a little too far with my note, what with saying I was dying. I am sorry about that." He rubbed the back of his neck sheepishly. "You were really worried about me?"

"Of course I was!" Horribly, Jasen felt tears prick behind his eyes. The whole day had been a jumble—first the meeting with the minister, then learning that his dad was dying, only to find out he wasn't after all, and now Rilvor here, looking not like a king, but a man—a man whose heart he might break. It was too much.

Rilvor rubbed his hand. "We've given you a shock. That was thoughtless of us."

"But for a good cause!" his father protested. "And see, your old dad is perfectly fine! And wait until you hear what Rilvor has in store for you."

"I was going to have it be a surprise," Rilvor said. He dipped his head so that Jasen was forced to meet his eyes. "Although I expect you have had enough surprises for one day, yes?"

Jasen made a faint sound of agreement in response—it was the best he could manage.

"I want to take you to Rakon—to show you all the things I told you about from my childhood. One of the draeds I've known since I was a child has offered his home to us—it's little more than a cottage, but comfortable, and more importantly, quite isolated. We won't be able to stay long—two or three days, at the most. But I thought it would be a welcome respite from the madness of Court."

"And you'll get to ride a dragon!" his father butted it. "Let me tell you, son, it is an experience like no other!"

Rilvor smiled. "Tasenred is most anxious to see you again. Would that please you?"

Jasen didn't know what to say. A day ago, it would have pleased him quite a lot. But so much had changed since then. He knew he ought to say no—his mind was made up that he could not accept a marriage proposal. But if he refused him now, that would be it. He would never see Rilvor or the dragons ever again. Jasen's heart lurched at the thought—every part of him cried out *no, not yet!*

"I would like that," he said quietly, which was true enough.

Rilvor smiled then, looking happier than Jasen could remember ever seeing him. He cursed himself for a coward, knowing how devastated he would be later on.

"This calls for champagne!" his father proclaimed. The champagne, however, had been knocked over, so his father went downstairs to get some more, leaving Rilvor and Jasen alone.

Rilvor peered at him. "Something still bothers you."

Jasen forced a smile. "It's nothing. Just still getting over the shock, like you said."

"Did he really tell you he was dying?"

Jasen pulled out the note from where he'd tucked it inside his cloak and handed it to him. Rilvor's eyebrows raised as he read it. "I see. That is rather dramatic."

"That's my father for you. I should have guessed, really. This isn't even the first time he's pretended to be dying."

Rilvor's eyebrows raised even further. "Oh?"

"It's a good way to get out of situations where you've gambled more than you have. He does a very good impression of a plague patient."

Rilvor laughed. "You must be joking."

"I wish I was." Jasen sighed. "How much money has he asked from you?"

Rilvor blinked. "He mentioned some debts. I told him I would be happy to help—"

"Don't. Giving him money makes it worse. If you want to help, pay his creditors directly and don't tell him about it. It's good for my dad to be worried about debt collectors. Not that there's much left for them to take if they do track him down. If he weren't an earl, he'd probably be in debtor's prison."

Rilvor considered him for a moment before speaking again. "It seems that I have acted hastily, without a good understanding of your relationship with your father. I am sorry."

Jasen shrugged. "What for? You can't help the way he is."

"But I did not speak with you about seeing him. I should

SERA TREVOR

not have presumed." Rilvor let go of Jasen's hand and rubbed his face. "This was all presumptuous. You must forgive me— as king, I am too used to having my way. If you do not wish to come with me, I completely understand."

Jasen smiled at him weakly. "You don't have to apologize. It was a nice idea."

"You'll come, then?"

"Yes."

"Wonderful!" Rilvor kissed his hand. "And I should hope it goes without saying that I do not have any…expectations."

Jasen cocked his head. "Expectations?"

Rilvor blushed a little. "I would not impinge your honor."

Of course. He'd forgotten he was supposed to be diligently guarding his virginity. He was saved from having to respond when his father entered the room, carrying not one but three bottles.

"It's time to celebrate, boys! I got a bottle for each of us!"

Jasen rolled his eyes but accepted his bottle.

"On the count of three," his dad said, getting his cork ready. "One, two, three!"

The corks popped simultaneously. His dad made as if to drink directly from the bottle, but seemed to think better of it when he saw Rilvor and Jasen pouring themselves glasses like civilized people. Once he filled his glass, he lifted up. "A toast to my son! May you have all the happiness in the world. You deserve it, after putting up with me your whole life."

"Don't talk like that, Dad," Jasen said.

"No, no—it's the truth. I know I was a shit dad, but I do love you, son, and I want you to be happy. My only regret is that your dear mother couldn't be here to see it." He waved his glass in Rilvor's direction. "And a toast to my future son-in-law! I'd be happy to have you in the family even if you weren't the king. I knew from the moment I met you that you were more than just a monarch!"

Rilvor raised his glass. "Thank you, Draul."

"Please—call me Dad."

"Don't encourage him," Jasen said before Rilvor could respond.

Rilvor just laughed, with his dad soon joining in. After a few moments, Jasen began laughing himself.

They spent the rest of the day and evening listening to his father reminiscing about his own marriage, which segued into many stories about Jasen's childhood. The champagne blurred out some of Jasen's sadness, and for a while he even forgot about Minister Adwig and the horrible decision that awaited him.

Instead, he allowed his father's stories to bring him back to his childhood. It was true that his parents weren't perfect, and he still felt the loss of his mother keenly. But the one thing he could say for his dad was that in between all of the drinking and the gambling and general irresponsibility, he had also been enormously affectionate, especially when Jasen was a child. And he seemed genuinely happy for Jasen, and not just happy that he'd snagged the king. It was a pity his happiness was misplaced.

Eventually, the champagne ran out. Rilvor went to his room, swaying a little. Jasen was to stay with his dad, who fell fast asleep before Rilvor was even fully out of the door. Sleep didn't come quite so easily for Jasen. He still had no idea what he was going to say to Rilvor, or indeed what he wanted for himself.

CHAPTER 15

$\mathcal{R}$ ilvor and Jasen woke early the next morning. His dad roused himself enough to murmur a bleary good-bye. He was going to stay at the inn for the few days that Rilvor and Jasen would be gone, after which they would bring him back to the palace with them. Or rather, that was Rilvor's plan. Who knew what would really happen.

Since they were traveling to Rakon via dragon and horses did not do well around dragons, he and Rilvor had to walk to the nearest draemir. Jasen didn't mind—it had been a long time since he'd gotten in a decent hike. They left their belongings at the inn, as all their other needs would be provided for once they reached Rakon. The one special item they brought was Rilvor's Drae's cloak, which was also hidden with magic. Wearing it made communion with the dragons easier.

The walk lasted about an hour. When they reached the draemir, Rilvor put his hand on the jewel of the Drae's cloak. "They shouldn't be long. I reached them earlier this morning."

"What does it feel like?" Jasen asked. "Communing with the dragons, I mean."

Rilvor thought for a moment. "Like fishing."

Jasen blinked. "Fishing? How do you mean?"

"Have you ever been fishing?"

"Of course I have! It's practically a national pastime in Grumhul."

Rilvor chuckled. "Forgive me. You have become such a creature of Court that I sometimes forget that you aren't a typical noble. So as you know, when you fish, you put out your line, and you wait. Eventually, you feel a tug. Once you do, you begin to pull it in. Instead of a fishing line, you use your attention. It requires some concentration, and most of all, patience." Rilvor patted the jewel clasp of his cloak. "This helps."

"So you just—think it?"

"In a sense, although I wouldn't call it 'thinking,' since you need to set your thoughts aside."

"Set your thoughts aside?" He scoffed. "Where on earth are you supposed to put them?"

Rilvor laughed again and then gave Jasen a thoughtful look. He took off his cloak and put it on Jasen's shoulders.

"What are you doing?" Jasen asked as he clasped it.

"I am going to teach you how to call the dragons."

Jasen furrowed his brow. "That isn't possible. I don't have any magic."

"But you have a connection with Tasenred, and I have felt the power in you, ever since you first arrived."

"You have?"

"Don't you remember, when we first met in the draemir?"

He did. It seemed like a lifetime ago, when in reality it had only been a few months, but he remembered that warm feeling when he wore the cloak. As soon as he thought of it, he felt it again. He sucked in a breath.

"You feel it again," Rilvor said. It wasn't a question.

Jasen nodded.

"Sit down with me."

They sank to the ground and sat, cross-legged. "Close your eyes," Rilvor said. "And draw your attention to your breath."

"I thought I was supposed to draw my attention to the dragons."

"You need to gather your attention first. Think of it as getting your fishing rod ready. Once the line is in place, you can cast it out."

"How will I know I'm ready?"

"You'll feel it."

Jasen was still skeptical, but he shut his eyes and tried all the same. But every time he managed to focus on his breath, his attention would shatter a moment later. He wasn't sure how long he sat there—long enough for him to be uncomfortable.

Sighing, he opened his eyes. "It's not working."

"Let us try another way." Rilvor put his hand on his back. All at once, Jasen felt a warmth in his chest. "Do you feel that?"

Jasen nodded. "It's warm."

"Close your eyes again and put your attention there, with the beat of your heart."

Jasen did as he was told. One by one, his thoughts and worries left him until all that was left was Rilvor's hand on his back, and the beating of his heart.

"Good," Rilvor said, his voice low. "Cast your mind out now. Look for Tasenrad. He's searching for you."

Jasen thought of the dragon. Before long, he felt a tug on his mind, just as Rilvor said he would. He tugged back. And then he "saw" Tasenred in his mind's eye—not just a memory or an imagining, but as clearly as if the dragon were already there, with his red scales gleaming in the sunlight as he flew through the air. He saw Woria, too, flying right beside him. The image grew more and more intense, realer than real now, as if he both saw Tasenred and was seeing through Tasenred's eyes as he swooped downward—

It became too much. He gasped and opened his eyes—and there the dragon was, standing in front of him. Woria was there, too. He hadn't even heard them land.

Rilvor removed his hand from Jasen's back. "Well done."

Jasen felt dazed, but managed to get to his feet. He moved to Tasenred's side, almost feeling more like he was floating than walking. The dragon lowered his head to meet him. Jasen leaned his forehead against the dragon's cheek, shutting his eyes and breathing in.

"I've missed you," he whispered.

He felt something stir in the dragon and in his own heart —he could feel that Tasenred felt the same. A loud snort from Woria startled him. He left Tasenred to approach the other dragon. "It's good to see you as well," he said, giving her a bow. She let out a snort and rumbled toward him, lowering her head until they were face to face. Jasen put his hand on her cheek, which seemed to please her.

He turned back to Rilvor, whose eyes were sparkling. "Shall we?" Rilvor said.

Both of the dragons laid their bodies on the ground. Jasen found it a little difficult getting onto the dragon's back, but once he was there, he knew precisely where to sit and how to hold himself. As soon as he was settled, Tasenred began to move, first at a lumber, and then more and more quickly, until at last, they were in the air.

The view from the air was breathtaking—he'd never imagined land could look like that. The higher they got, the smaller things seemed, until Jasen felt as if he were a giant, or a god. All of his doubts and sorrows vanished. Here in the sky, he felt as if he could breathe at last. Rilvor and Woria kept pace beside them. Even though he couldn't see him very well, Jasen felt a connection with Rilvor that was strong and strange and full of a joy he didn't know it was possible to feel.

Some time passed, although it was impossible for Jasen to determine how long. They passed over several rocky peaks until they reached a valley. Jasen gasped at the beauty of it. There was a lake, so perfect and clear that it reflected the sky as clearly as a mirror. Surrounding the lake was a field of flowers, so numerous and varied that it was as if seeing a rainbow painted on the ground. Along the edges of the valley were woodlands—the trees continued from the valley and up onto the mountain side, like a green blanket.

The dragons landed amongst the wildflowers. Jasen slid off of Tasenred's back and saw Rilvor dismounting as well. As soon as they had deposited their passengers, the dragons took off again, dancing around each other in the sky just as Jasen had seen them do on his arrival to the Draethenper so many months ago.

"Welcome to Rakon," Rilvor said.

"It's beautiful." That felt woefully inadequate. No wonder Rilvor missed this. His heart felt lighter here, almost like he had stepped into a dream.

Rilvor held out his hand. "Come—let me show you where we'll be staying."

After a brief walk, they reached a cottage at the edge of the woods. A charming little vegetable garden was off to one side. The interior consisted of only one room. There was a small, clay-lined pit in the center of the room that held the ashes of a fire. Over the pit was a small pot, suspended by a crude tripod. The walls were hung with a few tools that would prove useful for life in the woods, some herbs, and what looked like a side of salted meat. A small table sat off in one corner. Two wooden bowls and two chalices had been placed on the table, as well as a large basket, which was covered by a cloth. Another corner contained a straw mattress lying directly on the floor, beside which was a large trunk.

The furnishings may have been simple, but they all seemed well-crafted, and the cottage was clean, with fresh-smelling rushes on the floor.

"This is the home of Brother Vyncis," Rilvor said. "He's a childhood friend of mine."

"It seems a bit small in here for three people."

Rilvor laughed. "He won't be joining us. Brother Vyncis often makes journeys into the wilderness, to better commune with the natural world. He was delighted to lend us the use of the cabin for a few days—he's always admonishing me to take some time away from the palace. I haven't been able to do that in quite some time." Rilvor hesitated. "I hope this isn't too rustic for you."

Jasen smiled. "It's perfect."

Rilvor flushed with pleasure. He went to the table and took the cloth off of the basket. "Ah, he was able to find them!"

"Find what?"

Rilvor picked up the basket and brought it to Jasen. Jasen peered inside at red fruit.

"Strawberries," Rilvor said. "Just for you."

It took Jasen a moment before he remembered their first conversation, all the way back in the draemir when Jasen hadn't known he was speaking to a king. He laughed. "I did say I wanted strawberries, didn't I? I've only ever had them once."

"These are more tart than the ones that grow in the lowlands."

Jasen popped one into his mouth. It was more tangy than sweet, but somehow he liked it even more. "It's delicious."

Rilvor seemed pleased. "We'll bring them with us."

"Where are we going?"

"You mentioned you enjoy fishing. We can catch our lunch."

Jasen grinned. "Sounds good to me."

The fishing rods had been hung on the wall beside the rest of the tools. They retrieved them as well as a few additional supplies before setting off. Jasen was a bit tired from their early morning hike, but the prospect of fishing by the beautiful lake energized him. They moved at a slower pace than they had that morning, enjoying the beauty of the surroundings.

Finally, they reached the lake. It was just as lovely as it had been from the air, although it felt more real now, not just some impossibly beautiful but distant image. Rilvor dropped to his hands knees and began sifting through the rich soil.

"What are you doing?"

Rilvor gave him a wry look over his shoulder. "Looking for bait, of course."

Jasen laughed. "I wonder what people would think if they saw their king digging for worms."

"No doubt it would cause a worm-digging craze. Now, are you going to help me or not?"

Jasen gladly got into the dirt with him. They both laughed a little, as if they were overgrown children. "This is much more fun than Court amusements," Jasen said.

"I whole-heartedly agree."

Soon they had several big, juicy worms to bait their hooks. They cast their lines out into the water and settled in to wait for the fish to bite. Jasen breathed in the musty smell of the lake and shut his eyes, enjoying the sunshine on his face. It was heaven.

"What happened in Westrona?" Jasen asked after a little while. In all the excitement, he had forgotten to ask.

"It is going to take some time before things are set to order, but I believe the dragons have chosen the new ruler wisely."

"Is it a king or a queen?"

"Neither."

Jasen cocked his head. "What do you mean?"

"The young lady upon whom the dragons called has decided that there will be no more kings and queens in Westrona. She has agreed to preside over the transition of power, but has not committed to maintaining her position indefinitely."

"But if there's no king or queen, who will be in charge? The new nobles?"

"She is disinclined to appoint new nobles as well."

Jasen stared at him in bafflement. "That sounds like complete chaos! How does she plan for them to keep order?"

"She has an idea—a rather radical one, but I think it has the chance of working. She is collecting the money that would normally be paid in rent to the nobles and starting a fund to appoint justices and a protection force to protect the people from wrongdoers. Other decisions will be put to the people." The look on Jasen's face much have been comical, because Rilvor laughed a little. "You seem scandalized. Is that not how Grumhul works? You've said yourself that Grumhulians have a say in the law."

"Yes, but not the final say! What if the people choose unwisely?"

"I imagine the same thing as when the nobles choose poorly."

Jasen shook his head. The idea seemed incredible to him. "And the dragons are for it?"

235

"The dragons chose who they thought would be the best leader. They defer to her."

"And what if the dragons decide that there's to be no more kings and queens at all?"

"There may come a time when there are no kings and queens, but that is something that we will face when we come to it. As you know, I have no great love for being a king, although I will never shirk from my duty as long as I am needed." Rilvor peered at him. "I believe we have similar feelings on the subject, yes?"

Jasen wasn't sure how to respond. "What happened to the nobles who were deposed?"

"They were sent to provinces different from the ones they had presided over and given homes and a choice of professions to learn."

"That's going to be difficult for them, I imagine."

"Yes, but it is preferable to being demolished in flames."

"I suppose so." Jasen felt a tug on his line. "Oh! I think I've got something!"

Sure enough, Jasen had snagged a fish. Rilvor made quick work of it, preparing it with a knife they had brought from the cottage, and then strung it up. They waited a little while longer until they'd caught a few more fish before heading back to the cottage.

By then, Jasen was starving. He'd snacked on the strawberries while they were fishing, but it wasn't enough to satisfy him. They roasted the fish outside over an open flame, along with some vegetables from the garden. They ate stretched out on the grass beside each other.

Jasen put aside his plate with a contented sigh. "That was delicious."

"Agreed."

Jasen reached into the basket and pulled out a couple of the remaining strawberries. "Would you like one?"

"Certainly."

On impulse, instead of handing it to him, Jasen pressed the berry against his lips. Rilvor froze for a moment, his eyes wide, but then he accepted the fruit, his tongue licking briefly at Jasen's fingers. A wave of desire flooded through Jasen. From the heavy-lidded look Rilvor was giving him, it seemed he felt the same way.

Rilvor moved forward slowly, as if in a dream. He put his hand on the back of Jasen's neck, threading his fingers through his hair. Their faces were so close that Jasen could feel his breath on his cheek. "I want to kiss you," he murmured. "But if I do, I won't want to stop."

"Then don't stop."

"Are you sure?"

In response, Jasen put his lips against Rilvor's, who eagerly returned the kiss. Soon they were wrapped up in each other, falling back on the grass as they kissed again and again. All thoughts of the Court and its intrigues dissolved from Jasen's mind, given at last the full consideration they deserved—that is to say, none at all.

They shed their clothes and found pleasure with each other right there in the grass, beneath the bright blue sky. There was nothing they could do together that would be new to Jasen—his body fell into the familiar motions, the kisses and caresses, the feel of mouths and hands moving together to bring each other to climax. But while the mechanics of it were familiar, the feeling behind it was not. Jasen had always approached sex as a respite from boredom and loneliness. It was different with Rilvor. His whole self—body, heart, and soul—was swept away in utter bliss, so sweet that he never wanted it to end.

Rilvor must have felt the same way, for they moved into the cottage and did it again. When they were at last too spent to do more, they lay together under the furs, with Jasen's head against Rilvor's chest. Rilvor was stroking Jasen's hair languidly. It felt so good that Jasen could have drifted off then, even though the sun was still up. Unfortunately, his mind started up its usual chatter. He sighed. They needed to talk.

"I've done this before," Jasen said before he could think better of it.

To his surprise, Rilvor chuckled a little. "So I gathered."

Jasen frowned. "It doesn't bother you?"

"Of course not. Did you really think it would?"

"Well—yes. I'm supposed to be a virgin."

"You are 'supposed' to be many things, all of which I am very glad you are not." He kissed his forehead. "You should have told me sooner. I would have not been so worried about scandalizing you."

Jasen felt relieved—and then something occurred to him. "You've done this before, too."

"Surely you didn't think *I* was a virgin. I am a father."

"Yes, but your wife was—well, a woman. You seemed to have a pretty good handle on the differences."

Rilvor laughed. "I'm glad you think so." He kissed his shoulder, moving toward his neck.

Jasen pulled away from him and sat up. He wouldn't let himself be distracted. "But you were married when you were seventeen." All at once, Jasen remembered the conversation he'd overheard between Adwig and Rilvor—how Adwig had said he wouldn't interfere with the king's 'pleasures.' "You weren't faithful to your wife, were you?"

Rilvor sat up as well. He rubbed his temple. "No. I was not."

"Did she know?"

"Yes. We had an agreement. My preference has always been for men. I told her that before we were married. We agreed that we could both seek other lovers while still fulfilling our duties."

"So it was a loveless marriage."

"Not loveless, no. Quendra was the mother of my children, and a dear friend. But I did not love her as a husband should love his wife."

"So infidelity is something you are willing to live with?"

"Only because we had no other choice. I certainly wouldn't want that again." Rilvor frowned. "Would you?"

Jasen put his hands over his face and gathered himself. "When I said I've done this before, I mean that I've done this *a lot* before."

Rilvor looked at him blankly. "And you don't think that I could...satisfy you?"

"No! That's not it at all!" There was little sense in delaying it—he might as well get it over with. "Minister Adwig spoke to me yesterday morning. He knows about my past. An ex-lover, who tried to blackmail me a few days ago, took his story to Adwig when I told him I wouldn't pay."

Rilvor grew still. "And he dares to think that the word of a blackmailer is sufficient to stand against my choice of a spouse?"

Jasen bit his lip. "There's more. He claims he has proof that I've been having an affair with a guard. It isn't true," he added quickly. "But the guard in question is a friend of mine. He has witnesses to seeing the two of us together. And another friend of mine, we—well, we don't always behave as proper consorts should. He has witnesses to that, too."

Rilvor said nothing for a few agonizing moments. When he spoke again, his voice was cold with barely restrained fury. "The minister has grossly overstepped his authority. The approval of my marriage by the council of ministers is a formality, not a law. I am their *king*. I will not tolerate such insubordination. Any minister who speaks against my choice will be dismissed."

"What if they all do? Will you get rid of them all?"

"If I must."

"And how will that look? The entire council of ministers thrown out over their objections to the marriage of their king to a promiscuous, penniless young lord—from Grumhul, no less?"

"It does not matter what anyone thinks!" Rilvor nearly roared.

Jasen winced at the anger in his voice, but he couldn't let the matter go. "That isn't true, and you know it. Everyone's already on edge because of the situation in Westrona. Having their king debase himself and make a whore the king consort isn't going to help matters."

Rilvor looked as if he'd been slapped. He took Jasen's hands in his own and kissed them. "How can you speak of yourself in such a manner?"

"It's what the Court will say. You know that's true."

"I won't allow it."

"You can't control what people think. The more you fight against it, the worse they'll think of me. They'll assume I'm egging you on and they'll hate me all the more. Worse yet, they will lose faith in you. I can't let that happen."

Understanding dawned on Rilvor's face. "What are you saying? Are you refusing me?"

Jasen took a deep breath. "Adwig made me an offer. I could be your official paramour—"

"—and I would marry someone else?" Rilvor cut him off. "No. It is impossible."

"Why? You've done it before."

"And it killed Quendra!"

A shock of cold pierced his heart. "What? How?"

Rilvor held his head in his hands. When he finally looked

up, Jasen was shocked to see tears in his eyes. "We had an arrangement, as I said. And it worked well enough for many years. I had my lovers, and she had hers. But then I fell in love. His name was Gileon. We met two years before my wife's death. I was always very upfront with my lovers, making sure they understood that I was not looking for anything beyond someone to share my bed on occasion. But somehow, in spite of my best intentions, we fell in love. And that was when Quendra's health began to fail.

"None of us made the connection immediately. Why would we? But the marriage between the Lord of the Drae and his spouse is so much more than a simple marriage. The bond between Quendra and I had to be strong enough to bear the burden of the connection between humanity and the dragons. And it was—as I said, we really did care for one another. I loved her as a friend, and it was enough. But when I fell in love with Gileon, that bond was strained." His voice became so soft that Jasen struggled to hear. "By the time I realized it, it was too late. No healers could save her. And so she died." He put his face in his hands again. "And it was my fault."

His shoulders shook, although he barely made a sound. Jasen put a hand on his back, unsure of what else he could do. He only spoke again once Rilvor had calmed. "And you're sure that's what happened?" he asked gently.

Rilvor wiped the tears from his eyes. "What else could it be? None of the healers were able to find a cause."

"But you don't know for sure."

"I am not willing to risk another life in order to prove my theory." Rilvor took Jasen's face in his hands and kissed him desperately. "Jasen, I love you with all of my heart. I cannot marry another. Please say that you will marry me—*please*."

Jasen pulled himself away gently. "I need time to think."

Rilvor's gaze hardened. "If you were going to refuse me,

then why did you agree to come here at all?"

"Because I love you, too!" Jasen said miserably. "But what happens if our marriage weakens your reign? How would you feel about me then?"

"I would never hold you accountable for what is not your fault—"

"What happened to Gileon?" Jasen interrupted.

That stopped Rilvor short. It took him several moments to reply. "I asked him to return to his home kingdom."

"Because you blamed him for Quendra's death?"

"No. Because I blamed myself."

"But you still couldn't bring yourself to look at him any more, could you? How would it be different between us if our marriage causes a crisis in the Allied Realms?"

They lapsed into silence. Outside, the sun was setting, and the cottage grew dimmer and dimmer. At last, Rilvor heaved a great sigh and drew Jasen into his arms again. "Your caution speaks well of your character. I agree that there may be some difficulty with Court at first, but I also think that the scandal will pass. You are more popular than you realize. I am willing to take the risk—but it is unfair of me to ask you to do the same, if you feel you cannot bear it. Will you at least give the matter some more thought before you give me your final answer?"

"All right," Jase said quietly.

"Very well. I think you should return to Grumhul with your father. I can give you a month to decide, but no longer."

"I understand."

Rilvor kissed him. "Then let us speak no more of it tonight, and try to get some rest."

Before long, Rilvor's breath steadied as he slipped into sleep. Jasen clung to consciousness a little longer, wanting to savor every moment in Rilvor's arms. He had a feeling these moments might be their last.

CHAPTER 16

*J*asen woke up alone. Dawn had only just broken, and he was cold. He tried to remember where he left his clothes—were they still outside? Just as he was contemplating how he was going to retrieve them without freezing, he saw that they'd been folded neatly on the edge of the mattress. Shivering, he pulled them on and went to find Rilvor.

It didn't take long. He was sitting in the middle of the field of flowers, wearing the Drae's cloak. Jasen sat down beside him. Rilvor's eyes were shut, and he didn't acknowledge him. "So you're calling the dragons," Jasen said, not sure of what else to say.

"Yes. There's not much sense in staying longer."

Jasen winced. He sounded so cold, but he supposed he couldn't blame him. "Are you angry with me?" He was embarrassed at how pitiful he sounded.

Rilvor turned to him at last. "I'm disappointed, but I cannot blame you for your doubts. It is not a small thing to marry a monarch." He smiled sadly. "That you take it so seriously is yet another reason why I want you by my side."

Jasen looked down. "I'm sorry."

Rilvor put a finger on his chin and tilted his face upward until their gazes met. "Do not be sorry for listening to your heart." He sighed. "I am the one who should apologize—I'm acting like a spoiled child who didn't get his way."

"No, don't—I let you believe that I would say yes and sprung it on you out of nowhere. It's my fault."

Rilvor put his arm over Jasen's shoulders and squeezed. "Clearly, we are both have many flaws. Maybe neither of us should sit on the throne."

Jasen smiled a little. "You should just abdicate. Then we can move here. Surely the dragons will understand."

"And leave my poor son to take over the kingdom?"

"Of course not—the children will live here too."

"The cottage is rather small for six people. And Brother Vyncis will want it back."

"We'll build a new one, just for us."

Rilvor kissed Jasen's cheek. "If only we could."

Before Rilvor could turn away, Jasen captured his lips in a gentle kiss. When it was over, Rilvor rested his forehead against Jasen's. "The decision is yours to make, but know that I am willing to fight for you, come what may."

"I know," Jasen said quietly.

Rilvor put his arms around Jasen from behind and encouraged him to lean back. Jasen breathed in the smell of him, trying to memorize it. He savored the feel of Rilvor's embrace, so strong and yet so gentle. Would he be able to remember this years from now, or would it fade? Would the hurt of losing him ever heal? He didn't know.

They sat there, entwined and silent, until two shadows passed overhead—the dragons had arrived. Since they had brought nothing with them, there was nothing to carry away. It seemed wrong somehow, leaving empty-handed, as if they had never even been there. Jasen climbed on Tasenred's back and held on tight as the dragons took off again, and then they were soaring through the sky, and soon put Rakon far behind them.

They landed in the draemir not far from the inn. Once they had dismounted from the dragons, Jasen and Rilvor just stood there, staring at each other. Jasen didn't want to say goodbye; it seemed Rilvor felt much the same way.

Rilvor reached into a small purse that was tied on his belt and removed a few coins. "For your carriage home," he said, handing them to Jasen. "In case your father misplaced some of the money I gave him earlier."

Jasen snorted. "That is a possibility. Thank you."

Rilvor took off the Drae's cloak and draped it over Jasen's shoulders. "Take this as well. It is for you to keep, no matter your answer."

Jasen touched the jewel clasp. "Thank you."

He kissed Jasen's hand. "Good-bye, my love."

Jasen fought back tears. "Good-bye."

Rilvor climbed onto Woria again, and then they were off. But Tasenred didn't follow. He flared his nostrils and stomped his feet.

"I can't go with you right now," Jasen said.

Tasenred made a strange, keening sound and stomped his feet again.

"It's complicated. I'm sorry."

The dragon brought his face close to Jasen and regarded him with one giant eye. He made the sound again.

Jasen put his hand on Tasenred's cheek. "I'll call for you, I promise. I just have human things I need to work out first."

Tasenred snorted again, clearly annoyed, but it seemed Jasen's answer was good enough. He took off, soon catching up to Woria.

Jasen took a moment to collect himself before beginning the long trek back to the inn. When he arrived, his dad was not there. The innkeeper mentioned something about him going to the city. Jasen arranged for a carriage to take them the border of the Draelands. After that, they would be forced to find different transportation. A carriage was nice, but only on the better maintained roads.

With that settled, Jasen bought a light breakfast, although his appetite was poor. Once he'd eaten, he went up to their room. It was just as well that his dad wasn't there—he still hadn't decided what he was going to tell him. Besides, he was tired. He curled up on the bed and fell asleep.

He was awoken some time later when his dad burst into the room. "The innkeeper said you had returned—I wasn't expecting you for several more days!" He didn't sound particularly worried—in fact, he was very cheerful.

Jasen sat up and rubbed his face, still groggy from his nap. His dad sat down beside him. "Had a nap, did you? The king tire you out, eh?" He elbowed him in the ribs.

Jasen couldn't even muster up the energy to be annoyed. His father continued on, oblivious as usual. "A fellow traveler gave me a ride into the city. What a marvelous place it is— the shops alone are like nothing I've ever seen!" He fumbled under his cloak and pulled out a small box. "Now I really ought to keep this a secret since it's a gift and all, but I'm too excited! Just don't tell Rilvor."

He held out the box, clearly expecting Jasen to take it, but Jasen just stared at it dully. His father, never one to pick up easily on cues, opened it himself instead. "Look! Dragon necklaces!" He took the necklaces out of the box. "You see, if you hold them together, they look like they're dancing. You each can wear one—what do you think?"

He opened his mouth to reply, but no words came out. Instead, to Jasen's horror, he started to cry.

His father dropped the necklaces on the bed. "O my son! What's happened?"

Jasen still couldn't say anything, so he just shook his head. His dad put his big arms around him and held him close. "Has he cast you off? Done something to you? Blast him! I never liked him—from the moment I saw him, I knew he was no good! He thinks because he's king, he can treat the rest of us however he pleases?"

"No," Jasen said, finally finding his voice. He pulled back and wiped the tears from his eyes. "It's nothing like that." And then the whole story came tumbling out of him.

When he was finished, his dad pulled him into another hug. "We'll just go home. Back to Grumhul, where life is honest."

"What about the money? We're still broke."

"Never you mind about the money. What do I care about money when I can have my only son back home where he belongs!"

Jasen smiled a little. "Thanks, Dad."

"Of course, the king *did* make certain promises, which I think is only fair that he honor, given the circumstances."

Jasen rolled his eyes, but he couldn't bring himself to be too annoyed. His dad was his dad—he couldn't really be anyone else. Strangely enough, the thought was comforting. "Let's go home, then."

Jasen's appetite had recovered, so they went downstairs and had a hearty meal. The carriage wouldn't depart until tomorrow, so they had another night to rest at the inn. Jasen fell asleep easily, even with his father's snoring. He was still miserable, but there was something very freeing about being away from Court. He didn't have to worry about people finding him out. For the first time in months, he felt like himself.

They set off early the next morning. Jasen wasn't feeling quite as bleak as he had yesterday—he still didn't know what he planned to do, but a good night's sleep and a hearty breakfast made his problems seem more surmountable. Besides, a part of him was happy to be going back to Grumhul. It was funny to think of how eager he had been to leave just a few months earlier. He wondered if he would change his mind yet again once he got there.

They traveled for a little while. Jasen almost dozed off, enjoying the feel of the sun on his face. But that warmth vanished suddenly. Jasen frowned. The sky had been almost free of clouds.

But it wasn't a cloud, which was made abundantly clear when the ground shook as something very large landed in front of them. The carriage stopped dead in its tracks as the horses reared up, neighing wildly. The coachman let out a string of curses as he tried to get them back under control.

"What in the blazes is going on?" his dad bellowed, sticking his head out of the window.

Jasen didn't reply, because he already knew what had happened. A dragon had arrived.

It was Tasenred, to be specific. Jasen lept out of the carriage and approached him. The dragon flicked his enormous tail when he saw Jasen. It was always hard to tell with dragons, but he seemed pretty pleased with himself.

"I'm not going back!" Jasen shouted at him. "I told you I have human things to take care of."

Tasenred roared—a heart-stopping sound. The horses panicked further, and the coachman seemed on the edge of panic himself. "I can't control them!" the coachman called out. "Ask the dragon to leave, please!"

His father stumbled out of the carriage, looking up wide-eyed at Tasenred. "I will never get used to how big they are," he said in awe. Tasenred let out a smaller roar in reply.

The horses seemed to have had enough. The coachman pulled the reins and turned them around, and the carriage was tearing off down the road before either Jasen or his father could say a word. He wasn't too upset about losing their trunk, but how were they supposed to get to Grumhul now?

As if reading his mind (which he might very well have been), Tasenred stooped down in clear invitation.

"I told you, I'm not returning to Strengsend!"

A picture of Grumhul flashed through his mind—specifically, that of Castle Gumptar, where Queen Urga resided.

"You want to take us there?" Jasen frowned. "Can't you just take us home?"

Tasenred let out a huge stream of steam from his nose. His father jumped backward.

"I think we better do what he wants," his dad said. "What if he decides to toast us?"

"He's not going to toast us." He rubbed his temple. What if Tasenred was trying to trick him? But he didn't think that dragons had the same impulse to lie as people did. And it wasn't as if they had much of a choice, now that their carriage was gone.

He took his father's hand and gave it a tug. "Come on, then."

They climbed onto Tasenred's back, and soon they were soaring through the air—in the direction of Grumhul, thankfully. It was only a matter of hours before they reached Queen Urga's castle. Tasenred circled around it several times, as if looking for a place to land. But the castle was precariously situated on an island in the middle of a swamp, with nothing like the fields of a draemir anywhere near it.

Jasen tried to communicate to Tasenred that they should search for a landing place further out—generally, Castle Gumptar was reached by boat. But Jasen did not have a lot of experience communing with dragons, and Tasenred did not appear to get the message. He touched down in a huge splash that left Jasen and his father completely soaked. As Jasen and his dad tried to get themselves together, Tasenred let out a rather undignified squawk. It seemed as though he was stuck.

"What do we do?" his dad asked.

Jasen slid off Tasenred's back, directly into the swamp. The water came up to his thighs. He waded around until he was in front of Tasenred. "Are you all right?"

The dragon dipped his head and made a pitiful sound.

Jasen laid his forehead against Tasenred's snout. "It would have been easier if you let us take our carriage," he murmured. He still didn't understand why Tasenred had come for them, but dragons were often inscrutable, as he was learning.

"Well?" his dad called out. "What are we doing?"

Jasen looked to the castle. It wasn't that far off. "I suppose we're going for help."

His dad slid off the dragon and landed with a splash. Jasen gave Tasenred an encouraging stroke, trying to communicate that they would be back.

They waded through the swamp. Fortunately, they didn't have to make it all the way to the castle—a group of guards were waiting for them on solid land. They must have seen the dragon and come to investigate. Standing at the head of them was Queen Urga herself.

The last time Jasen had seen the queen was after his mother's death, but she was exactly as he remembered her: a stout woman with stringy red hair. Her olive green dress was well-made but rather plain. Just from her attire, it would have been difficult to tell that she was royalty. However, once she opened her mouth, there was no question who she was. She was a queen, and she *would* be obeyed.

She seemed none too pleased with them, her arms crossed and her eyes narrowed into a glare. "Lord Draul.

Dare I ask why you've brought a damned dragon into my kingdom?"

His dad took off a boot and dumped the water out of it. "Well, Your Majesty, I'd say that it's more the dragon that brought us!"

The queen rolled her eyes. She signaled to her guards. "What are you waiting for? Help the poor beast! And to be clear, I mean the dragon. I don't think there's much helping *this* one," she said with a nod to Jasen's dad. The guards saluted and head off to the dock that was not far away, where a longboat was waiting for them.

"It's not his fault, Your Majesty," Jasen said. "The dragon came for me."

The queen narrowed her eyes again, although it was more of a squint than a glare. "Little Lord Jasen? Is that you?"

"Yes, Your Majesty."

"Come closer, my boy—my eyesight isn't what it used to be."

Jasen obeyed. She looked him up and down with seeming satisfaction. "You've grown. You look so much like your mother."

"Yes, Your Majesty," he said with a bow.

She snorted. "I had heard you'd gone off to Court in the Draelands. Your manners certainly are fine." She reached up to wipe some mud off his face. "But you're back in Grumhul now, so why don't you give your old Urga a hug?"

He did as he was told. With her arms around him, he felt like a child again. A memory surfaced of her holding him after his mother's funeral. "It's good to see you again."

"I am glad to see you too, although I am less than pleased at your choice of transportation. What in blazes are you doing with a dragon?"

"It's a long story." Jasen looked back to Tasenred. The guards had reached him and were trying to get a rope around his neck. Tasenred, for his part, seemed like he was cooperating, but the rope kept falling back into the swamp.

"What are they doing?" Jasen asked.

"They're going to try to haul him out. It's been awhile, but it's not the first time a dragon has gotten stuck in our swamp. You'd think the beasts would learn."

At last, the rope was secured. The guards rowed with vigor, with Tasenred straining along with them. Slowly, he extracted himself, moving his legs one by one as he made his way to the shore. When he lumbered up onto the bank, he shook like a wet dog, spraying water everywhere.

Urga waged a finger at him. "Don't think we'll come to your rescue a second time, you wretched beast! Swamps are no place for dragons!"

It was shocking to see someone talk to a dragon that way, but Tasenred didn't seem to take offense. In fact, he caught Jasen's eye and winked. Or perhaps Jasen was imagining it. Tasenred ran along the bank, picking up speed, until he was in the air again.

They all watched until Tasenred disappeared over the horizon. Urga huffed. "That's one thing taken care of. Let's get the two of you dried out, and then you can tell me your long story."

Within the hour, Jasen and his father were clean and dry. Queen Urga saw to it that they were well-fed as well. His father retired to the room Urga had given them, claiming exhaustion, although Jasen suspected that he wanted to avoid Queen Urga. Jasen couldn't entirely blame him—the queen made no secret of how much she disliked him. It was the reason Jasen hadn't been back to the castle since his mother's death.

Castle Gumptar was much smaller than Strengsend and far less magnificent, but the relaxed atmosphere more than made up for the fewer material comforts. Jasen felt as if he could breathe, and it wasn't just because he no longer was wearing a corset. He'd spent a lot of time here as a child—his mother had been a favorite of the queen's. In a way, it seemed homier than home. Jasen and his father were so isolated in their dilapidated old castle in Hagas. Gumptar, while not very grand, was well-kept and well-attended, with people who Jasen had known from childhood.

Jasen joined the queen for a walk in the courtyard. The day was nice, if a bit muggy. Some children were playing with Hogort, the queen's enormous pet hog, squealing like piglets themselves.

"Do you remember Borgus?" the queen asked him.

"Of course I do." Borgus had been her pet when Jasen was a child. "I remember riding her around the courtyard, just like that," he said, gesturing to the children. "I always had fun."

"You were her favorite, I think. You were such a scrawny little thing, but tough, and you never pulled her tail. She was a good hog. Of course, Hogort is a good hog, too. Haven't met a hog I didn't respect. Can't say the same for people." She sniffed. "So did they chase you out, or did you escape?"

"Both, I think."

She snorted. "Just as well. A pit of vipers, that place is. Not a decent person among them. I suppose there's Rilvor. He was always a decent lad. Did you have the chance to meet him?"

"You could say that." Jasen fidgeted with his cloak. "He wants me to marry him."

Urga stopped in her tracks. "Well, now. That sounds like a story that would go best with a cup of mead."

They sat down in the queen's corner of the courtyard, where she had some comfortable chairs arranged around a table. Jasen waited for the mead to be served before he started his story. By the time he was through, they'd polished off the bottle and then some.

Urga said nothing for what seemed like a long time. "Well," she said at last. "It was very sensible of you to refuse him."

"But I haven't refused him yet. I told him I would think about it."

Urga pounded the arm of her chair with her fist, startling Jasen. "What's there to think about? How can you even imagine going back there, after how you were treated? Nasty snobs, the lot of them. Don't fool yourself that it would change—you aren't one of them, and they'll never let you forget it, not for a moment!"

Her sudden fury left Jasen perplexed. "But I love Rilvor. I really do."

"Bah!" She waved her hand dismissively. "What good is love? I know you're swept away with it now, but those feeling will fade, and by then you're trapped. Look what happened to your mother, may she rest in peace. Your dad comes along, addles her senses with his charm, and then he proceeds to ruin her."

Jasen didn't think that was fair. It was true that his mother and father didn't have the most harmonious of marriages, but he was sure that they loved each other. His dad's drinking and gambling only got out of control after her death. But Urga was his queen—even though the Grummish were less formal than the rest of the Allied Realms, it still wasn't good manners to argue with your monarch.

"You are Grummish," the queen continued. "And the Grummish put practicality over flights of fancy—or at least, they should. It's who we are as a people. We don't need magic, and we certainly don't need dragons and their meddling."

Jasen frowned. "You think the dragons are meddling?"

"Of course they are! You think it was just happenstance that the first thing that happened when you arrived was some dragon demanding an audience? They want to bring Grumhul under their sway—that's why they singled you out, made sure you met with the king. And once you married the high and mighty Lord of the Drae, they could start sneaking their influence into our kingdom. They'd probably want us to drain our swamps to make one of their draemirs, as if having them in every other kingdom weren't enough!"

Jasen blinked. "That hadn't occurred to me." Was that really the only reason that Tasenred had called to him? That there wasn't anything special about him after all? His heart sank.

His unhappiness must have shown in his expression, because the queen's tone softened. "Now there, don't take it so hard. I'm sure that Rilvor's affections for you are sincere, but he must see that it's impossible. His heart will mend in time."

Jasen's eyes stung. "And what about my heart?"

"That will mend, too, my dear."

Jasen shut his eyes and pressed his fingers to them, trying to discourage any treacherous tears from falling. He took a deep breath in through his nose before speaking again. "You're right. I will tell him no."

Urga patted his leg. "There's a good lad. It will work itself out, you'll see. Tell you what—why don't you move in here? I hear things are not going so well in Hagas, and let's face it— your dad is a shit earl. He can stay here, too. Between the two of us, we can make him clean up his act. You won't have to worry about a thing."

Jasen looked around the courtyard, which only moments before had seemed so safe and welcoming. But now that it might be his permanent home, it felt like a trap.

The queen frowned. "Well? Aren't you pleased?"

Before Jasen could answer, a scream rang out from where the children were playing. A little boy with messy blond hair lay on the ground, screaming his head off. All the adults in earshot hastened to him, including Jasen and Urga. The boy's leg was bent at an unnatural angle, clearly broken.

The children and the servants had crowded around him, speaking all at once. Some of the littler one were crying, too. "Stand back, all of you!" Urga shouted. "Give the boy room to breathe!"

The children backed away. Urga pointed at one servants. "Go find the royal physician and bring her here at once." She pointed at another. "And you—go find his mother. It's Lady Bora, if I'm not mistaken."

As the servants rushed off to do as she commanded, Jasen knelt beside the boy, who had stopped screaming but was still sobbing. "It hurts, it hurts!"

"It's all right," Jasen said soothingly, patting the boy's hair. "What's your name?"

The boy wiped his nose on his sleeve. "Tinnerand, but my friends call me Tin."

"All right, Tin." Jasen took his hand and squeezed it. "The physician will be here soon, and then will have you all fixed up."

Tin started to cry again. "She's going to crack my leg! My sister broke hers, and that's what they did! I don't want her to crack my leg!"

As the boy's cries washed over him, something strange happened. Jasen's chest grew warm with the same feeling that came over him whenever the dragons were near. Almost as if in a trance, he put his hand on the boy's leg. Everyone stared, dumbfounded, as his hand glowed. Gentle blue flame flickered into existence, licking silently along his hand, and from there, down to the boy's leg. The flames flashed a bright blue before dying down.

Tin's sobs had stopped completely. "It doesn't hurt anymore," he said with wonder.

Jasen snatched his hand away. All of the children were quiet now, staring at him with wide eyes. Queen Urga's mouth was hanging open in a decidedly unroyal gape, and her face had grown bone white. She snapped her mouth shut and glared at the children. "Not one word of any of this to anyone, do you hear me? That is a command from your queen!"

The children all nodded emphatically. She leveled her finger at Tin. "And you—that leg will be better when I say it is and not before, understand?"

Just then, the servants arrived along with two women—the physician and the mother, presumably. They were all out of breath.

"Oh my precious baby!" The mother ran to Tin and threw her arms around him. "Are you all right?"

"Seems it was not as bad as it looked," the queen said. "Merely a sprain. I expect it will be better in a day or two. Don't you think so, boy?"

Tin leaned on his mother as he got to his feet. "Yes, Your Majesty." He did a good job of faking a limp as his mother led him away.

Urga waved her hands at the children. "Shoo, the lot of you! Find something else to do!"

The children scattered. Jasen remained kneeling on the ground, still numb with shock. What had just happened? Did he heal the boy?

He dared a glance at the queen. Urga's face was no longer white—in fact, it was now a deep red, and she was quivering with barely suppressed rage. "You didn't tell me you were dragon-blessed!"

"I didn't know." Now that he had gotten over his surprise, he found himself more curious than anything else. He got to his feet and looked at his hands again. They didn't seem any different now, although a faint warmth lingered in them.

The queen cursed. "Wretched dragons! Foul, interfering beasts!"

He didn't see what was so horrible about being dragon-blessed, but he didn't think it wise to question her. Hogort nuzzled her hand with his enormous snout. It seemed to calm her a little, although her lips were still pressed together in a thin, angry line.

"Come on, then," she said. "To my chambers—this conversation requires more privacy."

Once in her chambers, Urga shut the door. Jasen made himself comfortable in one of the chairs. Instead of sitting, Urga paced the room, her hands clasped behind her back and a deep frown on her face. It seemed as if she were debating something with herself.

At last she stopped in front of a basin of water. She waved her hand over it, and the water shot upward. With another wave of her hand, the water gathered into a ball in mid-air. The ball whipped around the room before returning to the basin and settling in.

Jasen's jaw dropped. "You're dragon-blessed!"

"Dragon-cursed, more like." Urga sank into one of the chairs and rubbed her temple. "When I was several years younger than you are now, a man fell off a dragon while flying over Grumhul. I was sitting on the bank when it happened, fishing. It was a dreary, drizzling day, but the wet never bothered me. Since it was the rainy season, the waters were quite high. He was struggling mightily in the water—it was clear to me the poor sod couldn't swim. I stripped off my dress and dove in.

"No sooner had I rescued him than the damned fool dragon plunged into the water as well. There was no risk of the beast drowning, but it did get stuck. I wanted to ask the man what had happened, but he had fainted. So I slung him over my shoulder and went back to the castle to get help. My mother sent her men out to help the dragon while I tended to the man. He was really more of a boy—quite scrawny. He came to eventually—told us he was a draed who had gotten lost in the rain. He wasn't, though. He was Prince Gyles."

"Prince Gyles?" Jasen frowned. "Wait—Gyles as in King Gyles? Rilvor's father?"

"The very same, but he wasn't the king yet, just as I was not yet a queen. He had run away, you see, because his parents had told him he had to marry. The fuss he caused! All of the Allied Realms were in a panic searching for the lost prince, but no one ever dreamed he would end up in Grumhul. And so he was able to hide away for a couple of weeks, during which time he became quite besotted with me. His ruse was eventually found out, and he was shipped back to the Draelands. I figured he'd forget about me, but he didn't. He kept sending me letters, begging me to come visit him. I should have thrown those letters into the swamp. Instead, I relented and agreed to come to Court.

"Well, I don't have to tell you how I was received. Did it matter that I was a princess? No! I was Grummish, and that's all that mattered to the rest of them! They mocked me behind my back and belittled me directly to my face. Gyles couldn't see it. He said I was being too sensitive, and besides, it didn't matter what anyone else thought. He got it into his head that he was going to marry me! Have you ever heard anything so ridiculous?"

"You didn't love him?" Jasen asked carefully.

"I had a certain amount of fondness for him," she admitted grudgingly. "All right, perhaps more than that. Yes, I loved him. But what of it? Love is all well and good, but it won't solve your troubles. Indeed, it often makes them worse."

"So when were you blessed by the dragon?"

"It was after I came back to Grumhul. I'd refused Gyles's proposal. It broke my heart, it did. I always thought myself too practical to weep, but I cried enough to fill a swamp afterward. One night, I had a strange dream about Gyles's dragon. A few days after that, Gyles showed up again on the back of that same dragon. He'd had a dream, too, that I had been dragon-blessed. Turned out that I was. He was so excited. He was sure that meant that the Court would accept me with open arms now. But I knew it wouldn't matter. I had to break his heart again. And still the dragons plagued me in my dreams, so insistent that I give in." She pounded the arm of her chair. "How dare they! They had no right!

"It took a full year for the dreams to stop. And then Gyles found someone else, as I always knew he would. It seems they were happy enough, until they died. And when he lay sick and dying, did the dragons intervene? The same dragons who wouldn't leave me in peace didn't deign to save his life! What good are they, if not for that?" She furiously wiped at her eyes.

Jasen wasn't sure his sympathy would be welcome, but he had to offer it, all the same. "I'm really sorry that happened to you."

She removed a handkerchief from some hidden pocket in her dress and blew her nose. "Thank you, lad." She gave him a watery smile. "You must forgive me. It seems I have grown sentimental in my old age." Her smile faded abruptly. "And I will not stand idly by and let you be bullied as I was! We will make damned sure those dragons leave you alone, and if Rilvor shows his scrawny arse around my kingdom, I'll pitch him into the swamp myself!"

Jasen bit his lip. Rather than cementing his resolve, her story made his feelings even more complicated, but it didn't seem prudent to say as much. "Thank you for looking out for me," he said instead.

"You're welcome. Now, go on—I need some time to myself."

Jasen gave her a kiss on the cheek before leaving the room. It was clear that she wanted what was best for him. But was refusing Rilvor really the right thing to do? Rilvor was willing to fight for him, just as Gyles was willing to fight for Urga. But she had refused him—and had spent the rest of life in bitterness.

Was this why Tasenred had brought him here—to show him what his life would be if he turned Rilvor down? All of the doubts he had before about accepting Rilvor's proposal were still there—but he was now realizing that running away had perils of its own.

CHAPTER 17

Several days passed, and Jasen was no closer to making a decision. On the one hand, every concern he had expressed to Rilvor still held. Accepting his proposal would throw the Court into chaos. Perhaps Rilvor was right that the scandal would pass, but he couldn't know that for sure. Rilvor said Jasen was more popular than he knew—but then again, Polina had been popular, too, and look what happened to her.

If Jasen said yes, he would have to steel himself for intense humiliation. He would like to think he was brave enough to face it, but Queen Urga was ten times stronger than him and it broke her. And his wasn't the only humiliation he had to take into consideration—his friends would have to face it, too, although he was certain Rilvor would protect them from legal consequences. Larely was most likely to escape the worst of it anyway, especially since his family cared very little for the law and would be unlike to turn him over if he was summoned. And despite Adwig's threats, Risyda hadn't really done anything other than indulge in kara weed—she was hardly the only noble who shared that vice.

But she was his friend, and if his reputation was ruined, hers would be as well. Risyda made a big show of not caring what people thought, but did Lady Wessor feel the same way? She was Risyda's last hopes of a respectable marriage. The loss of Risyda's reputation would force her to go back to her father's home for good—and that was if she was lucky and her father decided not to turn her out.

But on the other hand, if he refused Rilvor, he would regret it for the rest of his life. Staying in Grumhul with Queen Urga was safe, but that didn't mean it would shield him from pain. Already, he missed him terribly. The thought of never seeing him again made him feel hollowed out. He didn't know if he would ever love another. And the thought of passing the rest of his life in this castle in the swamp, growing more and more bitter with each year, was as frightening as the Court's humiliations in its own way. He felt like his only decision was between a sharp, intense pain, and a slow, dull one.

Jasen did his best not to spend every minute brooding. There were nowhere near the amount of diversions as there were at Strengsend, but he began to settle back into the quieter pleasures of Grummish life. He especially enjoyed spending time with the noble children, who adored him, Tin most of all. Once the queen decided that Tin was "recovered," he insisted on including Jasen in all of their games.

One afternoon on an unusually sunny day, they decided to go frog catching in the swamp. Tin had just netted a large specimen when he dropped the net and pointed at the sky. "What's that?"

Jasen shielded his eyes from the sun and looked where Tin had pointed. He was right—something was moving toward them—a bird, perhaps? But as it grew closer, it became larger and larger until it was very clear it wasn't a bird at all.

"It's a dragon!" Tin shouted.

All of the children starting jumping and running around, screaming their heads off in a mixture of giddiness and fear. Jasen tried to settle them down, although his own heart was racing. Had Rilvor come to demand an answer so soon?

But as the dragon grew closer, it was clear it wasn't Woria or Tasenred. The dragon was smaller than either of them, sleek and green. Someone was riding on its back—actually, it looked like two someones, but Jasen couldn't make who they were.

The dragon circled around the castle, no doubt making the same calculations Tasenred had. It came to a similar decision and splashed into the swamp. One of the riders cupped her hands around her mouth and shouted. "Jasen! Is that you?"

He still couldn't make out her face, but he'd recognize that voice anywhere. "Risyda!"

"And Polina!" The little figure behind her waved. "We can't swim!" Risyda shouted, but she didn't sound particularly concerned. In fact, she was laughing.

By then, the commotion had caught the attention of the castle. Queen Urga headed up a group of guards, just as she had when Jasen arrived.

"Is that Rilvor?" she bellowed when she caught up with Jasen. "If it is, he can stay in that swamp for all I care!"

"No, it's my friend—" He looked again at the two figures. "My friends," he corrected himself, for if Polina was with Risyda, that must mean that she'd come around after all. Jasen's cheeks hurt from how hard he was smiling. He had no idea what they were doing here, but he was happy to see them, nevertheless.

The guards took two boats out this time—one to retrieve

the girls, and one to help haul out the dragon. This dragon, however, did not require assistance. It was small enough that the swamp didn't have the same amount of pull and was able to extract itself. Soon it was in the sky and soaring away.

Urga shook her fist at it. "And don't you come back, wretched beast!"

The boat containing Risyda and Polina docked. As they got out of the boat, Jasen noticed they were both barefoot. Risyda ran toward Jasen just as he started to run toward her. They grabbed each other into a fierce hug. But after a moment, Risyda pulled back and punched him hard in the shoulder. He staggered back with a cry. "What was that for?"

"That's for running away without telling me."

Jasen rubbed his arm. "I guess I deserve that."

Queen Urga seemed impressed, for once. "You are a strapping young lady—I thought all consorts were weak."

Jasen turned to the queen. "Your Majesty, may I present the Lady Risyda."

Risyda gather up her soaking wet skirts and curtsied. "Your Majesty."

"And this is Princess Polina," Jasen continued as Polina made her way to them.

She curtsied as well. "If it pleases Your Majesty, just 'Polina' will do. I have renounced my title."

Jasen looked back and forth between the two of them. "It seems like a lot has happened since I've been gone."

Risyda grinned. "You have no idea. So I take it your dad isn't ill?"

Jasen blinked. "How did you know?"

"I guessed when—well, you really need to hear the whole story."

"Let's get you dried off first, and then you can tell us about it," the queen said. "Wretched dragons, disturbing my peace," she added under her breath.

When they reached the castle, servants whisked Risyda and Polina away, and within the hour, they were clean and dry, dressed in Grummish attire. It was so strange to see the two of them dressed so plainly. It suited them. Polina, in particular, had never looked better, although that probably had more to do with the absence of her usual scowl.

The queen called them to her chambers to give them the most privacy. Jasen's dad joined them as well. After introductions had been made and everyone had settled, the queen turned to Risyda. "So what in blazes happened to bring the two of you here?"

"You tell it, Polly," Risyda said. "You're the hero after all."

Polina looked down at her lap. "I would hardly say I'm a hero."

Risyda gestured to the others. "Why don't we let them decide?"

Polina smiled weakly. "All right, then." She took a moment to collect herself. "The day after the the king returned to Strengsend, Minisiter Adwig took me aside and explained that you—" she nodded to Jasen, "—were 'defeated.' I asked him to tell me more, but he refused. He went on to tell me of his plans to bring the king and me together—he had some plan to put me in distress so that Rilvor could 'rescue' me and advised me to be clumsy and vulnerable, since he is sure that's how you 'fooled' the king into loving you."

She touched Jasen's hand. "He had been telling me that all along, you see—that everything you did was a calculated move to endear yourself to the king. I used to believe him, but now I knew better. And the king looked so heart-broken. Adwig wouldn't tell me what he had done, but I knew it had to be a dirty trick of some sort. After all, he'd been helping me pull dirty tricks myself."

Realization struck Jasen. "The cursed shoes!"

Polina nodded. "He was the one who told me how to

contact the person who did enchantments for a price. He didn't tell me precisely what to do, but he encouraged me to do whatever was necessary to eliminate you." She paused. "I'm really sorry. I didn't want you to be seriously hurt."

Jasen waved her off. "I already said that I forgive you. Did you go to the king?"

"I considered it. But I reasoned if I did, the king would take care of it privately. I felt like there needed to be a more...public discussion of the issue, not via the usual Court gossip." Polina paused, twisting her hands in her lap.

"Go on!" Risyda said, grinning. "This is the best part!"

"It was the day of the Sun Ball. That's the event that starts in the morning, in the Bedrose gardens. Everyone was there —the consorts, the suitors, the ministers, and the king. It was the perfect time. So I climbed up on a table and started talking. I told everyone everything the minister had told me, including his plans to cause Jasen's downfall." She smiled a little. "Needless to say, it caused a bit of a stir."

Urga slapped her knee and laughed. "Well done, lass! I wish I could have seen the looks on their faces!"

Risyda's grin grew even wider. "It was one of the best moments of my life."

"But what happened then?" Jasen asked. "How did you get a dragon?"

Risyda took over the story. "After Polly made her speech, I felt this tingle in my chest, pulling me toward the draemir. I'd felt it before, so I knew it was a dragon calling me. I wasn't about to leave poor Polly stranded, so I helped her off the table. We kicked off our shoes and ran."

"Didn't anyone try to stop you?"

"Oh, they tried." Risyda snapped her fingers, causing a flame to spark into existence.

"She didn't hurt anyone," Polina interrupted. "She just... made a demonstration of her abilities."

Urga was laughing so hard by now that she nearly fell out of her chair. "Now that's the use of a dragon blessing that I can get behind!"

"Anyway," Risyda continued, "once we reached the draemir, the dragon was waiting for me—the same one who blessed me all those years ago. I could feel that she wanted us to get on her back, so we did, and then she took off."

"Did you know she was bringing you here?" Jasen asked.

"No, but I trusted her." She spread out her hands. "And here we are!"

"And the king?" Jasen asked quietly. "He didn't try to follow you?"

"He might have. It was all a bit of a blur. But we didn't see any other dragons."

If Rilvor wanted to follow them, he supposed they would find out soon enough. "How did you know my dad wasn't ill?"

"Once Polly made her speech about Adwig's tricks, I figured it was a ruse to get rid of you. Was I right?"

Jasen's father burst in. "No, that ruse was mine! And it was a very good one, if I do say so myself."

Risyda raised an eyebrow. "All right, now it's your turn to tell us what you've been up to."

Jasen told them his story. When he finished, Jasen's father was the first to speak. "But now that this minister has been disgraced, there's nothing stopping you from accepting the king's proposal!"

"It changes nothing," Urga snapped. "Kill one viper in a nest of them, and you still have a nest of vipers. Besides, even one viper is not so easy to kill. I have no doubt this Adwig has talked his way out of it." She turned to Risyda and Polina. "And I am happy to offer you refuge from those vipers. The two of you are young people of considerable honor and common sense. I would be honored if you would join my court—my court is not a grand one, but I think you would be quite happy here."

"Or there's Hagas," Jasen's dad said. "We could all live there, if it please Your Majesty to perhaps give a bit of coin to make it suitable to house such brave and noble persons as these two fine young ladies."

"You aren't going anywhere, you old scoundrel. You've proven yourself a poor steward of the land. But it's not a bad idea. What do you say, girls?"

Risyda and Polina exchanged looks. "You mean...us, together?" Polina said, blushing.

"Why not?"

"Would we—" Risyda broke off. Her cheeks reddened, too. "Would we have to...wed?"

"Of course not! Unless you want to."

They blushed even harder and said nothing, looking everywhere except at each other.

"Well, there's no rush," the queen said when it became clear she wasn't going to get an answer. "Sleep on it, if you like."

"We will," Risyda said, standing. "Thank you, Your Majesty."

After that, they dispersed. His dad went back to whatever he had been doing before. Polina slipped away to the room the queen had given her without so much as looking at Risyda again, leaving Jasen and Risyda in the main hall.

"Do you want to tell me what's going on?" Jasen asked.

"I would love to." She gave him a wry smile. "I'll let you know as soon as I figure it out myself. And what about you? Your dad is right—I'm almost certain that Minister Adwig will lose his position, especially with what you already told the king. It gives him the perfect excuse to get rid of him."

"But Queen Urga is right as well. He may have found a

way to save his skin, and I know for a fact that he wasn't alone in his disapproval of me."

She squeezed his hand. "Whatever you choose, you have my support."

He squeezed back. "And you mine."

They went their separate ways. Jasen went back to the swamp, alone this time. He had hoped some time to himself would help clear his head, but it all seemed as hopelessly muddled as ever. He gathered up some rocks to skip along the water.

"It's nicer than I thought it would be," a voice from behind him said.

He turned to see Polina standing there. "The swamp, I mean. I always thought it would be dreary, but it's actually quite beautiful." She twisted her skirt in her hand. "Do you mind if I join you?"

"Be my guest."

She sat down and picked up a rock. She attempted to skip it, but it plunged into the swamp. "Oh dear. It seems I'm not very good at this."

"It takes practice. Here, let me show you."

They skipped rocks for a little while until the pile ran out. They sat in uncomfortable silence for a little while. "Do you think the king will have me arrested?" Polina asked eventually.

"He wanted to, before," Jasen said. "As Lord of the Drae, I'm almost certain he knows where the dragon was taking you. He could have followed you, if he wished it. But I don't think he will."

"Because you talked him out of it," she guessed. "I don't deserve your protection, but thank you, all the same."

He nudged her with his shoulder. "You paid me back already. It was very brave what you did."

"It was the least I could do." She turned to him, her eyes wet. "I am so sorry for what I put you through."

"You don't need to apologize."

"No, I really do. I was horrible to you, and there's no excuse for it."

"Apology accepted. I don't think there's any need to dwell on it further."

She smiled. "The king loves you, you know. You should have seen the look on his face when he returned. I didn't know the full story at the time, but I could tell his heart had been broken. For any argument the ministers may make, it seems evident that no good can come by breaking the king's heart." She touched his hand. "I remember what you told me about this not being a game, and you were right. I had trained my whole life to 'win,' and all it ever did was make me miserable. But at the same time, if I had a fighting chance at real, true love like you do, I would do whatever it took. You deserve to be happy." She stood up. "And I won't say anymore. It's your decision."

"Thank you. And I hope you take your own advice—you deserve happiness, too."

"I'm sure I don't know what you mean," she said, turning red. She excused herself in a hurry. Jasen couldn't help but laugh a little. At least he wasn't alone in being confused. Love was difficult. Or maybe it wasn't love itself—the truly confounding thing was that the world seemed so intent on thwarting it at every turn.

～

JASEN WAS IN THE WATER, *floating on his back. He determined that it was a river, and he was being carried gently with the current. The sky above him was a deep purple—a night sky, but not a night sky he'd ever seen before. Stars twinkled, but they were larger,*

271

brighter than he thought possible. There were no clouds—instead, ribbons of color floated in the sky, pink and blue and violet, bright against the dark sky.

Eventually, the river carried him to a lake, and from the lake, gentle waves pushed him to a shore of sparkling white sand. He lay on his back for a while, blinking up at the sky, trying to understand what was happening. A dream, surely, just as before.

A cool breeze passed over him, and then he felt a presence behind him. He got to his feet and was not entirely surprised to see a blonde woman standing before him, dressed in a simple white gown, her long tresses floating around her as if they were underwater.

"Queen Consort Quendra," he said.

She inclined her head. "Lord Jasen. We have much to discuss." She gestured. "Come—let's take a walk."

They walked along the shore as the waves lapped quietly at their bare feet. Although Jasen was wet, he was not cold. His own hair floated around him, and his movements felt weightless. "Where are we?"

She thought for a moment. "It's difficult to explain. It's a place in between."

"In between what?"

"In between everything—dreams and wakefulness, life and death, imagination and reality."

"Oh," Jasen said, which hardly seemed adequate. "It's nice."

Quendra laughed. "Indeed it is. More importantly, it's a place where we can talk." She folded her arm with his. "We don't have much time, so let's get down to it. I hope to convince you to marry my husband."

"That's not something I ever thought I'd hear."

"Much about our situation is unusual."

Jasen's stomach churned. "Are you going to tell me that the fate of the Allied Realms lies in my hands?" he asked miserably.

Quendra pursed her lips as she considered him. "We can't start this way," she said at last. She released his arm and took a few steps forward—and up. Jasen gaped as she floated above him. "Come with me."

"I don't know how."

"Yes, you do. Jump."

Jasen hesitated. "This is allegorical, isn't it? A leap of faith?"

"If you say so. Mostly, it's just fun."

Jasen screwed his eyes shut and pushed with his feet. When he opened his eyes again, he was floating beside Quendra.

"There," she said. "Was that so hard?"

"I guess not."

She floated up further. "Come on, then. There's something I want to show you."

"I still don't know how," he said helplessly.

"One foot in front of the other—the same as anything else."

Jasen tried it, and to his surprise, he began to move upward, as if he were walking on invisible stairs. He followed the queen consort as they made their way across the sky, over the lake that was growing smaller and smaller the further they went. They came to a mountain peak. With one fluid step, she floated her way to the top, her feet touching down silently. Jasen was considerably less graceful, but he managed to land beside her.

She sat down, and Jasen followed suit. The view was spectacular, even if he wasn't quite sure what he was viewing. There were so many swirling colors and bright lights, all bathed in a milky glow.

"What do you see?" she asked. "And really take a look before you say 'nothing.'"

Jasen squinted at the swirl. Gradually, shapes appeared. "Mountains," he said. "And oceans, and rivers, and forests—"

"—and swamps?" She smiled.

"It's the Allied Realms."

"Yes. And now tell me what you don't see."

Jasen was at a loss. He looked out again, but how did you describe something you couldn't see?

"I'll give you a hint," she said. "I don't see any ministers."

Jasen rubbed his neck. "No, I suppose I don't either. I suppose this is supposed to teach me to take things into perspective."

"If that's what you think."

"It's all very well and good to point out that out when we're up here, but living in the midst of it is much harder."

"Perhaps. Living often seems very difficult. But being dead gives you a different perspective."

Jasen startled at that. "And what perspective is that?"

"The problems that seemed so important to me while I was alive faded to nothing. Instead, what I remember is the love I had. My love for my family, for my children. The friendships I cherished. And yes, the love I had for Rilvor as well, imperfect though it was." She met his gaze. "You seem to believe that by casting off love, you will be quick enough to escape the storms of life. But those storms are unavoidable, Jasen. Love is not a weight holding you back—it is an anchor. And without that anchor, you are doomed to drift aimlessly through life."

Jasen dropped his gaze. "I've never thought about it that way."

"Of course you haven't. You're young." She cleared her throat. "Now, then, let us get back to the matter at hand. You love Rilvor, don't you?"

"Yes," Jasen said quietly. "But what if it isn't enough? The fate of the Allied Realms rests on the strength of his love for me, doesn't it?"

Quendra sighed. "You really are young, aren't you? The Allied Realms existed long before you were born, and will exist long after you're dead."

"Right. And if something in our marriage goes wrong, that death will come sooner rather than later!"

Quendra furrowed her brow. "What do you mean?"

"Isn't that what happened to you?"

"I became ill. It happens."

"But Rilvor said—"

"Rilvor is very fond of responsibility. It's a fine trait in a king, but he can be overzealous as to what he takes responsibility for. Perhaps our imperfect marriage did lead to my death. Perhaps it didn't."

"You don't know?"

She smiled wryly. "The afterlife doesn't offer many answers, unfortunately."

"But the magic of the realm weakened because you two were not —well, compatible. Or is that untrue, too?"

"That's true, but what of it? Rilvor will die one day. Perhaps my son will have better luck and magic will recover."

Jasen frowned. "I don't understand why you've brought me here if the fate of the Allied Realms isn't at stake."

She raised an eyebrow. "And the fate of my children and my husband are not important?"

Jasen snapped his mouth shut.

She touched his arm. "I'm not saying that your position is not unique. Being joined with the Lord of the Drae is a strain, and yes, magic will depend on you. It isn't an easy life. But your life will pass, as all things must. What I'm trying to say is that the world is much bigger than you." She gestured to the landscape. "Look again. It's beautiful, isn't it? But nothing is perfect. Beauty does not require perfection. Neither does love. The dragons understand this better than humans do. They have felt the love in your heart, and that is what is important to them—not the pedigree of your family or the kingdom of your birth."

Jasen scoffed. "Try telling that to the ministers."

"That's a splendid idea. Why don't you?"

"They wouldn't listen."

"How can you be so sure?"

Jasen opened his mouth to reply and shut it again. "I suppose I can't," he admitted sheepishly.

"Then it's worth a try, don't you think?"

"And what if they still oppose me? What if Rilvor defies them *and it sets off a political crisis? What if he grows to resent me because I caused all that strife? What if—"*

"You want reassurances from me," she interrupted. *"But I can't give them to you. I can't see the future. But I can tell you that you will regret living your life in fear."*

Jasen held his head in his hands. *"I need more time."*

"That, alas, I can't give you, either. You must make up your mind, Jasen. Life is fleeting. You cannot wait forever."

A dragon circled overhead and dipped down, passing close to them. *"Are these dragons dead, too?"*

"Dragons can travel in the spaces in dreams and the afterlife in the same way as they move in the waking world. Life and death are a little different for them than they are for us. It isn't quite as final."

"What do they want? Tasenred called me when I first came to the Draelands. Queen Urga thinks that he was trying to get Grumhul under dragon control by using me, just as she thinks they tried to use her."

"Queen Urga makes the same mistake many humans do. They ascribe human motivations to the dragons. The dragons don't care about control."

"Then why did they intervene in Westrona?"

"The dragons are more in tune with human hearts than humans are themselves. When humans and dragons first connected, the humans gave dragons the gift of knowing themselves in a way other beasts never can. They are eternally grateful and want only for humans to be happy. They are perplexed by human tendency to bring misery upon themselves and try to intervene where they think they can. That's why they call humans to their service—they know they can never truly understand the complexity of human society, so they seek humans to act for them."

"Is that why they called me? Because they knew I would make Rilvor happy?"

"I believe so. I was blessed, but never called. The dragons

accepted our marriage well enough, but I think we confused them. They aren't match makers in general, but since humans got it so hopelessly wrong the first time, they might have felt the need to intervene more directly." She squeezed his hand. "I agree with them. I think the two of you are a good match. You have a good heart, Jasen. That's what he needs, and what my children need."

She stood. Jasen got to his feet as well. "Call to the dragons, when you are ready," she said, taking his hands in hers. "You have their support, and mine. And if that is not enough, there is nothing more I can do for you."

She kissed him on the cheek. With a push of her foot, she launched herself off of the mountain top and floated onto the back of the dragon. She waved good-bye—

—and Jasen's eyes flew open. He sat up, breathing heavily as he looked around. He was in his bed, safe and sound, although his thoughts still felt slow and dreamy. He got out of bed and opened the window shutters. The sun was creeping up over the horizon, banishing the darkness of night.

He watched until the sun was fully risen. As the morning began in earnest, the fog of Jasen's dream faded. The light here was harsher than it had been in the dream world. His body was heavier. The ground beneath his feet was hard and cold. And the breeze coming off the swamp was chilly, and didn't smell very good, either.

It wasn't perfect. But it was life.

He shut the window and went to get dressed. After picking out something sensible and comfortable, he donned the Drae's cloak. He had made his decision.

CHAPTER 18

"*Y*ou're going to regret this," Urga said as they boarded the small rowboat.

"Maybe," Jasen agreed.

"*I'm* going to regret this," she added under her breath. "But a promise is a promise. Take us out."

Jasen began to row, and soon they were making their way across the swamp. After some time, they reached the small island that was just out of sight of the castle. They landed the boat and got out.

"How near is that dragon of yours?" Urga asked.

Jasen put his hand to his throat, feeling the jewel. It was warm. "Close, I think." He'd been calling out to him ever since he had awoken.

"He'd better be." Urga crossed her arms and scowled. "I don't plan on waiting around on this island forever!"

"Thank you again for doing this," Jasen said. "I know you don't agree with my decision, but it means a lot to me that you're supporting me anyway."

"Well, what was I to do? Order you to stay? You're Grummish, and in Grumhul, unlike some other kingdoms I could mention, our citizens have the right to make whatever decision they please, no matter how stupid." She softened a little. "And remember that there's always a place for you here. I won't even say I told you so."

Jasen tried not to laugh. "I appreciate it. Truly."

Jasen felt a flutter in his chest. A moment later, the sky darkened. Tasenred had arrived, and was circling above them.

Urga cracked her fingers. "Now it's been quite some time since I've called upon my blessing at all, so I'm not making any promises. If this doesn't work, you'll have to get yourself to a proper draemir." Urga sucked in a breath and raised her hands. The waters of the swamp parted. She moved her hands slowly outward, parting the water further, until there was enough room for Tasenred to land.

As soon as the dragon landed, Jasen ran up to him. Tasenred lowered his head in greeting. "Thank you for coming for me," Jasen said, placing his hand on the dragon's snout.

"You can talk with the damned beast later!" Urga shouted. "Get on—I can't hold this forever!"

Jasen did as she said and soon they were flying through the air. He waved to the queen but wasn't sure if she saw him. He resisted the urge to look back again.

It was hard to think of much when riding on the back of the dragon—the experience overwhelmed the senses. It was only when the Draelands came in sight that Jasen's nerves started to act up again. He had no idea what was going to happen.

He wasn't surprised to find Rilvor waiting for him in the draemir—he was the Lord of the Drae, after all. Rilvor swept him into his arms the moment he slid off Tasenred's back.

"Your answer," Rilvor said breathlessly. "Please tell me it is yes."

In response, Jasen threw his arms around Rilvor's neck and gave him a kiss, which led to another, and another. When at last they pulled away from each other, Jasen asked, "So what happens now?"

"Right now? We get you back to the palace and let you rest. We can make plans for tomorrow."

Jasen shook his head. "I would prefer to get answers now. I'm not sure how much more my nerves can take."

Rilvor kissed his forehead. "As you wish. I will call for an immediate meeting with the ministers."

"Is Adwig still among them? Polina and Risyda told me what happened."

"Unfortunately, he is. I believe your friend, but her accusations are unsubstantiated. He has cast doubt upon her testimony, dismissing her as embittered and seeking revenge because he told her she wasn't suited to be queen consort. I have put out a search for the person who put the enchantment on the shoes, but have been unable to find them. Until I have another witness, I don't want to move against him."

"It's just as well. I want to face him—get everything out in the open."

Rilvor raised an eyebrow. "Everything?"

"I can't marry you pretending to be someone I'm not, and I won't spend my life in fear of blackmail and gossip. If I'm to be king consort, it will be as myself, warts and all."

"Well put. I completely agree."

Jasen kissed him again. "Let's get this over with."

Rilvor had guards waiting for them at the edge of the draemir to escort them back to his chambers, but even so, word of Jasen's return had already spread. It seemed as if everyone in the palace had arrived to gawk at him. To Jasen's surprise, he found it didn't matter that much to him. Quendra had been right about perspective.

As soon as Jasen stepped foot into the royal chambers, he

was tackled by Rilvor's children. "I knew you would come back!" Erada said happily. "Papa wasn't sure, but I knew you wouldn't just leave us."

Jasen smiled. "You're very clever—much cleverer than me or your papa."

Erada beamed. Ados, however, looked more serious. "I wish you luck with the council," he said. "I would be happy to testify as to your good character."

Rilvor put a hand on his shoulder. "Thank you, son, but I do not think that will be necessary."

The children's governess gathered them up and took them away. Once they had left, Jasen noticed someone lingering in the doorway to the king's inner chamber. Rilvor motioned to him. "You can come out now."

Jasen was shocked to see that it was Larely, who gave him a shy wave. In a few swift steps, Jasen crossed the room to clasp his hand and pat him on the back. "It's good to see you! I thought you were with your family."

"Well, the king came and found me. Can't very well ignore the summons of the king, can I?"

"I brought him here to testify on your behalf, if you decided to accept my proposal," Rilvor said. "I wanted to keep his presence a secret, so he has been staying in my chambers."

"I'm sorry for all the trouble I caused," Larely said. "It's the least I can do to come help clear the air."

"It's not your fault," Jasen said. "But aren't you worried about being exposed? Your true identity is sure to come up."

Larely waved a hand dismissively. "The crimes of my family aren't my crimes—the king knows that. And I don't plan on staying in the Draelands anyway, so it isn't as if it will hurt my opportunities." He cleared his throat. "In fact, the new Prosider of Westrona has asked me to be on her council, at the recommendation of King Rilvor."

"My recommendation was only part of it," Rilvor said. "Your efforts to make an honest life for yourself despite your family's history is admirable. The Prosider and I both agree that your family background makes you ideal to help her mend the rifts in Westronan society."

Jasen patted Larely on the back. "Congratulations! I'm sure you'll do well."

"There will be time for you to catch up later," Rilvor said. "But for now, I must ask Larely to come with me to prepare for his testimony. I will send Rotheld to help in your own preparations."

Shortly after Rilvor left, servants came with some refreshments for Jasen. And soon after that, Rotheld arrived. "My lord," he said with a bow.

Jasen grinned. "It's good to see you, Rotheld."

"I am pleased to see you as well, my lord. The king thought you could use some help preparing for your audience with the Council." He waved in a rack of clothing. "I have take the liberty of selecting an outfit—"

"Thank you," Jasen interrupted. "But I won't be changing."

Rotheld puffed out his cheeks in surprise. "My lord, I most humbly suggest you change your mind. The council is very particular about proper etiquette."

"Believe me, there is no outfit that I can wear that's going to make them more amenable to my arguments. I'd rather be comfortable."

"As you wish, my lord," Rotheld said, although he didn't seem happy about it. "But would my lord at least consent to some styling of his hair?"

Jasen tried to run his fingers through his hair, but couldn't manage it since it was so tangled by the wind. "That might be a good idea," he admitted.

Rotheld set to work brushing out the tangles from Jasen's hair. Jasen was afraid he was going to try one of his fancier hair styles, but he merely tied it back in a simple bow. He also convinced Jasen to allow him to wash his face and hands. By the time Rotheld was finished, Jasen still didn't look fashionable, but he was put together, at the very least. As he looked himself over in the mirror, he noticed a change in himself that had nothing to do with his clothing or his grooming. Up until now, he hadn't realized how nervous he used to look all the time. A calm had settled over his features. He looked…dignified.

Jasen took his time finished his meal, sipping at his tea thoughtfully as he went over his arguments. He didn't have any control over how the council would respond, but he was optimistic. He had been called by the dragons to speak to their hearts. When he was finished, he wiped off a small knife and tucked it into his waist coat. He would need it for the demonstration he was planning.

Before long, Rilvor arrived. He put his arms around Jasen. "The ministers have convened and are awaiting us."

"We should go then."

"Yes," Rilvor agreed, his arms still around him.

"You should probably let me go."

Rilvor pulled back, his cheeks a bit flushed. "My apologies. I have only just gotten you back—part of me is afraid you will slip away again."

"I won't," Jasen promised.

"And I meant what I said—even if the ministers do not give their blessing, I will fight for you. It would go better for us if they agree, but do not be disheartened if they do not rule in your favor. There is nothing to be worried about."

"Yes, I know," Jasen said mildly.

Rilvor tilted his head. "You aren't nervous?" Rilvor rushed to correct himself. "That is to say, of course there is no need to be nervous, but it's…" He trailed off.

"Not like me?" Jasen finished for him with a grin.

"I would never say that, but it gladdens me that you are not distressed." He offered his arm. "Shall we go?"

Jasen took his arm. "Yes."

They made their way to the Chamber of Justice. Jasen had never been inside, but he knew what to expect. As a part of his consort training, he had received lessons in the system of justice in the Draelands. The Chamber of Justice was where the royal ministers debated matters of law, and where the king dispensed justice to subjects who came to him with disputes. The king's throne sat at the opposite end from the entrance, raised to be well above the rest of the room. Ten podiums were situated in a semicircle around the perimeter of the room, five on each side of the throne. While not as high as the throne, they were also on a raised level. The center of the room was empty—this was the floor, where those seeking to bring a matter to the ministers' attention were to stand.

The set-up was meant to be intimidating, and it was. Even with his newly earned confidence, Jasen felt a flutter of nerves, which only increased when Rilvor left him to take his seat on his throne. The ministers were all at their stations, dressed in ceremonial white robes. Ministers were not aristocrats—they were dragon-called to serve the cause of justice. That included Minister Adwig, Jasen realized, who was currently giving him a look that one might give a viper that had sneaked its way into an otherwise perfectly maintained garden. It was something Jasen would keep in mind.

A page appeared to announce Jasen's arrival. "May it please the ministers to receive Lord Jasen of Grumhul, who comes to plead his case to be made king consort of the Allied Realms through marriage to His Majesty King Rilvor." The page bowed, ceding the floor to Jasen.

Jasen cleared his throat. "Honorable ministers, I know that I am not the person many of you would prefer to be at the side of the king. I'd be happy to address any concerns you might have."

Minister Eveth, an elderly woman, was the first to speak. She wore a purple mantle, indicating her status as the senior minister. "Your lack of pedigree, as you put it, does concern many of our members, but you would not be the first person of humble origins to ascend to the level of consort to the monarch. The larger concern is your scandalous conduct. Do you deny that you have engaged in carnal relations with a host of men, including those of common stock?"

"No, Your Honor."

"You are aware that consorts are expected to be pure of heart and of body, are you not?"

"I'm aware that it's the expectation, yes."

"Then by your own admission, your very presence at Court is fraudulent."

"I disagree. I was not asked to take a vow attesting to my virginity. The so-called 'purity' of a consort is an unwritten rule, as I understand it."

Minister Eveth turned to one of her colleagues. "Minister Droge, is that true?"

Minister Droge—a short, bald man—flipped through an enormous book. "He is correct. There is no written rule that a consort must be a virgin."

Adwig butted in. "It may not be the letter of the law, but it is its spirit. The role of consort to the king requires impeccable moral character. Lord Jasen not only lacks the dignity of a proper consort, he is also a liar who has deceived the king!"

"This is untrue," Rilvor said. "I am well aware of Jasen's past."

A murmur rippled through the ministers; Minister Eveth waved a hand to quiet them. Adwig's jaw had dropped in shock, but he composed himself quickly. "But it is not just his past, Your Majesty. He has been conducting an affair right under your nose! I have evidence that Lord Jasen had carnal relations with a guard, who he then had sent away to cover his crimes."

"I am aware of your accusations," the king said. "But your evidence is lacking. I have done my own investigation." He nodded to the page, who left the room. He returned a few moments later with Larely by his side.

"If it pleases the ministers, I present Larely of Westrona to give testimony."

The ministers' murmurs were even louder this time. Minister Eveth had to call for order several times before the room quieted again. "Young man, you may give your testimony," she said.

Larely wiped some sweat from his brow before speaking. "It's true that I had romantic feelings for Lord Jasen, but he firmly rejected them. I have made a dragon-sworn written testimony to that effect."

Eveth gestured to the page. "Let's see it." The page approached her and handed her an envelope. She opened it and scanned the contents before passing it to the minister beside her. "This all looks in order."

"And what if he's lying?" Adwig said, who had grown quite purple with rage.

"He has sworn directly to a dragon, in presence of draeds and draedesses," Eveth countered.

"That does not guarantee the truthfulness of his testimony. It is not impossible for a hardened criminal to lie to a dragon."

"Are you suggesting that this young man is a hardened criminal?"

"He comes from a long line of criminals!" Adwig said triumphantly. "His family is the most notorious in all of Westrona."

"I do not believe a man should be judged by the actions of his family," Rilvor said. "The dragons are convinced of the sincerity of his testimony, as am I. Do you doubt my judgment?"

Adwig hesitated. "Of course not, Your Majesty."

Eveth raised her hand, drawing everyone's attention. "All those in favor of accepting Larely's testimony, say aye."

Adwig was the only judge who remained silent. Eveth nodded her head. "Then it is settled. You are dismissed, young man."

Larely bowed and left the room. When he was gone, Eveth turned her attention to Jasen again. "You may not be technically in violation of the law, but what do you say to the accusation that you lack moral character?"

"Kindness and humility are more important than sexual purity. Those are both qualities that I nurture in myself. And if sexual purity was the most important judgment of character, then I'm afraid the Allied Realms are in a great deal of trouble."

Several of the ministers laughed, including Eveth. "True enough. Let us move on to the next point. While your humble origins do not disqualify you from taking on the role of king consort, it is still of some concern to several members of this council. In particular, your nationality makes you an unusual choice. A Grumhulian has never ascended to the throne, and the Grummish are known for their distrust of dragons. Magic in the realm has suffered as of late, and there is concern that your lack of connection with the dragons will worsen it. Can you speak to that?"

"Yes, Your Honor. I may be Grummish, but that doesn't mean I don't have a connection with the dragons. As you are no doubt aware, I was called by a dragon on my first day in the Draelands—"

"So you say," Adwig interrupted. "Or perhaps you sneaked

off to the draemir without permission and happened to encounter a dragon. That isn't the same thing."

Jasen met Adwig gaze and continued as if he hadn't been interrupted. "I've also been blessed."

Several people gasped, including Rilvor.

"Were you aware of this, Your Majesty?" Eveth asked.

"No," Rilvor said, the surprise evident in his voice. He looked to Jasen. "Why didn't you tell me?"

"I only found out a few days ago."

Adwig looked skeptical. "And what blessing did the dragons supposedly give to you?"

"Do I have permission to demonstrate?" At Eveth's nod, Jasen took out his knife. Before anyone could respond, he drew the blade over the back of his hand, deep enough that he began to bleed. Several ministers shouted; Rilvor sprang to his feet. But before any of them could make a move, Jasen called forth his ability. For a moment he was afraid it would fail, but soon the same blue flames that had healed Tin flickered from his fingers. The wound closed. Jasen wiped the blood from his hand and held it up for all to see.

The room erupted as the ministers all started talking at the same time. The only one who wasn't talking was Adwig, who had grown quite pale. Once again, Eveth called them to order. "How did you discover this power?"

"When I was in Grumhul, a child injured himself. I was able to heal him, just as I've healed myself now."

"And why are you only just now aware of it?"

"I think because I didn't have occasion to use it. Fortunately, the life of a consort usually doesn't involve bodily harm." That got a few laughs. Jasen waited for them to quiet before continuing. "But beyond that, I think I wasn't ready to accept it yet. Whatever doubts you have about me, I have had about myself—maybe even more. I couldn't imagine why on earth a dragon—or a king, for that matter—would choose me, out of all the more accomplished lords and ladies of the Court.

"My head was telling me that I wasn't worthy. I was too busy thinking to listen to my heart. I was told by someone very wise that the dragons know our hearts better than we know them ourselves. Right now, the heart of humanity is changing. That's why the dragons interfered in Westrona, and it's the same reason they called to me."

He turned to Minister Adwig. "I know that you only want what's best for the Allied Realms. That's what I want, too. However, the world is changing—clinging to the rituals of the past for their own sake is not the right way to move forward. I think we can both honor old traditions and move toward a future that increases the happiness of the people of the Allied Realms."

Adwig still seemed shaken, but slowly, he nodded.

Jasen addressed the rest of the room. "My manners still aren't the finest. I probably will make a lot of mistakes. But I promise I will always lead with my heart." He met Rilvor's gaze. "And the king and I are madly in love, which I hope counts for something." He bowed. "And that's my case. I await your judgment."

Eveth folded her hands. "Well, you have certainly given us much to discuss, Lord Jasen. We will inform you of our decision when we reach it."

The page led Jasen to another room where petitioners of the court were sent to wait as the ministers debated. Now that it was over, his nerves finally caught up to him. He collapsed into a chair, wondering how long it would take. His hands shook as took out a handkerchief to wipe the sweat off his brow. A few tears slipped from his eyes, which he wiped away, too.

The door opened, but it wasn't the page—it was Rilvor. Jasen rose to meet him, and he was by his side in an instant.

"Have they made their decision?" Jasen asked.

"Not yet, no. I stepped out to give them time to debate." Rilvor smiled. "But it is decided, either way. You will be my husband, no matter what they say." Rilvor reached into his waist coat. From it, he removed a ring with a bright red jewel. "The jewel is from Tasenred," he said. "And the ring is from me." He got down on one knee.

Jasen laughed nervously. "What are you doing?"

"I need to hear it from you, unequivocally." He held the ring up. "Lord Jasen, will you marry me and rule by my side?"

Jasen's voice caught in his throat for a moment. "Yes," he finally managed to say.

Rilvor slid the ring on his finger before standing up and embraced Jasen again, and then they were kissing passionately.

They only pulled apart when they heard a polite cough. It was the page. "Your Majesty, the council requests your presence."

"Already?" Jasen asked. "Is that good news or bad news?"

Rilvor grinned. "Good, I think." He kissed his hand. "I will see you in a moment."

Rilvor and the page departed. Jasen sat down again, dazed. It all felt unreal. He looked down at his ring, which was sparkling far more than an ordinary jewel. The metal against his skin felt real enough, at any rate.

A few minutes later, the page returned. "They will see you now, my lord," he said with a bow.

As soon as Jasen took his place on the floor, Minister Eveth spoke. "Lord Jasen," she began. "You said that you were not the candidate any of us would have chosen, and you are correct. You are unusual in many ways. But it is the opinion of this court that you have pled your case with the grace and humility that we would expect of a king consort. We give you our full endorsement. Congratulations."

Jasen's knees felt weak. Fortunately, Rilvor was there by his side in a moment, sweeping him into his arm. And then they were kissing—it probably wasn't proper decorum, but Jasen couldn't bring himself to care. All his fears and insecurities melted away, at least for the moment. He was still apprehensive about taking on such a huge responsibility— but all love was responsibility, no matter if your partner was royalty or a peasant.

Jasen felt a now-familiar warmth in his chest, only it was ten times as strong as he'd ever felt it. He pulled back slightly. "Do you feel that?"

"Yes." Rilvor took Jasen's hand. "Come with me." He looked over to the ministers. "All of you."

Rilvor and Jasen led the procession of ministers outside, heading toward the gardens. Overhead, two dragons circled, then three, then five, and more, until soon the sky was thick with them. All of the members of Court and the servants had come outside too. They were laughing and shouting as the dragons dipped and swirled above them, the sun shining on their colorful scales, making the sky sparkle as if it were full of jewels.

Rilvor and Jasen left the rest of them behind and made their way to the draemir, where Tasenred waited for them. Jasen threw his arms around the dragon's neck. "Thank you for believing in me."

The dragon just snorted, the warm air tickling Jasen's skin. Tasenred bowed his head in obvious invitation.

Jasen turned to Rilvor. "Do you want to go for a ride?"

Rilvor kissed him again. "There's nothing I would like better."

They climbed onto the dragon's back and soon they were sailing through the sky. Tasenred joined the other dragons. Jasen laughed as they flew, his heart so full of joy that he thought it might burst. When he had first come to the Draelands, he never imagined it would end like this. He leaned back against Rilvor's chest, relishing the feel of his arms around him, and of the dragon beneath him, and of the sun shining down on him, his lover, and the whole of the Allied Realms.

From here on out, there would be no escaping responsibility, but the thought no longer filled him with dread. He was bound, yes—but not chained. In fact, he had never felt so free.

EPILOGUE

*J*asen examined himself in the mirror with satisfaction. His white frock coat was simple but elegant, with a subtle pattern of golden dragons; his red hair fell in waves over his shoulders, freed from any ribbons for once; and best of all, his shoes were extremely sensible.

"Is my lord pleased?" Rotheld asked.

"I am," Jasen said with a smile. And he *was* pleased—not only with his wedding outfit, but with how well everything had turned out. Minister Adwig had resigned, saving Rilvor from the unpleasant task of putting him on trial. The rest of the Court accepted him immediately, as Rilvor had predicted. It was amazing to Jasen that he had been so blind to the support he had gained. He had always believed all the other consorts were merely attempting to curry favor with him and would turn on him the moment he slipped. Perhaps that was still true of some of them, but once Jasen's engagment became official and his position was secure, he began to see that many of them truly liked him. More than once, he was taken aside by a consort who mentioned some kindness he had done them, and how much it had meant to them. Rilvor very gallantly did not gloat, although his look of satisfaction when Jasen told him about it was a tad on the smug side.

"You look very regal," Risyda piped in. She and Polina were to be his groomsmaids. Their dresses were gorgeous, although not as ostentatious as what they used to wear. Both of them had adapted a more Grummish sensibility, which ironically made them very fashionable in Court. A few days after Jasen's engagement was announced, Lord Banither had debuted his new, Grummish-inspired wardrobe. After that, the rest of the consorts fell in line. Gone were the corsets and impossibly tight breeches, as well as the eloborate wigs and enormous skirts. In truth, Jasen missed some of the opulence, although he was certain that fashion would find a happy medium after he had been on the throne for a while.

The thought still made his stomach flip, although not quite as much as it used to. He still wasn't looking forward to the ceremony, although there was no helping it. Whenever he got too nervous, he imagined the trip to Rakon that they would take once the wedding celebration was over. They were bringing the children this time; he could hardly wait.

Polina fussed over Risyda's dress, smoothing it out in the back. "I still think you should have gone with a different dress—it's too long for you! You're going to trip."

"I'm not the one prone to tripping," Risyda replied, although there was no irritation in her voice. Jasen still wasn't sure what was going on between the two of them. It seemed as if they weren't sure themselves, although it seemed they had settled into their new estate well enough. He was looking forward to visiting.

There was a knock at the door. At Jasen's nod, Rotheld opened it. Larely stepped into the room, looking quite dashing in his official Westronan minister's uniform. "I managed to sneak away to say good luck," he said. "But I can't stay long—she's bound to notice I'm not there eventually."

"Who—the Prosider?" Risyda asked.

Larely nodded. "Hopefully she won't commit some diplomatic disaster in the meantime." He shook his head. "And I thought that you and Risyda were trouble!"

Jasen grinned. "You seem to attract troublemakers."

He grinned back. "I wouldn't have it any other way. The Prosider is a good woman. Just rather...blunt. It causes an awful lot of trouble."

Risyda laughed. "You'll have to tell us about it some time."

"I will." He turned to Jasen and smiled wider. "You look amazing. I'm so proud of you."

"And I'm proud of you, too." Larely had become the Prosider's closest advisor, and the two of them were slowly untangling the knots in Westronan society.

There was another knock on the door; this time, it was a page. "The ceremony is ready to begin, Your Majesty."

Larely squeezed his shoulder. "I should go, then. Good luck!"

After Larely left, Jasen turned to look at Polina and Risyda, who were both beaming. Waves of love and gratitude washed through him. He couldn't believe how lucky he was.

Once they left the chambers, they were flanked by guards, all dressed in ceremonial uniforms. They made their way down the halls of the palace and out to the Bedrose gardens, where the wedding was to take place.

As Jasen and his wedding party appeared at the edge of the largest garden, hundred of pairs of eyes turned to them as the musicians began to play. The sheer number of guests was overwhelming—Jasen almost stumbled, but Risyda caught him, as she always did. Jasen shut his eyes briefly and took a deep breath. When he opened them again, he looked not at the crowd, but at Rilvor, who was waiting for him at the altar. He kept his gaze steady on his husband-to-be as he made his way down the aisle, with Polina and Risyda spreading rose petals ahead of him. Once he was near the altar, he caught a glimpse of the children, who were sitting with their new Granddad Draul. They all had identical grins on their faces. Queen Urga sat beside them. It had taken some conjoling to get her to the Draelands again, but she had at last relented and seemed genuinely glad to be there. Jasen gave them all a little wave before he joined Rilvor.

The rest of the ceremony was a blur, as was the grand feast afterward. There were so many people to greet and so many congratulations to receive. Jasen fielded them as best he could, although all he wanted to do was retire to the royal chambers (which were his now, too) and fulfill the promise in Rilvor's gaze.

"This must be the happiest day of your life," Lord Banither said, and hiccuped. He was more than a little drunk.

"Yes," Jasen said, nodding absently, but he knew it wasn't true. It was a good day, yes, but he was sure it would be far from the best. Who knew what wonders the future held for them?

THE END

ABOUT THE AUTHOR

Sera Trevor is terminally curious and views the 35 book limit at her local library as a dare. She's a little bit interested in just about everything, which is probably why she can't pin herself to one subgenre. Her books are populated with dragons, vampire movie stars, shadow people, and internet trolls. (Not in the same book, obviously, although that would be interesting!) Her works have been nominated for numerous Goodreads M/M Romance Reader's Choice Awards, including Best Contemporary, Best Fantasy, and Best Debut, for which she won third prize in 2015.

She lives in California with her husband, two kids, and a cat the size of three cats.

For more books and updates:
http://www.seratrevor.com

Do you need more romance in your life? Sera Trevor has you covered!

If you're in the mood for a paranormal story, try...

Curses Foiled Again

One cursed witch. One witless vampire. One last chance...

Felix is a vampire--a fierce creature of the night who strikes terror into the hearts of everyone unlucky enough to become his prey. Or at least, that's what he thought was true, until he met John. John is completely unimpressed with Felix, much to his dismay. Felix becomes fixated on proving his ferocity to John--and when that doesn't work, he strives to make any impression on him at all.

John is a witch, and as all witches know, vampires are notoriously stupid creatures who only have the power to hurt those who fear them. Besides, he's under a curse much more frightening than any vampire. Felix's desperate attempts to impress him annoy John at first, but gradually, they become sort of endearing. Because of his curse, John has pushed everyone in his life away. But Felix can't be hurt, so there's no harm in letting him hang around.

Felix is technically dead. John has nothing left to live for. But together, they might have a shot at life.

If you're looking for high fantasy, check out...

A Shadow on the Sun

Light cannot always illuminate—sometimes the truth lies in Darkness...

Prince Theryn and his loyal knight, Sir Atrum, are both bound by duty: Theryn serves the kingdom of Glinden, and Atrum serves his prince. Although they harbor a secret love, a relationship between a prince and his servant is forbidden. Things change when the king promises Theryn's hand in an arranged marriage to the volatile Prince Lyar of the Soltaran Empire, who needs Theryn's Light magic for some sinister religious rite. Theryn and Atrum's struggle to discover Lyar's scheme brings them together at last, but there is more at stake than their happiness. Atrum discovers Dark magic of his own, but neither his love nor his power may be enough to save Theryn from Lyar's dangerously seductive pull. And if

Atrum loses Theryn, the world as they know it may be lost as well.

And if you want a contemporary tale with a lot of laughs, you'll love...

The Troll Whisperer

Oscar Lozada is repulsive, and he likes it that way. His apartment is always a wreck, he works at a sewage plant, and he's an abrasive jerk to just about everyone. When he's not out drinking and hooking up with strangers, he trolls people on the Internet for lulz. His life changes when he finds out a victim of his trolling lives right next door. Noah is super hot and disarmingly nice. In spite of himself, Oscar starts to fall for him. All he has to do is make sure Noah never discovers the truth behind his trollish ways.

Made in the USA
Monee, IL
06 January 2022